The DeFord Chronicles, Part I

This book is a work of fiction. With the exception of historical happenings and individuals, the characters and events contained herein are the product of the author's imagination. Any similarity to persons living or dead is coincidental.

ISBN 978-0-6151-5084-0

The DeFord Chronicles, Part I

By Kate Warren

Collier Bluff Books

Warrens, WI

Author's Note: In writing this novel I have done a great deal of research in an attempt to make the story as historically accurate as possible (with the exception of dialogue). If I have made any mistakes in that regard, I apologize and I will do better next time. If, in reading, you come across terms with which you are unfamiliar, I recommend contacting your local Society for Creative Anachronism group or visiting their website http://www.sca.org or visiting Fandia, the official fan site for my novels http://www.lifeandstuff.com/fandia I am certain that members of both groups will be happy to answer any questions you might have.

Prologue

She slipped quietly through the darkened woods of eastern Frandia muttering to herself. "Well, I'm in for it this time."

"That you are girl." Came a voice from the shadows. Three men approached from behind the trees, surrounding her, and giving no chance of escape. "Such a pretty little thing."

"What are you doing out in the woods at night? Don't you know it's dangerous for a young girl like you?"

"Why there's no telling who you might run into." At that remark from the one she took to be in charge, they all laughed. The sound sent a chill down her spine. She could only stand there, wide eyed and frozen with fear.

They circled her like wolves moving in for the kill—taunting her, and enjoying the fear that played over her face. To these three villains torture was half the fun. The apparent leader was tall and dark. The other two were shorter, blond and blue-eyed—brothers by the look of them. Even in her fright and the darkness the girl could see the similarity, and note the quality of her captors' clothing.

You would think the rich could find other ways of amusing themselves than accosting young girls at night. She thought, but remained silent knowing anything she said would only make matters worse. She almost laughed at herself. Just a few moments before she had been so worried about the scolding she would receive from her parents. Now she just hoped to get home alive.

One of the brothers lunged toward her then suddenly stopped. He fell to the ground, moaning and holding his head. The girl and her attackers were startled by a voice.

"Leave her alone."

A new face emerged as a streak of moonlight broke through the clouds. Red-haired and fierce, the newcomer picked up his victim and held him against a tree. "If you ever touch her again I'll kill you. Do you understand?" The bleeding man nodded, and was released to slide to the ground.

The girl stood trembling as the red-haired man approached and said: "Come. I'll take you home." Recognition dawned when she saw him up close, but she was too astounded to speak. The man who had rescued her was none other than the infamous William DeFord.

Seeing no better alternative, she followed him into the forest toward a horse tethered several yards away. He mounted and reached down to pull her up behind him. They rode in absolute quiet for several minutes as the horse headed toward the main road. She wanted to break the uncomfortable silence, but could not think of a single thing to say. Why on earth would this man have come to her aid?

"What is your name?" William asked, interrupting her thoughts.

"Moreen Kelly." She replied, grateful that he had chosen to speak first.

"How old are you?"

Moreen thought that a rather odd question and of little importance, but she answered anyway. "Fourteen."

"What were you doing in the woods after dark? And by yourself?" His tone held reproach. Whether it was directed toward herself or her non-existent companion she could not tell.

"I was visiting neighbors and lost track of time. I thought if I went through the woods I might make it home sooner, and avoid whatever punishment might be in store for me."

He seemed to think about that for a minute before reminding her: "You neglected to tell me why you were alone. Surely your father and mother would not let a child such as yourself travel so far unaccompanied."

"I am not a child!" Moreen responded angrily. "I've visited the Sinclairs often and always returned before sundown. The main road is safe enough in the daytime. My father and mother never had any cause to worry about me."

"But they do now. How is it you managed to stay so long on this particular visit? There is the road. Which way should we turn? And do not think you can avoid my other question. I expect an answer." At twenty-one William had already mastered that authoritative, 'do as I say or else' tone.

"To the right." She was finding his attitude rather irritating. "The Sinclairs have a new babe." He chuckled and she continued. "I don't expect someone like you to understand."

"You are right, I don't understand the female obsession with babes. What are they good for? I do agree that in time they can be of some use, but from what I see the first several years are a complete waste." He could almost hear her jaw drop, and feel her eyes boring into the back of his head. He smiled. It always pleased him to infuriate people who depended on him for something. Even if that something was merely to be escorted safely home. "You are very ill-mannered, Moreen."

"What do you mean by that sir?" She demanded, completely thrown by both the rapid change of the subject and his use of her Christian name.

"You have not thanked me for ripping you from the jaws of terror." He could not resist the opportunity to build himself up. "What kind of maiden is plucked from danger by a handsome young nobleman, and does not bother to thank her savior?"

Without missing a beat she shot back: "Jesus is my savior. You merely rescued me." That should teach him, she thought. "And I don't recall ever hearing the word noble mentioned in connection with your name, Master DeFord."

So she knew who he was. That left an interesting question. "What *have* you heard about me?" Normally he wouldn't care. He was proud of the legend he had become.

Without thinking Moreen replied. "That you are a vile, self-centered, untrustworthy scoundrel, who would as soon cut off his own hand as help someone in need. And that dissipation comes as naturally to you as breathing."

"Is that all?" He was certain a legend such as his would inspire more contempt than that.

"There is also your tremendous greed, unforgivable arrogance, and thoughtlessness of mythic proportions. Aside from your salacious appetites, I believe that covers most of it." Moreen was certain her description would leave him speechless. But she was mistaken, for he responded immediately.

"You forgot my infamous temper. Are you afraid of me?"

"No."

"Why not? If I'd heard those things about me I would be afraid of myself. If I was a girl, that is." He said casually.

"If you meant to do me harm you wouldn't have come between me and those..." She searched her mind for the word, "...miscreants. You simply would have joined in the fun." She emphasized the last word with unmistakable sarcasm.

William wondered at the remarkable vocabulary that Moreen possessed, but decided against asking her about it. It would not do to know too much about this girl. He already liked her far too much. Innocent maidens were not generally his type. He spotted a cottage in the distance, with a light burning in the front window. "Is that your home Moreen?"

"Yes it is." She would have been relieved except that she expected a lengthy lecture on safety and consideration of others' feelings. Plus she had the strange feeling that she didn't want this ride to end. Unusual that she should feel safe with the most notorious reprobate in the country. "Please. Let me get down here. My father would kill you before I got a chance to explain."

"Very well. I don't wish to die quite yet." He stopped the horse, helped her down, and dismounted. The sweet smell of lilacs permeated the air. He grasped her hand and lifted it to his lips for a fraction of a second, never breaking eye contact. "See that you are more careful in the future Moreen. Goodnight." He mounted again and turned the horse back toward the forest. She watched him gallop off and disappear into the darkness, then walked the remaining distance to the cottage door. She lifted her chin, took a deep breath, and stepped inside.

Back in the forest, William's first priority was to locate the three miscreants, as she'd called them. He came upon them around a fire in a small clearing. The blond man he'd injured earlier looked up at his approach and shot him a hateful look. "What was that all about Will? You nearly killed me back there." He rubbed his head for effect.

"Oh come now, Jack!" he replied. "It's just a scratch. A bit of blood and perhaps a slight bump."

Jack continued to pout and shoot poisonous glances at Will from his seat on a fallen tree's trunk. Ignoring him, Will turned to the tall dark one. "Is there any ale left for the great one, Stan?"

Stanley St. Robert replied good-naturedly. "Of course. But I've had enough for now, thank you." As Will took a seat and accepted a flask from the remaining "miscreant," Stanley continued. "Now what *was* that little incident about? You've never interfered in our sport before. Is there something special about this particular maiden that we should know?" Will remained silent and continued drinking his ale. "Come your *future* lordship, it is not like you to injure one of your friends over some little chit who doesn't have the good sense to stay home at night. You owe us an explanation."

Will adopted his best tone of superiority to reply: "I owe you nothing! The lord's son does not answer to anyone but his father and the king. If you persist in this, I shall have to report you for your barbarous and illegal behavior."

The third member of the little band finally spoke up. "Now Will, you wouldn't really do that, would you? You know your father don't care about our harmless fun."

"Gilbert, your grammar is an embarrassment to all nobility. And if you'll recall, father has been under a great deal of pressure from the crown to remedy the recent crime wave in the area."

Stanley knew William well enough that he could tell his friend was merely trying to distract them from the subjects of the girl, and his uncharacteristic intervention on her behalf. He also knew that Will had been acting strangely since his youngest sister had been married off earlier that month. "As you wish Master Will. But before you turn us in, do allow us the hospitality of your father's wine cellar. What do you say gentlemen? Shall we stay in the damp, dark forest all night, or shall we adjourn to the comforts of Thornhill?"

Gilbert and Jack immediately gave their assent, and took Will's lack of objection as a sign of his approval. The four men rose and departed the clearing, leaving the fire to die on it's own. They gathered horses from the surrounding shadows and headed toward the ancestral home of the DeFords. Jack and Gilbert chattered and sang boisterously along the way. Stanley alternated between joking with them and trying to divine what was wrong with Will, who rode in contemplative silence.

Will's mind wandered from one subject to another, always coming back to settle on Moreen Kelly. For the life of him, he couldn't figure out why she continued to occupy his thoughts—a mystery he would ponder often in the future.

Chapter 1

May 1396

A soft breeze blew and lifted the fragrance of lilacs through the air to where William DeFord stood, idly watching the townsfolk. Lilacs; the air had been heavy with their perfume the night he'd rescued Moreen Kelly from his friends. As if summoned, a vision of Moreen danced in his mind—lovely and smiling. She had been pretty four years before, and had grown more so with each passing year. He had seen her in the village from time to time, always chaperoned, always unapproachable.

Why he was so entranced by a common girl was puzzling to him. Numerous titled maidens had been paraded before him in the hopes that he would marry well. He had rejected every one on the basis of unsuitability—at times inventing deficiencies where none existed. Had he allowed himself to think as far, he would have realized that the standard against which he measured all prospective brides was Moreen.

He would wait just one more minute and then leave. She was always here by this time on Wednesday mornings. Just as he was beginning to get annoyed, she appeared. His previous irritation fled at the sight of her. Every time she came in view his mind ceased to work. It took nearly a full minute for him to recover sufficiently to notice that she was alone. He stood motionless and gazed at the enchanting sight that Moreen provided. He watched her interact with the villagers, as she always did. Chatting with an elderly widow, stooping to answer a small child's question, going about her day as usual. But this time she was alone. No father or mother preventing Will from approaching.

He was just starting toward her when a young boy came rushing into the market calling for her. She tried to calm the boy, but his agitation would not subside. Between gulps of air the boy managed to deliver his urgent message. Will watched as Moreen's rose-petal pink complexion turned ashen. She stood frozen in place. He felt a sudden urge to go to her, comfort her. Then she was gone. And Will was left to contemplate what news could have such an effect. What could be so terrible as to make her look like a porcelain doll on the verge of shattering?

He did not have long to wait for an answer to his unspoken question. The news spread through the market swiftly and Will was able to hear snippets of whispered exchanges: *"Poor child. All alone in the world." "To lose both of them at once!" "Did you hear how they died?" "...cart was overturned...just off the road." "What will she do now?"* It took him a moment to put it all together.

In four years of observation Will had noted the bonds of affection between Hugh and Mary Kelly and their only child. He had envied their warmth. His own family was glacial in comparison. The thought crossed his mind that he wouldn't be so shocked to hear of his parents' demise—it was a wonder they hadn't killed each other in more than 30 years of marriage. The world would be well rid of them. But Moreen...

She would grieve deeply. Her whole world was gone. She had no family to turn to. She would be alone—all alone in that cottage and in need of comfort. For a sad event it was working well to William's advantage. He finally had an excuse to speak to Moreen, she would need a shoulder to cry on, and there would be no one to keep him from her.

He smiled as he walked home. He would wait until evening, when the flow of visitors was slowing. Then he would appear on the very horse he had ridden all those years ago, to save her once again. It was a perfect plan. He began to whistle as he quickened his pace.

Moreen received visitors at her home all day. As was the custom in Frandia, the deceased had been buried right away. A funeral mass would be held as soon as the priest came to the village on his usual circuit. In the mean time, the whole village came to pay their respects. There were the Andersons and the Kirks, the widow Eldridge and her daughter Kate, the Burtons, the Petersons, the Duncans, the Sinclairs, and countless others.

Thomas and Anna Sinclair were Moreen's greatest help and comfort. Thomas had gone north to retrieve the remains of his nearest neighbors as soon as he had heard the news. Little Tommy had been sent to find Moreen. Anna and the other children were waiting at the cottage when Moreen arrived home with little Tommy at her side. Eleanor, who was now four years old, climbed up into Moreen's lap and offered to share her mother and father. Moreen kissed the child's head and held her tightly, but said nothing.

All sense of time disappeared for Moreen. It seemed mere moments ago that she was standing in the market hearing the awful tidings from Tommy, and yet it felt as if she'd been sitting in the cottage for an eternity when Thomas came through the door. "Anna, we'd best be getting home. Have to tend the stock, then I'll come back for you Moreen."

"What?" Moreen asked. "What do you mean?"

Anna replied gently. "We would like you to come and live with us, dear."

Moreen looked from Anna to Thomas and back again. "Oh thank you! You've always been so very kind to me. But...I can't leave my home."

"But Moreen. Child, you cannot stay here alone." Anna protested. "It's far too dangerous."

"Anna's right." Thomas agreed. "Why don't you come with us, just for tonight, and we'll sort the rest out tomorrow."

"No." Moreen stood firm. "I thank you for your offer. I understand your concerns. You've been like family to me my whole life. I just can't think of leaving now. In truth I cannot think at all. I know I'm not being sensible, but...how can I leave? I...I can't believe they're gone! I look around this room and I see them so clearly: Mother at the hearth starting to get supper; Father here by the window, writing the accounts." The first tear she had cried all day fell as she picked up her father's quill. "All the evidence of their lives, of *my* life, is here. I can't bear the thought of leaving! Please don't ask me to." she begged as more tears fell.

Thomas looked at Anna and said "Alright. We won't force you, Moreen. If you insist upon staying though, be sure you bar the door."

Moreen nodded as she wiped tears from her cheeks. "I will. Thank you."

Anna embraced her and murmured quietly: "I'll be praying for you, dear." Moreen nodded and thanked her.

"Come along Anna, children. Time to go home. I'll be by in the morning to look in on you Moreen." Thomas herded his family toward the door. Moreen followed. Her tears had ceased and she looked calm once again as she watched their cart drive away.

She stood in the doorway a long time, almost afraid to turn and face the empty cottage. Just as she was preparing to go back inside, she saw a horse and rider approaching. Her first thought was that she should go in and bar the door, but something stopped her. Something held her there on the threshold. As the horse came nearer it seemed familiar to her. In a few moments it was near enough that she could recognize its rider. Her breath caught as she struggled with yet another shock.

William's first glimpse of Moreen standing in the entrance of the cottage disturbed him. She looked lost. He had never seen that look of despair on her face. She had always been happy when he'd observed her. He cheered himself with the ego-enhancing thought of rescuing the damsel in distress. Not really his style, but he had done it once before, so he could see no reason why he could not do it again. William DeFord to the rescue of the sweetest maiden in the country! He nearly smiled before he remembered the circumstances and his opening line. He stopped his horse several feet from the cottage and sat gazing at Moreen. She was even more beautiful up close, but the light was missing from her eyes.

She watched as he dismounted and walked slowly towards her. William DeFord was the last person she would have expected to appear on her doorstep. His gradual approach gave her ample time to wonder why on earth he was there, but try as she might, she could not account for his presence.

His voice pulled her from her contemplation. "Miss Kelly...I heard of your parents' accident and I wish to offer my condolences."

"Thank you Master DeFord." She replied quietly.

"If there is anything I can do for you...anything you need..."

"That is very kind of you, but there is no need for you to trouble yourself." Moreen looked into his eyes and was surprised to see genuine concern. She had not spoken to him since that night four years before. His reputation had remained intact subsequently. She never had been able to reconcile what she had heard about him with his behavior toward her that evening.

"It would be no trouble." He said softly. "Do you have any other family? Some place to go?"

Moreen remembered her manners and forgot propriety. "Please, come in. How rude of me to make you stand out there." It was a convenient way to change the subject.

William nodded his acceptance of her request and they both entered the cottage.

No sooner had the door closed behind them than William again took up the topic Moreen had thought to avoid. "Have you any place to go?"

She answered reluctantly. "I have no other family, but I have friends who have offered me the kindness of their home."

He had known she had no other family. Friends he hadn't counted on. He had to think fast. "Please allow me to escort you to their home."

"Thank you, but that won't be necessary. I will be staying here." Moreen continued before he could respond. "Please don't ask me to change my mind. The Sinclairs tried to persuade me to stay with them, but I can't even think of leaving."

Ah, here was the opening he needed. "Of course not." William inched closer. "How could you? Isn't it enough that you have lost your family? Why should you have to lose your home as well?"

"That is exactly how I feel. I am glad someone understands." Moreen offered him a weak smile. She felt tired. The day was wearing on her. She crossed the small room to sit on the bench near the hearth. "I would offer you something to eat, but I haven't even made anything for myself. Pray forgive me Master DeFord."

"Won't you call me William?" He crossed the room as well and sat next to her. "You look weary, Moreen."

"Master—..."

"William." He interrupted. Up close he could see the way her dark brown hair shone in the firelight. And her eyes, which he had thought gray, were actually a deep blue.

"William." She repeated. "I am weary. It has been a long day already. It feels like it will never end." Pain clouded her eyes, but she remained calm.

Will was at a loss for what to do next. Why wasn't she crying? He found her self-sufficiency irritating. Many times in his life he had been annoyed at silly women who became hysterical with grief and flung themselves into his arms. Each time he had wondered why women couldn't experience pain without dissolving into a puddle of tears. Now that he was in the presence of a sensible female who could maintain her composure and seemed to have no need of his comfort, he wanted nothing more than to take her in his arms and croon soft, soothing words to her. An exasperating situation if ever one existed!

"Sweet Moreen." He spoke softly. "How difficult it must be for you. I cannot imagine what pain you must feel. I hate to see this sadness in your eyes." He lifted a hand to her face, and ran his thumb down her cheek. She closed her eyes. He leaned toward her and touched his lips to hers. The kiss was soft, warm, and sweet. He pulled away and saw her look of bewilderment. Then it came: he heard the sound before he felt the impact of her hand hitting his cheek.

"How dare you?" She cried angrily as she leapt to her feet. "Is that why you came here? It couldn't possibly be the result of any tender emotions of yours."

"You slapped me!" Will was shocked. Sweet little Moreen had slapped him and was shouting at him—over a tiny kiss. He looked sincerely confused and Moreen almost took pity on him, but the events of the day had taken their toll and she no longer cared about her precious self-control.

"Leave my home this instant!" She commanded him with all the righteous indignation of a wronged saint.

Will was so surprised that it didn't even occur to him to protest until he was outside the cottage with the door slammed and firmly barred behind him. He stood staring at it for a moment, wondering what had just happened. His horse nuzzled his shoulder from behind. He knew Moreen wouldn't let him back in, so he mounted up and rode for the village tavern.

On the other side of the door Moreen stared into space, listening to the horse's retreating steps. She wasn't quite as angry anymore. *The nerve of that man!* She thought. *Thinking he could have his way with me!* What irked her the most was that she had responded to his kiss. For half a moment she had wanted more and would have given anything he asked. The man was dangerous, in many ways. It was a good thing she'd thrown him out when she did. Yet a mutinous part of her wished he would come back. She wanted him to take her in his arms and tell her that everything would be all right. *Curse you William DeFord. As if I didn't have enough to deal with already.*

Back in the village, William was indulging his tastes for ale and self-pity. No one had ever refused him—especially no female. He didn't know what to make of the situation. Apparently "sweet little Moreen" had quite a temper. For the life of him he couldn't figure out what had set her off. Obviously she had uncovered his true intentions in visiting her, but he didn't see why that would make her so upset. As he continued to mull over the predicament in the dark of the tavern, he became conscious of the voices at the next table.

"Are you saying it wasn't an accident?"

"That's what."

"But why? Did you have some score to settle with 'em?"

"Not them, their daughter. Can't hide behind 'em anymore, can she? If I know her she'll be all alone in that cottage, and no one around for miles to interfere."

"Aww that girl wouldn't tumble with the likes of you."

"She won't have much choice, now will she?" Raucous laughter followed that remark.

William's blood began to boil. His first thought was to beat the miserable creature within an inch of his life. However, though Will was a hotheaded scoundrel, he was not a fool: he knew that two of them against one of him did not give him the best odds. Pulverization was, therefore, not an option. That left his second and strangely even stronger impulse—get to Moreen before the other reprobate did. He dropped a few coins on the table, rose and left slowly, then mounted his horse and rode as though the king's army was after him.

Throughout the heart-pounding ride the sun's last dying rays gave a faint light. Will had plenty of time to contemplate everything he'd like to do to the ruffian at the tavern. The fact that *he* had gone to Moreen with the same intentions didn't bother him. But the thought of any other man touching her made him feel homicidal. By the time he reached the cottage, he had formed a plan. He tried the door and found it still barred. *Clever girl!*

"Moreen! It's William." He called through the door.

She peeked out the window before calling her reply. "Go away!"

"Moreen please! I came to apologize." Truth wasn't terribly important to him under normal circumstances and was even less so now.

"You can do that from where you are." She was a stubborn little thing.

"Please let me in. I can't leave without seeing your face. I have to know that you have truly forgiven me. Please Moreen!" *This had better work!* He was running out of ideas. Just then the door swung open and he stepped inside.

Without thinking he gathered Moreen into his arms and held her tightly against him. She was too tired to fight her own feelings. She gave into to the warmth of the embrace and relaxed in his arms. "Well, I'm waiting." She said. He looked at her blankly, so she continued "For the apology."

He looked down at her sweet face. "I didn't come to apologize."

"But you said…"

"I lied." He saw the anger building in her beautiful blue eyes. "Well if I'd told you the reason I came you wouldn't have let me in." He placed his hands on her shoulders and held her a little away from him. "When you threw me out earlier I went to the tavern. I overheard two men talking about your parents' death. It was not an accident, Moreen."

Her eyes widened. "What do you mean? Of course it was an accident."

"No. I heard them. It was deliberate." He kept his eyes on hers and cringed inwardly at the raw pain in them.

"But why? Why would someone do that?" She pleaded with him to make her understand.

"To leave you alone and defenseless. I didn't get a good look at them, but I don't think I know them. Though one of them seems to know you. He said he knew you would stay here by yourself." Will hesitated as Moreen's face paled, but she needed to hear the rest whether she wanted to or not. "He said you could not hide behind your parents anymore, and there would be no one for miles to interfere."

Moreen instantly comprehended the meaning in those words. "It would seem you and he had the same idea."

"*I* was going to be nice about it." Will protested. "I would never hurt you Moreen! I would never force you to do anything." Oddly enough, he meant it.

"How do I know you didn't make this up to get me to open the door?"

"I didn't have to make it up. You had already let me in. Although I appreciate the compliment." He smiled.

Her eyes sparked with fury. "It's not a compliment!"

"You're beautiful when you're angry."

"Then I'm about to become positively bewitching." She replied.

Will pulled her closer. This time he caught her hand before it hit him and pressed his lips to her palm. Stunned, she barely protested as he slid an arm around her waist and drew her closer still. The world receded as his mouth descended to hers. Neither of them heard the door open.

Chapter 2

"What in hell is going on here?"

William recognized the voice from the tavern. He stepped away from Moreen but kept her hand in his as he turned to face the intruder. "I'll thank you not to use such language in the presence of my betrothed. And as it's only just been decided, I see you shall be the first to offer congratulations."

The man stood perplexed. Will was waiting to see what he would do. Moreen was still reeling from the kiss. So the three of them remained for a moment.

"Who are you?" The man asked Will, breaking the silence.

"Oh, of course. Where are my manners? Please allow me to introduce myself. I am William DeFord." Will's voice held an unusual combination of courtesy and menace.

The man quailed visibly and stammered. "D-DeFord?

"Yes—son of Lord Geoffrey and Lady Constance DeFord. And you are?"

The man was clearly distressed. His eyes darted around the room repeatedly as if searching for another exit. Moreen recognized him. "His name is Rupert Andin." She began to look fearful.

"Then you know him, my love." Will slipped his arm around Moreen's waist.

"Yes. Rupert is the blacksmith's son." She leaned into Will.

Rupert's eyes were still flying about the room, as his mind scrambled for a quick explanation. He had seen Will leaving the tavern and had no doubt that his plan had been deliberately foiled. All his efforts had come to nothing. But his main concern at the moment was to remain alive.

Will stepped closer to him, blocking Moreen from his view. "Well since you've known my intended for some time, I presume you came here to deliver your condolences on her parents' untimely demise. I suppose you might have been anxious for her safety, but you needn't concern yourself. I am more than capable of protecting my bride. If *anyone* attempts to harm her, I will see to it that he's killed— slowly." He smiled to chilling effect. "If you've nothing else to offer, we wish to be alone."

Rupert turned and bolted out the door. William barred it behind him and went quickly to Moreen. She had begun to shake. There was no resistance this time as he pulled her to him.

"You were right. I know it. He...he killed them...and he...he...would have..." She began to cry, and Will who had wished for her tears before, was now torn apart by them. He would do anything to make them stop, but he didn't know how.

"He'll never come near you again. I meant what I said. I will kill anyone who harms you." Her tears did not cease, but they slowed a bit as she looked up at him. Her lovely face awash with tears, eyes tinged red and filled with pain and fear, wrenched his heart.

"I would never have believed that he would do something so terrible. He always seemed good and kind." She laid her head against his heart.

"Yes, well appearances can deceive, can't they my love?" He tightened his hold of her.

"Thank you, William. Thank you for rescuing me...again." She was silent a moment, then lifted her head to look at him again. "Did you mean it?"

"Mean what?" He asked.

"You called me your love. Did you mean it?" she repeated.

"I don't know. I haven't given it any thought." He shrugged as if it didn't matter.

"You told Rupert that we were betrothed. Do you expect us to wed?" She had stopped crying, but Will wasn't sure this was an improvement.

"Of course." Will looked puzzled when she pulled away.

"I cannot wed you." She said simply.

Shocked once again he exploded. "Why the hell not?"

"You wouldn't let Rupert use such language in front of me, yet you'll use it yourself?" She stared accusingly at him.

"That was when we were betrothed. If we're not getting married I don't care who says what to you."

"We were never betrothed." She retorted. "I cannot wed a man I cannot trust."

Will blew out an exasperated breath. "I promise never to lie to you again. Now we can be wed."

"It's not that simple, Will." Moreen began to pace. "First of all, how do I know that you won't lie to me again? Second, I hardly know anything about you at all."

"Ask me anything. I'll tell you." He stood back and waited. He was encouraged by the fact that she'd called him Will.

"Are the rumors true?"

"Some of them. Which rumors do you want to know about?"

She rounded on him at once. "Have you killed men?" She wasn't sure she wanted the answer.

"Yes. But always in fair fighting, and with good reason." He replied.

"What could possibly be a good reason to kill?" She demanded.

"In order to remain alive oneself. What else?"

"What about the women?" Moreen stared at the floor.

Will studied her carefully. "Any particular ones you're concerned about?"

"I have heard—I was not supposed to, but I heard—that you have...been with...more than fifty." Her eyes remained riveted to a knot in the wooden plank on which she stood.

"The numbers have been grossly overstated. But I've had my share." He admitted.

Moreen's stomach lurched, and her heart squeezed. The room was stifling all of a sudden. "Is it true that you have fathered children out of wedlock?"

"No. That is not true." He was relieved when she finally met his eyes. "I am not the only scoundrel in the country. Does that ease your mind?"

"Only slightly." She began to pace again. "You drink, gamble, fornicate, lie, steal..."

"I have never stolen. I don't need to steal." That was the sole charge on which William could defend himself. "And as for the rest...what is so bad about all that? No one gets hurt. It's not the 1350's!"

"Oh really? When did God change the rules? And people *do* get hurt. You may be too selfish to see it, but people get hurt, including you. You have no idea the harm you have done to yourself, and to others. Have you no care for that?" Moreen was passionate about her religion. It had sustained her through what was, so far, the worst day of her life. It was an integral part of her and William had to see that. She felt drawn to him in a way she had never been to anyone, but she could not separate her faith from her heart.

Will was speechless. He was not used to being censured, and this was the second time in the span of one evening that Moreen had taken him to task. The girl was infuriating, but he had to have her. Not given to introspection, Will did not understand his obsession. He wanted her. He would have her. That was all there was to it. He just had to figure out how to convince her.

"Do you even believe in God?" She threw the divine gauntlet. He had to answer this one. She lifted her chin ever so slightly in challenge.

He gave the question a moment's honest consideration before replying. "I think so. I'm not certain, but I think I believe God exists. I do not think He has much to do with matters here though."

She wanted to appreciate his honesty.

She didn't respond so he continued. "If God directed us in our lives, would he have allowed your mother and father to be killed, leaving you prey to less scrupulous characters than myself?"

"God gave men free will. He allows us to do evil or good as we choose." Moreen had found her voice and was not about to back down.

"But why? If men are so evil by nature, why allow us to choose? You, Miss Kelly, are lucky that I chose to come back here." He crossed his arms and awaited her reply.

"Then you do not believe that God sent you to rescue me?" She had unwittingly given him just the argument to use against her.

"God sent me to rescue you? Then saying we were betrothed must have been His idea as well. If you believe He sent me, you must also believe He intends for us to wed. Why else would He send *me*? Surely there are many other more suitable men to protect you. And why would God have allowed you to stay here alone when he knew Rupert's plans for you? Would he have allowed you to do so foolish a thing when you had a safe place to go?" He had her, and he knew it. She could not refuse him without denying the faith that meant everything to her.

She looked at him in astonishment. She was feeling a myriad of emotions: fear; doubt; confusion; anger at herself; anger at Will. She decided to focus on the last. "You tricked me. You've used my convictions against me. How could you be so despicable?"

"A lifetime of practice makes it easy." He replied casually. He could see that she was more upset than he had intended. Acting on impulse he crossed the distance between them, took both her hands in his, and looked straight into her eyes. "Moreen Kelly...if you will have me I vow never to mislead you again. I will do everything in my power to ensure your safety and your happiness. I cannot change what I have done before, but I give you my word that I will never mistreat you."

"Is your word worth anything?"

"Not usually." He answered truthfully. "But this time I mean it. Please Moreen."

"Why?" She asked. "Why do you want to marry me?"

"I'm not certain." He had promised not to lie to her again and he would keep his word, even if it meant he wouldn't say what she wanted to hear. If she expected a declaration of love, she was going to be disappointed. "I don't know why. I know that I have to have you—that you can never belong to any other man. But I don't know why. I am a selfish, wretched man, but I care more for you than I ever have for anyone. That is all I can tell you."

Moreen knew she had to make her decision. His words, while not the most romantic gesture, were quite a lot coming from a man of his background and character. His heart might never be attainable. She could not begin to imagine a life with him. Life without him she could imagine all to well—it would be empty. As she closed her eyes and pictured him walking out of her life forever, she felt a sense of loss and anguish that were foreign to her, even after the day she'd had. His presence brought her comfort. Even knowing what he was, she felt at peace with him. As of that morning her life had become a whirlpool of turmoil, but William was strong and steady. *Please Lord, tell me what to do!*

"Yes, I will marry you." Her answer surprised them both.

"Really?"

"Really." She smiled and he swept her up in his arms, twirling her about the room.

"Get your things. You're coming home with me." Will's statement startled her. "Moreen, you know you can't stay here. If you are with me I can keep you safe."

"I know." She looked around sadly. "I just...my whole life is here. Will, what will happen to the cottage now?"

"We'll worry about that later. First we must get you to Thornhill." He kissed her gently.

Moreen began to gather her meager belongings, as well as a few things that would remind her of her parents. A single tear spilled down her cheek. She wanted to go with Will, she felt happy about agreeing to be his bride, but the reality of the changes the day had brought was a heavy burden to her. She was wiping at more teardrops when they stepped out into the night.

"Dearest, please don't cry." Will said. He suddenly felt like the cad he was. "I'm sorry sweetheart. You've been through hell today, haven't you? I hate to see you hurting so. But if crying helps, then weep away."

Moreen stopped crying and threw her arms around him. "You are so sweet to me. I don't care what anyone says about you!"

"That's good, because you'll be hearing a lot of things." He smiled down at her. "Shall we go?"

"William, will you take me to the Sinclairs' first? I must tell them of our betrothal. Thomas means to come by tomorrow and I won't be here." She looked up at him with imploring eyes. "They are my dearest friends."

Although she didn't know it, he could deny her nothing when she looked at him that way. "Of course I shall take you to them." Her smile was worth any inconvenience it might cost him. He helped her onto his horse and mounted behind her.

Moreen leaned back against him and he smiled. She was comfortable in his arms, which was exactly where he intended to keep her. This day had worked out even better than he had planned.

Neither said a word as they rode on, each being absorbed in their own minds, each thinking back to the night they first met.

Will had been on his way to meet his friends for a bit of drunken reveling, but when he arrived at the designated spot they were noticeably absent. He followed the faint sound of voices and discovered Stan, Jack, and Gilbert surrounding a girl. He knew their intentions and would not have minded, but something in her innocent face compelled him to a protectiveness he had never before felt. And so he viciously attacked poor Jack, and delivered young Moreen from danger.

While escorting her home Will had been captivated by her mettle. Within minutes of being extracted from less than desirable circumstances, she was in a verbal sparring match with him, and she held her own quite nicely. Will was unused to females who were capable of matching wits with him, his mother being the sole exception. Moreen had won his respect that night, a feat no one—male or female—had accomplished up to that point.

"There it is." Moreen pointed to a light in the distance.

"Are you going to change your mind?" He was still uncertain of her feelings.

"No, of course not. They will understand." She wasn't as confident as she sounded.

As they neared the house the door opened. "Who is there?"

"It's me Thomas!" Moreen called back.

"Moreen!" Thomas sounded alarmed.

"Moreen?" Anna appeared in the doorway with her husband. "Child, are you all...?" The words died as she caught sight of William. "Goodness!" She whispered. Thomas, whose eyesight was not quite as good as his wife's, shot her a questioning look. The cause of her concern became all too clear as the horse drew near their dwelling.

Thomas and Anna thought of Moreen as family, and were shocked to see her with that scoundrel William DeFord. Thomas, who was not the coolest headed individual, and was known to be quite a talker, was so stunned that he remained both still and silent. Anna's own quietude resulted from a more laid-back temper, and her willingness to hear the facts before judging any person or circumstance.

William jumped down as soon as they had stopped and helped Moreen down as well. Anna noticed that his hands lingered a bit on Moreen's waist.

Moreen rushed over to them and embraced Anna. "I had to come and tell you everything. I could not bear the thought of worrying you."

Anna returned her embrace. "Tell us what dear?" She looked curiously at Will, who wisely let Moreen do the talking.

"Thomas, Anna, you know Master William DeFord. We are to be wed." Moreen beamed at Will, and the Sinclairs exchanged perplexed looks.

Chapter 3

Thomas found his voice. "Why on earth would you..." he trailed off as his wife shot him a warning glance.

"Won't you come inside?" Anna was bewildered as to how the betrothal had come to be, but Moreen seemed to be happy about it, so she was determined to act cordially.

"Are the children still awake? I wouldn't want to frighten them." Moreen was ever thoughtful.

"You've nothing to fear on that account. They are fast asleep." Anna replied as she ushered Moreen in the house. Will followed them past Thomas, who was looking eager to pummel him since Moreen had mentioned frightening the children. Thomas closed the door and made a show of barring it as well.

Anna made sure her guests were comfortable sitting at the small table. "Now dear, tell us how these...joyous tidings came to be."

Moreen did not believe in lying, but she was aware that William's reputation had preceded them, and she so wanted Thomas and Anna's blessing, that she decided not to tell them about his first visit.

"Master DeFord...William," she gazed softly at him, "overheard something dreadful about the accident. It was not an accident."

Anna inhaled sharply. Thomas stared at Will. "Overheard it, did he?"

Moreen looked at Thomas. "Please, it's not what you think. There was more. The...man...who did this...intended to...I don't know if I can say it. He meant for me to be alone so he could..." she couldn't meet even Will's gaze.

"It's all right, dear." Anna took her hand. "You don't have to go on."

Moreen looked at Anna with gratitude. "Thank you. But William saved me. He came to the cottage before Ru—I mean before that man could get there."

"I don't believe it!" Thomas shot daggers at Will.

"I didn't either at first, but then he showed up." Moreen shuddered at the memory. "Will made him leave."

"Will, is it?" Thomas still wasn't convinced. "And why would 'Will' go to all this trouble for someone he doesn't even know? I've heard plenty about you Master DeFord, and none of it good."

Will decided to use humor to try and defuse the situation. "I have heard some quite shocking things about myself."

Thomas was not amused. He didn't like Will's reputation, or his attitude. Idle rumors were one thing, but so far William DeFord did not improve upon acquaintance. He made up his mind then and there to have a little chat with "Will" as soon as possible.

Moreen pleaded, "Please Thomas! You don't know him at all."

"And you do?" he countered.

Unfortunately Moreen could not say that she truly knew Will. She felt that she knew him, but there was no way she could make Thomas understand. Anna looked at her with compassion, and patted her hand in sympathy.

She knew that she wouldn't be able to get Moreen to confide in her with the men in the room. She didn't quite feel safe sending them outside together, but there was no other alternative. "Would you excuse us for a moment? I wish to speak to Moreen privately." Her tone was mild, but firm. The men had no choice but to leave the room. As soon as the door closed behind them, Anna turned to Moreen. "There is more to this tale, isn't there dear?"

"I never could hide anything from you." Moreen felt almost relieved. She knew she could trust Anna no matter what. "I didn't mean to keep it from you, truly! I just—I want you to like Will. I don't want to disappoint the two of you."

"Child, you cannot live your life based on what others want or think. You are the one who must live with your decisions. Say you disappoint us. We'll get over it. We'll always be here for you—anytime you need us. Now tell me all about it."

Moreen began to tell Anna about the night of their first meeting, how she had waited and watched for glimpses of him ever since. Then she came to his first visit that evening.

"I was so surprised. He was the last person in the world I would have expected to see. He said he wanted to offer his condolences. He seemed truly concerned about me."

"Seemed?" Anna asked.

Moreen continued. "I'm not certain. He kissed me. I liked it, but I was so angry I slapped him and ordered him out of my home."

"And what did he do?" Anna was truly curious.

"He left." Moreen replied. "I suppose he could have stayed. I could not really have forced him out. But he left when I told him to. Then he came back to save me."

"Strange." Anna mulled it over for a minute. "No, not so strange considering that rescue years ago. Why did you not tell me of that before now?"

"Mother and father thought it best not to speak of it. And anyway who would have believed me?" She had a point. Kindness to others was not a DeFord family trait.

Anna did not want to put Moreen through any more trauma—she'd certainly had plenty for one lifetime, let alone one day—but she had to ask. "Moreen. Dear you must tell me where Master DeFord heard about this plot against your family, and who was behind it?"

"It was at the tavern. Will did not know the man." Moreen looked down.

"But you do, don't you dear?" Anna prompted gently. "You needn't be afraid to tell me."

"Oh, Anna! It was Rupert Andin!" Moreen cried. "I was so frightened when I saw him standing there. You should have seen the look on his face when Will said he would kill anyone who hurt me."

"He said that?" Anna smiled. "The boy must care for you a great deal. I can't say I'm all that surprised about Rupert. There always was something I didn't trust about that lad. But let's not talk about that anymore. I can see you have a certain regard for Master DeFord, but are you certain you wish to wed him?"

Moreen was glad to have the subject changed.

"Are you in love with him?

Moreen thought a moment. "I think I might be. I've never felt this way before. How can you tell if you love someone?"

"People will tell you different things. Some say it's when you can't stop thinking about the person. Some say it's the way your heart beats faster when you're near them. I've always thought that truly loving someone means putting their happiness ahead of your own.

"You can wish someone well and happy, or think about someone a lot of the time. That is not so special. But to truly put someone else first—that's what I call love."

"And that's the way you feel about Thomas." Moreen observed.

Anna smiled. "That's the way it is."

Meanwhile outside, Thomas and Will were having their own version of a heart-to-heart. They started with an abbreviated staring contest—Thomas trying his best to be intimidating, and Will refusing to be intimidated.

After several minutes Thomas spoke. "I don't know you boy. I don't know if what people say about you is true and I don't care. But if you hurt that girl in there, I will hunt you down and teach you all new meanings of the word pain."

Will believed Thomas would do just that. "I have no intention of hurting her."

"I don't give a damn about your intentions, boy!" Thomas snapped. "You see that it never happens."

"Mister Sinclair, I have a great regard for Moreen. I will do everything that is within my power to see that she is safe and happy." Will wasn't the slightest bit worried, and telling the truth took much less effort than lying.

"You'd better." He was warned. "Tell me DeFord, who was behind the accident?"

"Moreen said his name is Rupert Andin, the blacksmith's son."

"The little bastard!" Thomas wanted to string him up. "He's had his eye on Moreen for years. Hugh and I made certain he never got near her. How did you get him to leave?"

Will recognized that Thomas cared for Moreen more than even his own father cared for him. Of course she was well worthy of such devotion. "I merely explained that if anyone tried to harm my bride I would see to it that he was killed— slowly."

Thomas smiled. "You and I may be more alike than I thought. Let's go back in."

Moreen went to Will's side at once. She had a good idea of what Thomas might have said, but surprisingly Will didn't seem the least bit troubled. He merely smiled and said: "We must be going. It is growing late."

"Yes, of course." She replied obligingly. She turned to embrace Anna. "Thank you so much!"

Anna smiled warmly.

Thomas' words as William and Moreen headed out the door were less than gentle: "Remember what I said, boy."

Will nodded in acknowledgement.

Thomas and Anna watched as they rode off into the distance. Moreen turned back and waved before they disappeared from sight.

Will held the reins in one hand and put his free arm around Moreen. She leaned back and sighed. "Will, when shall we be wed?"

"Whenever you wish, love." He kissed the top of her head.

"But it will be weeks before the priest comes!" She contradicted.

"My father can have a priest here in a few days time. You see the advantages of marrying nobility?"

"I had not thought of advantages. I only thought of you. And I'm glad we won't have long to wait." She turned her head to look at him and he kissed her ardently. "Isn't it dangerous to kiss me like that? Who's controlling the horse?"

"The horse knows the way home." He replied and kissed her again.

And so they spent the ride to Thornhill alternating between comfortable silences and fervent kisses. Moreen turned her head as they rode past her home. William held her tighter and she closed her eyes. When she opened them again the farm was far behind them, lost in the vast expanse of black night.

They came upon their destination much more quickly than Moreen had expected. Her sense of time had diminished as she rode in Will's arms. Now that they were almost there, a thousand thoughts converged upon her: this would be her home now; she would be meeting Will's family; she would be living with these people from now on. What if they didn't like her?

Will was merely thinking how much better his life would be with Moreen in it. He gave no thought to whether his parents would like her or not. He would wed her regardless of their opinions. He knew they would not be pleased with her lack of dowry, but his mother had always made a show of doting upon her only son, so he felt certain that she would pretend to overlook the money issue in favor of his happiness. His father wasn't interested in anyone's happiness, but he would understand his son's appreciation for Moreen's physical charms.

"William?" Moreen sounded anxious. "Will your family like me?"

"My father and mother are the only family I have here. My sisters are all married."

"But will they like me, do you think?"

He looked down into her eyes and smiled. "How could anyone not like you?"

She smiled back at him as they approached the gates. A boy came out to take the horse and was stunned to find a girl with Master Will. Will had never brought a girl home before.

"Stop your staring, boy." Will commanded as he dismounted and helped Moreen down. "This is my betrothed."

The boy swallowed hard. "Beg your pardon, milady." He took the horse and quickly led it away.

Moreen was puzzled by the exchange between Will and the boy, but she had little time to reflect on it, for as she turned she got her first glimpse of her new home.

Thornhill had been built by the DeFord family 200 years before. It was part fortress, part palace. The stone walls were thick and strong and had withstood many attacks. Numerous windows adorned the exterior. It was a soulless edifice—at once splendid and stark. The keep looked as though it had once been the pride of the family, but over time had become nothing more to them than a residence: a grandiose pile of stones, devoid of any of the emotion that might have inspired its creation.

The DeFord banner flew atop one of the crenellated towers. In the daylight one could see that the green banner was emblazoned with the family arms. A griffin stood out against the black of the shield; it was the same golden color as the three suns embellishing the wide red stripe that adorned the top.

As she absorbed the sight, she became more and more nervous. Will took her hand and squeezed it gently as they started toward the immense oaken doors.

Chapter 4

Moreen had expected the interior of the keep to reflect the extravagance suggested by the exterior. When she stepped inside she was surprised to see the hall filled with dogs and unconscious men; empty flagons still clutched in their grimy hands.

Will had forgotten that there had been a very successful hunting party that day, and a celebration over the course of the evening. Had he not been otherwise engaged, he would have joined in the revelry. Instead he had brought his bride-to-be into a den of fools passed out drunk. Moreen's first impression of his home would forever be this scene. His embarrassment quickly turned to anger. He dropped Moreen's hand and began shouting at the sleeping men.

"Get up! Up I say! Go sleep off your stupor elsewhere!" Some of the men grumbled. Will picked one of them up by his tunic and growled into his face. "What was that you said?"

"N-n-n-nothing." The sot replied.

"I thought so." Will growled again before dropping him. Their steps were slowed by the significant amount of alcohol they had imbibed. Their straggling only inflamed Will's temper 'til finally he roared: "Out you dogs! And take your animals with you."

Just then an equally resonant voice bellowed "What the devil is going on here?" A tall, dark-haired man appeared at the far end of the room. "Well, is someone going to answer me?"

Will stepped forward. "Father, I believed the night air would help to clear the heads of those who might have over-indulged this evening, and have roused them to that effect."

"And that is why my rest was disturbed?" He barked.

Moreen, who had been observing the peculiar dynamic between father and son, stepped forward and Will continued "I did not deem the scene in the hall a proper welcome for my betrothed. Father, may I introduce Miss Moreen Kelly?"

Lord DeFord looked surprised for a moment. Then he smiled as he started toward them. He was an imposing figure, richly attired, well groomed, and graceful of movement. His mustache and beard were the same silver-streaked ebony of his hair, and closely trimmed. He stopped in front of them and looked Moreen up and down. "Such a disturbance is easily overlooked when such happy tidings are conveyed." His smile grew larger as he took Moreen's hand and bowed over it. "My dear. Welcome to Thornhill. I can readily see why my son has been so captivated. Such beauty as yours could enchant a king."

He still held her hand, and his eyes held something that made Moreen uneasy. She slowly withdrew her hand. "Thank you, my lord."

"Allow me to apologize for the spectacle that greeted your arrival. A few guests seem to have partaken too liberally of our hospitality. I assure you it is not an everyday occurrence. I apologize also for not being present to receive you. I was unaware that my son had chosen a bride." Geoffrey DeFord was a handsome and charming man, with a dangerous air about him. His manners, like his appearance, were impeccable.

"No apologies are necessary my lord." Moreen looked down.

"It has only just been decided this evening." Will informed his father.

"Ah, so that's where you were. You were missed at supper. Your mother was concerned."

"Indeed." The three looked up to see the lady of the house descending the staircase from the hallway above with majestic elegance. Will had inherited his mother's hair.

Lady DeFord's tresses streamed down her back like a river of flame. Her eyes, however, resembled ice. The gray depths held no discernable warmth.

"I am sorry mother." Will clearly preferred his mother to his father. "I was occupied by something of the utmost importance."

"And what could be so important as to keep my son from his supper?" She smiled, but the expression lacked feeling.

"The future, mother." Will once again took Moreen's hand. "May I present Miss Moreen Kelly, my betrothed."

Lady DeFord covered her shock well. "Betrothed? I had no idea. Miss Kelly."

"My lady." Moreen said meekly.

"Forgive my surprise my dear. I was beginning to think my son would never choose a bride. We must plan a celebration." Lady DeFord was less than pleased with her son's choice, but years of practice enabled her to bend the truth effortlessly, while concealing her real object behind a mask of courtly charm and flawless deportment.

"That would be out of the question." William objected.

"Oh, and why is that dear?" She was relieved that she would not have to celebrate the occasion.

"A celebration would be inappropriate given that Moreen has recently lost her mother and father." Will looked at her with concern while his mother abruptly changed tactics.

"Oh my dear!" She took both Moreen's hands in hers. "I am so sorry. Was it very recent?"

"Yes my lady." She replied as tears began to fill her eyes. "This very morning."

"How dreadful! Had I known I would never have…Please forgive me." Lady DeFord smoothed Moreen's hair and spoke in her best motherly tone. "If you need anything, anything at all, please come to me."

"Yes of course." Moreen was delighted to find such a friend in her soon to be mother-in-law.

Geoffrey, not to be outdone by his lawful wife, also volunteered his help. "Yes Miss Kelly, if we can be of any assistance to you do not hesitate to ask." A look of challenge passed between the elder couple, prompting Will to interject his own request:

"Actually mother, father, as Moreen has no other family I took the liberty of asking her to move to Thornhill. I hope you have no objections." Will knew his parents so well. Neither of them wanted Moreen there, but neither was willing to say so and allow the other the opportunity to play the saint.

They both spoke at once: "Of course not. Don't be silly."

"Moreen, you are as welcome here as my own daughters." Geoffrey said sincerely. To which his wife countered: "I shall direct my personal lady-in-waiting to attend you."

"Oh no. Please, don't go to any trouble for me." Moreen implored.

"It's no trouble at all my dear. Now it is decided, and we'll not speak another word about it. I shall have your rooms prepared directly. Poor thing, you have had such a hard day! A hot bath will do you good. Follow me dear." With that she performed a graceful turn and started toward one of the many passages adjoining the hall. Moreen looked to Will, and seeing he had no objection, she accompanied his mother from the hall.

As soon as the ladies were out of sight Geoffrey turned to his son. "William, would you accompany me to my solar?" Without waiting for a reply he started up the stairs. Will followed obediently.

They mounted the stairs and strolled the corridors in silence. Geoffrey closed the door, headed straight for the brandy on the table, and poured himself a good measure. "Now son, what have you to say for yourself?"

"What do you mean, father?" Will maintained an expression of innocence, he knew his father wasn't fooled, but he enjoyed the charade.

"Bringing home a maiden of no family, no connections— no dowry I'm sure—and announcing your intention of wedding her. That is what I mean! Need I remind you of your responsibilities to the family; to the crown?"

"I am well aware of my responsibilities, father. I must say I am surprised. I would have expected such a reaction from mother." After 25 years Will was adept at manipulating his parents. They both underestimated him, and that worked to his advantage.

Geoffrey frowned thoughtfully and Will knew he had him. "Your betrothed is charming to be sure. But will she be able to fulfill the duties required of her when you are lord of this keep?"

Will remained in control of his expression as he replied. "I anticipate that she will be fully competent in *all* respects of the title of Lady DeFord." Will allowed that to sink in before continuing. "Moreen might be uneasy in a new home. I wish to have her lodged close to my chambers. I'm sure mother will have her comfortably installed in the other wing."

"I quite understand your wishes. She is positively ravishing." He sipped his port reflectively. "I would imagine your mother will settle her in the third suite of rooms on the south end." That was where Constance always lodged unwelcome guests. It was the smallest suite in the keep. "What she does not know is that there is a hidden passage from that bed-chamber to your own."

Will looked surprised. "I didn't even know that!"

Geoffrey smiled. "This place has its secrets. I have shown you many, but *I* do not know all of them yet. You may go." He waved his hand in dismissal.

Will started toward the door but his father's voice stopped him. "And don't worry about your mother. I will handle her."

Will grinned. Things were going exactly as planned. But as soon as the door closed behind him, he had to extinguish his pleased look, for he saw his mother coming down the corridor. He put on his best expression of long-suffering vexation and readied himself for yet another grand performance.

"How now, my son? What has put you in such a humor?" She played the concerned mother so well one might even have believed she meant it.

Will added a touch of a pout. He offered his mother his arm and they began to walk out of Geoffrey's hearing distance. "I've just been speaking with father."

"Well that's enough to put anyone out of sorts. What has he done to upset you?" She had a few ideas. Her husband was less predictable than she, but she was far more adaptable. Constance DeFord could twist any situation to her advantage.

"He is in a huff over my choice of bride. Talking about dowries, connections, responsibility to the family—that sort of thing." Will seemed thoughtful.

"Darling, you know my opinion of your father's family. And money does not concern me either. But are you certain this is the girl for you?" Will made as if to protest, so she continued. "I know. She is a lovely, charming girl. I have grown quite fond of her already. But are you sure about her? Are you certain she will be happy here? This is a wretched family to bring such a sweet, unspoiled girl into."

Will respected his mother's tactics but he was about to astonish her. That truth thing had worked so well before, and truth was the one thing neither of his parents would expect, or be able to combat. "I am certain that I cannot live without her! She is the most adorable creature I have ever known. Mother, she is alone in the world. Her parents were killed so that she would be defenseless. If I had not overheard the plot at the tavern and gone to her..." he left the thought unfinished. "I won't leave her vulnerable to such machinations. I can protect her. I love her." It wasn't strictly a lie. He might love her. He just didn't know yet. "A more pure and perfect girl could never exist. I must have her!"

"And so you shall, my son." She smiled and patted his cheek affectionately. "Do not worry about your father. I'll deal with him. Now off to bed with you."

Will no longer needed to hide his delight. He bid his mother goodnight and went whistling down the corridor.

Constance started toward her own chambers. Pure and perfect—she meditated on that phrase as she ambled. By the time she had reached her suite she had formed her plan. Her lady-in-waiting had anticipated a discussion and had arrived ahead of her mistress. "Is Miss Kelly settled?"

"Yes milady. I saw to it that all of your instructions were carried out." Gertrude had been her lady-in-waiting since she was Constance Richelieu, before her marriage to Geoffrey. She was the only friend Constance truly had. There were others in the household who would do her bidding and swore their loyalty, but Gertrude was the only person she really trusted. Constance sat at the vanity and Gertrude began to brush out her fiery locks.

"Gertrude. You are to continue to attend Miss Kelly. My son thinks she's some sort of angel—the essence of perfection. Keep your eyes and ears open. Find something we can use to tarnish that image."

"Yes milady. She seems very sweet."

"Exactly." Constance replied. "No one is *that* sweet. There must be something, and you shall find it."

Gertrude was finished with the brushing. "I've already laid out your chemise milady."

Constance glanced toward the bed. "Not that one. The Venetian silk."

Gertrude blinked. She wasn't certain she had heard correctly. "Are you sure, milady?"

"Perfectly." Constance grinned viciously. "I'm going to pay my loving husband a visit."

In a matter of minutes she was opening the door to Geoffrey's solar. He was sitting in an ornate chair near the windows, savoring his best brandy. She entered quietly; her steps falling noiselessly on the luxurious Persian rug. She hesitated.

His voice startled her. "My darling wife." He stood and bowed mockingly. "What mission of affliction and treachery brings you to me at such a late hour? And in such fetching attire? I haven't seen so much of you in over 20 years." The Venetian silk chemise was sleeveless, form fitting, richly embroidered and rather low-cut. For a woman who had borne five children, she was holding up very well. His eyes took in the sight of her pale skin and her silken tresses set ablaze by the light of the fire. "Do you know something Constance? You look older in the firelight."

"Indeed my lord. If only the same could be said of you." She replied, unruffled.

"What's that? I don't look older?" He was confused. It was not like his wife to compliment him.

"Not merely older, but shorter as well. And gaining around the middle." The last was a lie but she had the satisfaction of seeing him glance at his waist to check. In this particular marital dynamic each victory, no matter how small, counted. She seated herself in the chair opposite his. "Won't you sit down?"

"Oh how gracious of you!" he scoffed. "Yes, I believe I will have a seat in my own solar. Now tell me, what is the purpose of your sudden manifestation?"

"I believe it is customary for married couples to discuss the events of the day." She replied innocently.

Geoffrey let out a mirthless laugh. "No, really. Tell me why you're here."

She was silent a moment. "What do you think of our son's betrothed?"

He eyed her carefully while formulating his answer. "A lovely young woman. I found her thoroughly charming."

She sniffed disdainfully. "Yes, I'd wager I know exactly what about her charmed you. You'd best stay away from her Geoffrey." He merely smiled in response. "She belongs to William."

"Surely you of all persons would scorn the idea of a woman being considered a man's property."

"Fathers, provoke not thy sons to wrath." She replied simply.

Geoffrey erupted into laughter. "How droll. The devil herself quoting the word of God."

"I'm surprised you recognized it. The Holy Scriptures do come in handy. But what makes you think the devil is a woman? It seems to me that most of the evils of this world are perpetrated by men."

"Because women are kept in their proper place. The world would be much worse if men did not rule. Ambitious females cause enough trouble when paired with weaklings who cannot govern them." He rose to refresh his drink.

She spoke to his back. "Perhaps if men were not weak, they would not need women to lead them. No matter your opinion it is certain that more perfidy is worked on this earth by bad men than by bad women."

He turned. "Come now, all this talk of good and bad is irrelevant. What care you or I for such terms? We both live by our own creed. We are much more alike than you admit."

"We are not alike!" Her eyes sparked with anger and he congratulated himself on having broken through her frosty exterior. She rose and continued: "However, we do have one common goal." She sauntered toward him until she was practically standing on his toes.

"And what is that?" He asked coolly.

"The prevention of this wedding." She let her wrapper slip from one shoulder.

"On the contrary my pet, I have no objection to our son's impending nuptials."

The room sizzled with tension—half lust; half hatred. Constance let the wrapper fall to the floor.

Chapter 5

Geoffrey's mind traveled back to the first years of their union. The marriage had come about for political reasons, but while tenderness was not part of the equation, there had been no shortage of heat between them. He knew that she had enjoyed their bed as much as he, but she would never admit it. The fact of her attraction to him only made her despise him more. She could not stand him, but there had been a time when she could not resist him either. The entire matter had been much simpler for Geoffrey: he found her enjoyable; emotion did not enter into it. He had no problem bedding someone he detested.

Once she had provided him with a son and heir he had been forbidden her favors. That was no hardship to him. Most women were easy prey to his charm, and he had not lacked for companionship. But there was something galling about not having access to one's own wife.

"Tell me you want our son to wed Moreen Kelly." Her voice jolted him back to the present. She presented a tempting picture, but he knew better.

He glanced at the pool of silk on the floor. "You dropped something."

"Answer the question." Constance snapped in irritation.

Geoffrey leveled a look of indifferent sarcasm at her. "I don't believe it was a question. But since you are being so unusually solicitous, I will tell you that I find Miss Kelly to be a happy addition to our loving family."

Constance played her high card. "Is that because of her mother?"

"What?" he snapped.

"Did you think I did not know about your former...*admiration* for her? Yes I know the whole story, my dear." There was a bite in her voice as she circled him slowly, and a hint of triumph in her eyes. "Young Geoffrey DeFord endeavored to seduce a simple peasant girl named Mary Brandt. Sadly, Mary did not return his ardor. She refused him, and chose instead to marry a free man not subject to the DeFord family's authority—a farmer by the name of Hugh Kelly." She paused for a moment, trying to gauge the effectiveness of her words. "Do you see this betrothal as some sort of second-generation fulfillment of your youthful desires?"

"Jealous, my pet?" He would not let her win this time. "She meant little enough to me. It was no hardship to replace her…nor you."

Her eyes filled with anger. "You dare to speak of me in the same vein as your whores?"

"I should think you would find it a compliment. I meant to compare you to Mary—both so virtuous and chaste. Well, chaste anyway. But you need not concern yourself, virtue holds little charm for me." There was challenge in his heated gaze.

"You waste your breath darling." She said in a venomous tone. "You shall never gain entrée to my bed."

His expression was one of boredom. "I shall never seek it. I much prefer fire to ice. Have you anything else to offer or shall I bid you goodnight?"

"Enough of this. Are you going to allow your son to marry beneath himself? A common girl with no money and no connections!"

"The boy's a DeFord—he can do whatever he pleases. I'll not try to dissuade him, and if I know you, you won't either."

Constance angrily retrieved her wrapper. "I will not have to. That girl will be gone within a fortnight."

"If you believe that then why are you here?" Geoffrey pinned her with a look of deadly conviction. "*That girl* will be your undoing. You've lost the power you once had over your son. She holds it now...and you'll never get it back."

She stormed from the room followed by the sound of his jeering laughter.

Moreen lay in bed drowsily contemplating the events of the evening. She knew she should feel terrible, but she could not help a certain measure of joy. She hoped her dear parents would understand and forgive her.

Lady DeFord had shown her some of the keep and taken her up a staircase and down a wide corridor to a set of rooms that Moreen was informed would be her own. She could hardly believe it. The whole cottage would have fit in the sitting room. She had her own solar. The bedchamber was spacious and richly decorated. There were fires laid in all three rooms. A large copper tub filled with rose-scented water was situated before the fire in the bedchamber, and a tray of food was set on a small table nearby.

She had been bathed, fed, and pampered. It was unlike anything she had ever known. Pleasant, but she hoped such treatment was merely for guests. She wasn't certain she could become accustomed to so much attention. Lady DeFord had sent her own lady-in-waiting, Gertrude, as promised. Gertrude had helped Moreen to wash her hair and brushed it after it had dried. Moreen had asked many questions and the response was always the same: "That's just the way things are."

Her borrowed chemise was made of fine linen and embroidered with delicate pink roses. She had never owned such a garment, and she thought it rather a shame that something so fine and so pretty would be worn only for sleeping.

She lay in the big, soft bed, under a goose-down comforter and drifted contentedly toward sleep until a sudden noise startled her. She was instantly wide-awake. She pulled the comforter up to her chin and tried to remain calm.

"Moreen?" William's voice whispered from the shadows.

"Will! You frightened me." She was so relieved she could have wept.

He came forward and sat on the bed next to her. "I'm sorry dearest. I didn't mean to." She looked different in the soft light cast by the glowing embers in the hearth, clad in a dainty chemise with some kind of flowers on it.

"How did you get in here?" She knew he hadn't come through the sitting room or the solar.

"There is a hidden passage between your chambers and mine." He stroked her cheek with one finger. "I couldn't stay away. Are you comfortable? Do you need anything?"

"I've never been so comfortable in my life. It's strange. Will..."

"What is it dearest?" He took one of her hands in both of his.

"I can't believe this is real. This morning everything was fine. Normal. Routine. Then my whole world collapsed. And then you were there to rescue me. And now I'm here in your home, and it's my home now." She spoke in hushed tones. She doubted anyone could here them, but she felt her words deserved the sanctity of quiet.

"You forgot the part where you struck me and threw me out." He teased.

"I can't apologize. You deserved that. But Will, I shouldn't feel so happy."

"I don't understand." What on earth was she talking about?

"I love you. I'm certain I do. And I'm happy to be here with you. But shouldn't I be more sad?" He still looked confused. "My parents died mere hours ago and I've barely thought about them. They loved me so, and were so good to me, and here I am surrounded by luxury and riches, and feeling happy about being with you."

She had begun to cry and Will did not know what to say. He had a feeling that she had shed few tears 'til now. She had been stoic when he had arrived. In the events that followed he supposed she had not had time to grieve. Everything had happened quickly and only now did she have time to think, and to feel. He gathered her in his arms and tried to think of a way to ease her pain.

"Moreen? I know that you believe in God. And so I must conclude that you also believe in heaven." She nodded against his shoulder. "I am certain your parents are in heaven. These past four years I've watched you from a distance. I've seen what good and kind people they were. Now if they are in paradise with God you needn't feel sorry for their passing." He stroked her back gently as he thought for a moment. "I've seen how much they loved you. They would want you to be happy. They would understand. As much as they loved you they could not possibly wish for you to continue in such pain."

"I know that, but I still feel so ashamed." She began to weep afresh. Her sobs tore at his heart. He decided to try something else. He brushed the tear-dampened hair from her face and kissed her soundly.

Her tears subsided instantly and she threw her arms around his neck. They remained locked in each other's arms for several minutes. Will's hands tentatively explored over the delicate chemise. Moreen merely hung on to him for dear life. He pressed her gently back into the pillows.

"Stop!" she could barely breathe, but she managed the half-hearted entreaty.

"Stop?" Will couldn't believe his ears. "Why?"

"Not yet." She pleaded.

"Why not?" *What is with this girl?*

"Not until we're married." She had that pleading puppy look.

She can't be serious! Will held his head in his hands and tried to calm down. Moreen had been through a lot. This was probably another religious thing. They would be married. He could wait, as long as he didn't have to wait very long. "Alright." He agreed. "We'll wait. I don't like it! But we'll wait."

She threw herself back into his arms. "Oh, Will! You don't know how much this means to me. Thank you!"

Her words gave him an unfamiliar feeling of warmth and contentment. This wasn't like him at all. He was either in love, or insane. "I must go, before I change my mind." He rose at once and disappeared into the shadows.

"Will!" Moreen jumped out of the bed and ran after him. She bumped into him, almost knocking them both down. Her hands found his face and she kissed him. "Goodnight."

"Goodnight, my sweet." He went deeper into the shadows, and she returned to bed.

She fell instantly into a deep and peaceful sleep.

Will did not fare quite so well. He was not much of a thinker, but tonight he couldn't seem to stop. Moreen had surprised him with that kiss. He was pleased, but astonished. His thoughts swirled back and forth between his lovely betrothed, and his vitriolic parents. He would have to be very careful about his handling of the situation. He'd been managing Geoffrey and Constance for years as a form of entertainment and never worried about being found out, but now he actually had something he would regret losing. Without Moreen he would most certainly end up like his father.

Geoffrey had everything a man could own, women aplenty, riches, leisure, power and influence, but he was miserable. So miserable in fact that he didn't even realize it.

He knew something wasn't right, but he couldn't figure what was missing. So he pretended his way through life, giving such a brilliant performance that he fooled even himself.

William didn't mind the idea of the riches and power, but those in and of themselves were not enough. He wanted to be happy. Somehow he knew that Moreen was the key to his future bliss. And he decided that he would be the key to hers. He didn't know how to be a good husband. His own sire was a pitiful example. He had only seen his sisters' husbands at their respective weddings.

One by one his sisters had taken their vows and vanished from his life. The only one he missed was Emmergene. She had been a mere eighteen months older than Will, and for the longest time they had been inseparable.

From the age of eight Will had not been allowed to play with his sisters. While they were instructed in all things domestic, his education was much farther reaching. In addition to being brought up to be lord of the keep, Will was raised to be a warrior. As heir to the family riches he was treated with a measure of importance that his sisters never received. Geoffrey told him that girls were inferior, and his sisters unworthy of his time. Will felt the injustice of the situation but had been powerless to change it.

At the age of twenty-two Emmergene had been sold in marriage to a Comte in France. Since that day four years ago she had never visited, never written. Will hoped that she was well and happy. He rather doubted it given his father's hand in the marriage, but he hoped just the same.

He was determined to ensure his own bride's happiness. She would have everything she desired and more. He would be generous to a fault; lavishing her with gifts of clothes, jewels, trinkets...*What else could she want?* He searched his mind. Although certain she would be pleased with the items he already planned to bestow upon her, he sensed that Moreen would hold them less important than most women of his acquaintance. She had a caring and sweetness about her that was unlike anything he had known.

A child! Of course she would want children. And what a mother she would make: kind and patient, loving and forgiving; unlike his own mother who pretended her affection as a means to control him.

Until then he had not thought about having children. But at that moment it became inescapably clear that he would be a father to someone, someday. That thought frightened him more than anything he could recall. He knew less about being a good father than he did about being a good husband. His friends' fathers were all very much like his own. He had seen other fathers in the village, but never paid them much notice. He suddenly remembered he had no experience with children. He had seen them, of course, but he had not been able to observe them up close.

Children start out as babes. His words of four years before came back to him. *"I don't understand the female obsession with babes. What are they good for...the first several years are a complete waste."* He groaned aloud and hoped that Moreen had forgotten that part of their first meeting. It wasn't that he disliked babes. It was just that he knew nothing about them other than that they were small and had to have everything done for them. *Not so very different from the nobility in the latter respect.*

His thoughts turned to his unborn children. Would they look like Moreen, or like him? Would they have her sweet temper, or his hot-headedness? Would they be boys or girls, or both? After years of hearing how inferior girls were, he wasn't sure how he would handle having a daughter. But he imagined that a smaller version of Moreen might be a quite charming addition to his life. A son would be different. He could not set a good example for his son. Moreen would be the standard to which any daughters would hold themselves, but a boy would look to him for guidance. Will could not bear the thought of his son feeling about him the way he felt about his father.

Well there's no use worrying about it now. He rolled over for the twelfth time and attempted once more to sleep. When he finally succumbed, he dreamed of a raging storm that left a mighty oak split in twain—one half green and flourishing; the other burned black.

Chapter 6

Moreen awoke next morning to the sunshine streaming into her bedchamber. She stretched her arms above her head and tried to determine the hour. Just then a young girl entered the room with a tray.

"Oh! Beg pardon milady! I didn't know you were still abed." The girl prepared to leave.

"Please don't go. I'm almost up anyway." Moreen smiled at the girl and she smiled back. "What is your name?"

"Agnes, milady." She set the tray on the table near the fireplace. "I'll be attending you this morning, as Gertrude is busy with Lady DeFord. If there's anything you need just say the word."

Moreen took an instant liking to her. She was pretty, with shining black hair, a ready smile and green eyes that sparkled. Moreen felt that she would find a true friend in Agnes.

The ensuing day was filled with activity. There was much discussion as to when the wedding would take place. Will was impatient. Moreen was concerned about the impropriety of having her wedding so soon after the funeral mass for her parents, which would be conducted as soon as the priest arrived. Constance, in an attempt to forestall the event indefinitely, took up Moreen's argument. Will would not wait any longer than he had to, and reasoned that his bride should have some joy after such tragedy. Geoffrey, who loved any reason to carouse, insisted that Will was right to be so thoughtful of his bride. Constance could not argue that point so instead she campaigned for a proper celebration, which of course would take at least several weeks to plan. Will protested that such a delay would be unacceptable. Moreen interjected that she would prefer a small celebration.

There were several minutes more of discussion during which everyone claimed concern for Moreen as their motivation, but she was beginning to wonder if that was really the case. She was saved the frustration of trying to please everyone when Geoffrey settled the matter by informing them that he had already sent for a priest to perform both the memorial and the wedding.

The wedding preparations began in haste. While Constance was displeased about not being able to postpone it, she took comfort in the fact that few people would be in attendance. Still she had to give the appearance of happiness and helpfulness. If she could not prevent her son's marrying this girl, she could at least see that the child was decently attired.

The village seamstress was sent for. Moreen was measured and examined and felt very much like a prize goose on display. She protested the cost of so much clothing. She felt that the money would be better spent helping people. Constance covered her irritation with an expression of soothing motherliness. "Do not think of it that way dear. You are marrying William DeFord. You will be the lady of Thornhill someday. People will expect you to dress a certain way. You would not want people to speak ill of William and say that he cannot keep his wife properly attired, would you?"

"Of course not." Moreen thought for a moment. "Could we perhaps reduce the number of gowns and give the difference to the poor?"

Constance was getting to truly dislike Moreen. "Think of it this way, dear: the money we pay the seamstress helps her to continue her work and pay other women in the village to help her; they use those wages to feed their families. It would be wrong to deprive them of what little income they have."

After that Moreen was silent and the planning of her wedding apparel and wardrobe continued without interruption.

Moreen's days were filled with discussions of clothing, food for the wedding feast, and learning about the keep. Her head fairly spun from all the new information. She sensed that Lady DeFord grew weary of her questions. There was so much she didn't know, and so much to do. Gertrude still attended her every night. She was becoming accustomed to the attentions, and began to relax. Gertrude seemed to be warming up to her. She even asked Moreen questions from time to time. Still Moreen was glad when Gertrude took her leave every night. Much as she appreciated the wonder of her new life, it made her somewhat uneasy.

She didn't see much of Will. He was always busy with one thing or another. There were whole days she didn't see him from sunrise to sunset. But every night he came to her. It was the best part of her day. In his arms she didn't think of everything she did wrong and everything she didn't know, she didn't feel awkward or ignorant, all she felt was loved. Whether he really loved her or not did not matter. He made her feel special and beautiful, and wanted.

The days and nights passed in much the same way for nearly a week and when the priest arrived everything was ready. That night a funeral mass was said for Hugh and Mary Kelly. Nearly the whole village attended. Rupert Andin was noticeably absent. Moreen decided against wearing one of her new gowns, and instead wore the very dress she had been wearing the day they died. The mass was held in the village church. The keep had a chapel, but it had not been used in more than two generations.

Will was at Moreen's side the entire time. He did not know the mass, but he had studied Latin and was able to fake his way through. Only Moreen knew the difference, and she didn't mind. It was enough for her that he was there and willing to pretend for her sake. She shed silent tears for her mother and father and wordlessly bid them farewell.

Anna and Thomas came up to them after the mass was ended, the children in tow. Eleanor rushed to Moreen, who swooped her up in a giant hug. They were all invited to attend the wedding mass, which would take place the next morning, and they promised to do so. Moreen wished them to be present for the feast as well, but Thomas would not commit to a definitive answer. Finally goodbyes were said and everyone went home their separate ways.

That evening when Will arrived in Moreen's bedchamber she was solemn.

"You haven't changed your mind?" Will asked.

"No, of course not!" She replied readily. "It's just...I wish they could be here tomorrow. Please don't worry Will. I will be well in the morning. I promise." She smiled, not as brightly as he would have liked but it was something.

Will stood as if to leave. "Sleep well, my love."

"Aren't you going to kiss me goodnight?" She looked genuinely disappointed. He smiled indulgently and placed one gentle kiss on her forehead. As he began to pull away, Moreen grabbed his tunic with both hands and pulled him to her. He hadn't expected her to protest quite so forcefully. Nor did he expect her begging him not to stop.

"You are the one who insisted we wait, darling." He reminded her.

"Oh Will," she pleaded, "the wedding is tomorrow. We're almost married. Isn't that close enough?"

He got up and started for the hidden door. "You'll thank me tomorrow, dearest."

She was pouting. "I'll curse you tonight."

"You wouldn't be the first person to do that. Farewell Miss Kelly, and may you have sweet dreams of me." With that he disappeared into the shadows as he did every night.

He laughed quietly to himself as he made his way back to his own chambers. He was sorry to leave Moreen so disappointed. Waiting had been killing him. But he was certain she would be much happier this way. She took this religious stuff so seriously. She might never have forgiven herself if he had acquiesced, and she might never have forgiven him. He had plenty in his past and current character to garner her disapproval without adding anything more to it. As it was, there would be no guilt or regret to interfere with their joy.

The day dawned clear and bright. It was late in May and summer was just beginning to spice the air with a hint of her sultry sweetness. No clouds marred the brilliant cerulean sky. The countryside was a sea of wildflowers dancing in a cool breeze that felt chill at early morning, but would be welcome by the heat of midday.

Moreen arose early, too nervous to sleep any longer. Agnes had anticipated her restiveness and poor appetite, and brought a small tray of bread, jam, and tea. Moreen had barely enough time to consume those few morsels before Gertrude and Lady DeFord appeared. From that point on she was too busy to be nervous. Her chambers were a flurry of activity. Moreen was bathed in scented water and carefully dressed. Great pains were taken to dress her hair in a style that was both elegant and simple: a single braid wreathed her head to form a coronet. The effect was angelic.

Constance felt a pang of jealousy remembering her younger days, and beauty she considered long-since faded. She knew she was an exceptionally appealing woman, but she was no longer the irresistible enchantress she had once been. Years of bitterness, anger and greed had stolen her radiance. What charm she still possessed was mere artifice. The only passion she had left was her struggle for control—

and this wedding put a chink in her carefully laid plans. She saw Moreen wipe at a tear. "Why what's the matter child?"

"I wish my mother was here." Moreen replied sadly.

"So do I dear." *It would have been wonderful to see Geoffrey miserably pining after her all day!*

At that very moment Geoffrey entered the room. Moreen was standing by the window, illuminated by a sunbeam. In her cloth-of-gold gown, with her halo of tresses, she looked every inch an angel.

"What are you doing here?" Constance asked, already irked by his presence.

"I have brought a gift for our new daughter." He handed a small package to Moreen. She gasped when she opened it, as did Constance. Moreen drew out an ornate necklace—glittering diamonds and sapphires set in luminous gold. "It has been in the DeFord family for centuries. I want you to have it."

"Oh, I couldn't! It's too fine!"

"Nonsense. I insist. My son's bride shall be the finest sight ever beheld. Turn around, my dear." As Geoffrey fastened the necklace Constance stormed out of the room.

"Have I done something to upset Lady DeFord?" Moreen asked quietly.

Geoffrey decided that half-truth would serve best. "It is not easy for her seeing her only son wed. She feels she is losing him, and even losing him to someone so sweet as you are is difficult. Don't worry about her. She'll be fine. Now let's have a look at you." She turned. "Ah! You look beautiful, Moreen. You do me proud."

She smiled gratefully. "Thank you my lord. May I ask something of you?"

"Certainly my dear."

"Since my father—God rest his soul—cannot hand me to William, would you?"

Geoffrey was stunned. That hadn't occurred to him. He should have thought of it himself. "I would be honored."

She took his arm and together they walked to the entrance hall where Will was waiting impatiently. At the foot of the grand staircase they paused as Will stepped forward. Geoffrey, taking Will's right hand and Moreen's left, uttered the traditional words: "I give this maid into your keeping." And placed Moreen's hand over Will's.

Thus they began the walk to the village church. It was a silent trek as the custom was that the bride and groom should not speak to one another on the wedding day until they said their vows. But there were many secretive glances exchanged. Will even dared to flash a smile at his bride. Luckily no one noticed—such a display would have been considered contrary to the solemnity of the occasion. Constance had recovered sufficiently, and was in the proper place at her husband's side. Thomas, Anna, and the children were there as promised, as well as a few other of Moreen's parents' friends.

The procession halted at the church doors, where the priest stood ready to conduct the wedding ceremony. He began with a short blessing of those assembled, then inquired of the couple if they had freely consented to be wed. The response being affirmative, the guests present were asked to proclaim any impediment to the marriage. Geoffrey shot a warning glance at Constance, but he needn't have worried, she knew that interrupting this wedding would not serve her cause. As there was no objection from the crowd, the priest asked if there were any rings to be blessed. Will produced two rings—one a thick and ornately carved gold band, the other smaller and delicate with brilliant sapphires set around its circumference.

The clergyman intoned in Latin briefly and then handed the rings to each of them. Will would go first. "With this ring I plight thee my troth, and take thee as my wife 'til death depart us." He slipped the ring on the fourth finger of her right hand. Then Moreen took his right hand. "With this ring I plight thee my troth, and take thee as my husband 'til death depart us." She slowly slid the ring to rest at the base of his finger.

They were so caught up in each other's eyes that they nearly forgot the next part of the ceremony. Will reached up to unfasten Moreen's braid and unwound it, then separated the strands gently. This was to symbolize the husband's authority over the wife. Some Frandians believed that if a man's fingers tangled in his bride's hair it was a sign from God that the marriage should not go forward. Fortunately for William and Moreen no such tangling occurred. One final blessing and a chaste kiss, and the ceremony was complete. There was a moment of quiet applause and then the assemblage streamed through the church doors for the mass.

Afterwards everyone proceeded to Thornhill for the wedding feast, with the exception of the Sinclairs. Thomas had wisely realized that the children would be overwhelmed by the experience and discontented with their meager existence thereafter. Instead he and Anna had wished Moreen happy at the church.

In spite of herself Constance had prepared an exquisite banquet. Garlands of greenery and flowers draped every crossbeam in the great hall. Minstrels, musicians, and players had been hired for the occasion.

Trestle tables groaned under the weight of a prodigious amount of food. There were roast suckling pigs; racks of lamb; pheasants; quails; partridges; turtledoves; chickens stuffed with mushrooms and rice; conies baked in a white wine and onion cream sauce; fifty beef and gravy pies, their fragrant juices bubbling up through golden crusts; sweet breads with raisins and currants; spiced cakes; tarts made of strawberries and gooseberries in cream; a green salad with violets; mountains of mashed turnips dripping with butter; corn pudding with honey; Seville oranges; fried apple fritters; sugared almonds; marzipan flowers; and a host of other tantalizing concoctions, all complimented by the finest Burgundy to be had.

Moreen had thought her meals at Thornhill exquisite before. It was all quite different from her usual simple fare. The wedding feast rendered her speechless. She'd had no idea that such an extravagance of food existed in the world.

Will was well pleased with the banquet. Constance prided herself on the fact that while certain important persons were thankfully absent from the celebration, none of those in attendance would be able to guess at her displeasure in her son's marriage. Geoffrey's pride was fully satisfied—he enjoyed his food, his wine, and the ability to claim the right of host for such an extraordinary feast.

There were toasts to the health and happiness of the bride and groom, as well as to their future fertility. The minstrels sang ballads, and recited epic poems. The players performed many sketches and, to the delight of all in attendance, a few tumbling passes as well. Halfway through the celebration some of the tables were removed to make room for dancing. The troupe of musicians played with such precision and skill that even Constance joined in a dance. Geoffrey—pleased by the events of the day, the lavishness of the feast, and plenty of wine—invited all of the servants to make merry with the assembly.

The festivities lasted all throughout the day and well into the night. The guests who lingered imbibed greatly and became somewhat noisome. There was a great deal of cheering and several raucous comments shouted when Will and Moreen retired for the night. Innocent though she was, Moreen had some knowledge of the activities to which the bolder guests referred, and blushed furiously at their remarks.

Moreen's pulse pounded in her ears as Will led her to his chambers. Gertrude would not be attending her tonight. She would have no need of a lady-in-waiting; she would be assisted by her husband. Husband—an odd word, at once exciting and soothing. She supposed Will was having similar thoughts about the word wife. She was wrong. The only words he was thinking about were the words they would whisper to each other all night long.

Some time later, as Will and Moreen lay blissfully asleep in each other's arms, Constance once again appeared in Geoffrey's solar. There was no pretense of seduction this time. Both were weary after a long day of reveling.

"Why are you here this time? Surely not to prevent the wedding." Geoffrey smirked as he poured his wife a bit of brandy.

She accepted the drink. "No."

Geoffrey indicated the chair she had occupied the last time she had condescended to grace him with her presence and she seated herself wordlessly. He took the opposite chair and pondered, watching his wife carefully. He was having trouble gauging her mood. She was generally easy to read. Although Constance was a master at hiding her true feelings Geoffrey had figured her out rather early in the marriage, and she him. They continued with pretense out of tradition and mutual love of the game. But she looked different tonight—much less guarded, and rather subdued. If any vestige of his previous feelings for her (limited though they were) had remained, he would have been concerned. "What is it Constance?" He almost sounded as if he gave a damn about the answer.

"Our youngest child is wed." She stared into her brandy.

"Yes. What of it?"

She glanced up at him. "Does it ever occur to you that we are growing old, Geoffrey?" He did not reply. "All our children are grown. Think how many of our friends and enemies we've outlived. Wars, famine, the plague...how did we manage to live so long?"

He set down his drink. "Because we are fighters, you and I. We've fought the world, fought each other, fought God and the Devil both. And we'll keep fighting to the very end."

"But what are we fighting for?" She questioned. "Do you know? I don't."

"The thrill of battle. The pride of victory. Or perhaps it's merely that we don't know any other way to live." He took up his brandy again.

"I feel as if the fight has gone out of me." She admitted sadly.

"You? Never! Truly my dear, you are as tempestuous as ever. This sudden melancholia is only the calm at the center of a raging storm."

She met his gaze through a slight sheen of tears. For once his bright blue eyes held no mocking gleam. There passed between them a moment of tenderness, all the more precious for its brevity. Neither of them would ever admit that moment's importance, but each would carry it buried deeply in their hearts just as many of us foolishly seek to conceal that which we consider our greatest treasure.

"Now my pet..." Geoffrey broke the spell. "I have some news that will lift your spirits." He paused to allow her a moment to consider what it could be. "There are rumors that there is to be a change of some import in Vallenburg."

"What? Our beloved king is replacing his queen?"

"Ah...replacement is the thing, but think bigger and with a bit more bloodshed."

She smiled. "A revolution!"

Chapter 7

"Precisely what we need." Geoffrey grinned.

Constance looked a bit surprised. "I was under the impression that you supported our king."

He rose to refresh his drink. "You misunderstand me, my dear. I swore an oath to the crown, and you know what a loyal creature I am." He grinned wickedly. "But things have been bloody boring in this kingdom far too long. I've been dying to get back into my armor."

She laughed softly. "And what traitor dares covet the throne of Gustave the Great? Is it anyone we know?"

"No one we know. I have heard... Of course one cannot be certain. You know how rumors fly." Geoffrey made a great show of savoring his brandy.

"Are you going to tell me who it is, or must I guess?" A list of possibilities ran through her mind.

"Phillip of Arbandeur."

Surprise registered on her face. "Phillip the bastard?"

"Now my dear, bastardy is a matter of perspective. There have always been rumors about Gustave's legitimacy. According to what I've heard, there may be something to it. Phillip claims to have evidence that our beloved late king Magnus already had a wife when he wed Lady Rowena."

"How does that change the circumstances of Phillip's birth?"

Geoffrey clucked in mock reproach. "Now, now my pet. Let me finish. It seems that Magnus married Phillip's mother. You see by the time Magnus and Katarina were wed, his first wife had died. The union with Rowena was not of any concern because it was never valid to begin with. It seems that in addition to being already wed, Magnus signed someone else's name on the royal marriage record."

"Hmm. If Phillip can prove it, he'll have the support of the church." Constance mused. "Gustave won't like that."

"I highly doubt he'll relish being proclaimed a bastard either." Geoffrey added.

"It should prove to be a most interesting summer." Constance smiled at her husband. "And have you decided on which side of the fence you will reside, my lord?"

"Not as yet." He admitted. "But I am leaning toward our current monarch. If the revolution should prove unsuccessful, I'd prefer to be on Gustave's good side."

"Are you certain that he has one?"

"Yes. It's slightly less malicious than his bad side. He is no fool. I'm afraid that this particular war cannot be played both ways." Geoffrey looked thoughtful, his brow furrowed.

"And if Phillip should prevail? What then?" She asked pointedly.

"It should not be difficult to convince him that my allegiance to 'Gustave the Grim' was purely for reasons of self-preservation. Then I shall pledge fealty ever so humbly to the new king."

"You? Humble?" Constance looked askance. "This I must see." She raised her glass. "To a mighty victory for Phillip of Arbandeur!"

Geoffrey lifted his own glass. "For our king."

She smiled. "Yes, for our king—whoever he may be."

Next morning Moreen awoke to find her new husband watching her. "So it wasn't a dream." She said with a sleepy smile.

"No. It wasn't." He pulled her close and breathed in the scent of her hair. "No more dreams from now on."

"Will," she protested gently, "I don't believe you can just proclaim something like that."

"Why not, love? I have no more need for them. What dream could ever compare to you?" He pulled her even closer and into a passionate kiss. Then there was a knock on the door. Will groaned in frustration. "What do you want?" He shouted angrily.

A page called out from the other side. "Lord St. Robert is here to see you, Master Will. He said to send for you at once."

Will sat up abruptly, as did Moreen. "Who is that, Will?"

"One of my friends. He'll likely only be here a few hours. I'd better go down." He kissed her soundly again and began to dress. Moreen lay back against the pillows. "What? What are you staring at?"

"My handsome husband." Her brilliant smile lit up his whole world. He crossed back to the bed and scooped her up in his arms. She giggled. "Will! Put me down and go welcome your friend. I must dress."

"You're right. You look far too fetching in that coverlet." He kissed her once more before departing.

Down in the great hall Stanley stood surveying remaining evidence of the previous day's celebration, and sipping some ale that one of the servants had brought.

"Stan! What are you doing here?" Will bounded into the room with a smile.

"I heard that my friend William had taken a bride. I thought it odd that I did not receive an invitation and so I determined that the only way to be sure of the facts was to come here and ask you in person." He gazed around pointedly. "But I see there's no need for that."

"Don't be put out Stan. It was all very sudden." Stan continued to feign hurt until Will added. "I'll make it up by sending you a case of father's best brandy."

"Sending? Why can't I just take it with me when I go?" Stanley loved brandy and didn't want to have to wait for it.

"Because that way if father discovers it missing he won't connect it with your visit. He'll think it was one of the servants."

Stan smiled. "An excellent idea. I have always had a great appreciation for your intellect Will. Now what about this wife of yours? Is it anyone I know?"

While Will was contemplating how to answer, Moreen appeared in the hall. She swept toward the "gentlemen" with a winsome smile that disintegrated when she recognized the man standing next to her husband. She stared in disbelief. Will looked distinctly uncomfortable. "Well Stan, may I present my wife Moreen? Moreen, dearest, this is Stanley St. Robert."

Stan stepped forward and bowed over Moreen's hand. "It is truly a great pleasure to meet you my lady. I must confess that when I heard that Will had married I was surprised. I simply had to meet the lady who could tame his heart."

At this point Moreen rather doubted that her husband possessed a heart. She was furious but managed to coolly reply. "How do you do?" Without breaking the fiery glance she was shooting at Will she continued. "Would you excuse us, my lord? There is a matter of some import I must discuss with my husband."

Stan agreed graciously and went off on the pretext of paying his respects to the Lord and Lady of Thornhill, and wondering what on earth was going on.

Moreen wasted no time with her husband. "How could you?!"

"What is it you think I've done?" Will was on the defensive already.

"It's not what you've done. It's what you haven't done." She clarified. "How could you marry me without telling me your connection to that…"

"Miscreant?" He supplied. Her venomous look made him instantly wish he hadn't remembered her first description of his friends. "I didn't see any harm in it."

"Of course not. How could you? You aren't the one who was accosted in the forest and scared half to death."

"They wouldn't have actually hurt you." He said knowing it wasn't completely true.

"Wouldn't they?" She pinned him with a look that made him feel transparent as window glass. "You promised you would never lie to me again."

"Alright, they might have. But they didn't, did they? And if they hadn't trapped you that night I never would have met you. I did not deliberately set out to keep it from you. It didn't even enter my mind—all I could think about was making you my wife."

The steel in her eyes melted. "Oh Will. When I saw him there I was right back in that forest, 14 years old again. I felt just as scared as I had then."

He gathered her in his arms. "Dearest, you know I would never let anyone hurt you. Stan is my best friend. He knows what I'm capable of, and I will make it quite clear to him not to offend my bride. You have nothing to fear from him."

Another thought suddenly occurred to Moreen. "What about the others?"

Will was puzzled. "What others?"

"The others in the forest that night? Are they your *friends* as well?"

"They were." He replied.

"But not anymore?" He nodded and she asked, "What happened?"

"They were killed two years ago." She looked curious so he continued. "They went out hunting together, as they always did. But that time they got separated while following stags. Each must have thought he heard his prey and loosed his arrow. They shot each other."

"That's terrible, even for them." Moreen murmured. "Their mother must have been devastated."

"Not really. She'd been expecting them to kill each other for years. She was just glad they hadn't done it in the keep." His eyes twinkled.

Moreen laughed. "Can you never be serious?"

"Only about this." He said as he lowered his mouth to hers.

They were interrupted by the sound of Geoffrey clearing his throat and looked up to find him staring at them rather pointedly. "Young St. Robert is sitting in my solar, William. Kindly remove him." Will acquiesced and Geoffrey called after him. "And keep him away from my brandy!" Turning his attention to Moreen, he seemed to be concerned. "Are you all right?"

"Yes, my lord. I was a bit startled to learn of Will's association with...Stanley, was it?" He nodded. "I had met him before under less than amiable circumstances."

"I'm not surprised. That one is a no account. Smart lad, but too undisciplined to amount to much."

"Oh surely there is hope for him yet." She exclaimed, unable to think of giving up on someone entirely.

"Certainly." Geoffrey replied. "He is young, but although it is possible, I don't think him likely to change. Hope misplaced can be a dangerous thing, Moreen. Well, I have some business to attend to." He excused himself gracefully and left Moreen to ponder his warning.

She had never thought that hope could be misplaced. She had been taught to love everyone, and with a few exceptions, she thought she had been doing quite well. Had not Saint Paul himself written that love bears all things, believes all things, hopes all things...? How then could it be wrong to hope for the betterment of someone with such potential as Stanley St. Robert had? If he was truly intelligent, as Lord DeFord had suggested, then he might be an excellent candidate for amendment. All that would be necessary would be to demonstrate that change was needed.

As Moreen continued to ponder the reformation of Stanley St. Robert, Stanley himself quizzed his friend as to his odd reception.

"What is going on here? Did you and your bride have a disagreement of some sort? She's lovely but she seemed rather put out with you. And I get the feeling she doesn't like me. Did I spill wine on her gown at a feast years ago?"

"No Stan. I'm afraid it's not that trivial." Will stared into the rug.

"Since when do women consider gowns to be trivial?" Stan was confounded, and Will was not helping to solve the mystery.

Will tore his gaze from the floor. "Stan, do you remember about...four years back...that night in the forest?"

Stan thought for a moment. "I'm afraid you'll have to be more specific."

"You, Gilbert and Jack had a girl surrounded." Will added.

"Once again, more specific."

Will filled in more of the picture. "I hit Jack with a branch and threatened to kill him if he touched her again."

"Yes, I remember that! Poor fellow couldn't see straight for three days. What of it?" He smiled at the memory, then immediately turned serious. "That was the girl?" At Will's nod he continued. "Oh. Well that explains it. I suppose she has a right to hate me then." He added nonchalantly.

"She doesn't hate you Stan. She doesn't like you. But I'm the one she's truly angry with."

"How's that?" Stan was confused again. "Aren't you the dashing young man who saved her from me?"

"Yes, but that also makes me the dashing young man who failed to inform her of our friendship. Moreen is rather particular about truth. She is very religious." He lamented.

"Hmm. Bad luck there." Stan sympathized. "But at least you won't have to worry about your wife plotting against you. That must be a relief."

"I would be more relieved if I was certain I won't be greeted with flying objects upon our next meeting. I certainly deserve it."

Stan was startled. "Will, have you developed a conscience?" Stanley was familiar with the concept of a conscience owing to his dear little sister Winifred, who had often berated him for not having one.

"No need to worry Stan. It's only where Moreen is concerned. In all other aspects I am the same man I have always been."

They both looked up as the door creaked open and Moreen stepped tentatively into the solar. "May I join you?" She asked quietly.

"Of course." Will exclaimed, puzzled by her sudden docility. He and Stanley both stood as she came toward them.

She lost no time. "Lord St. Robert I must apologize for my earlier behavior."

"Not at all my lady. I'm afraid I had quite forgotten our...first meeting. Please allow me to offer my sincerest apologies for that night's stupidity. And please, do call me Stanley." Stanley played humble rather well, with just the right amount of affability.

"Very well, Stanley. Perhaps I should thank you, for if it hadn't been for you, Will and I might never have met." Moreen conceded the point from her earlier argument with Will.

Stanley turned to address Will. "I've always told you I'm an excellent matchmaker. I do see why I was not invited to yesterday's celebration. Again, my lady, my most abject apologies." Stan was starting to over-do it a bit.

"What is past cannot be changed. If you would agree, I wish us to begin afresh." Moreen was anxious to see that that night was not brought up again, and to establish a kinship with her husband's best friend.

"Excellent!" Stan proclaimed. "I think this calls for a celebration in and of itself. More brandy Will?"

"Oh, no thank you." Moreen hurriedly declined. "I do not partake of spirits. I believe it can be harmful to the body and the soul."

Stanley smiled softly. "You sound just like my sister, Winifred. A saint if ever one did live."

Moreen smiled. "I should like very much to meet her." Stanley's smile dimmed. "Have I said something wrong, my lord?"

"Stanley." He reminded her. "Nothing wrong. Winifred died almost a year ago. She was always far too good for this earth. I suppose she is happier in heaven."

"Then you believe in heaven?" she inquired.

"Not for myself, but for my sister's sake I must believe it exists. It is too cruel to think of her in the dark earth. I much prefer to picture her with angels in a land of love and happiness."

"I cannot imagine what it's like to lose a sister. I have none, nor brothers. It is clear you love her very much."

"Winifred was the only good thing in my life—the only person who truly cared for me." Stanley could not bear unhappy thoughts for long. "Let us talk of something more pleasant. Tell me of your family."

Will spoke for Moreen. "Moreen's parents died but a week ago. She has no other family."

"Oh." Stan said simply. A moment of silence followed, during which Moreen fought back tears for her parents and Stanley's sister, Will glared at Stan, and Stan tried desperately to think of some clever remark to ease the situation.

Moreen saved them all by insisting on learning all about her husband's youth from Stanley. The remainder of the morning was spent in Stanley's somewhat exaggerated tales, with Will arguing the details, and Moreen alternating between fondly scolding her husband and bursting into laughter at the antics of his childhood.

Stanley was invited to stay to supper, and readily accepted. The rest of the day passed pleasantly. Moreen genuinely liked Stanley—he was the sort of person who is naturally agreeable, and she believed him to have a good heart. Stanley could not help but admire Moreen for her similarity to his darling sister. When Stanley left the next morning there was no tension between them—it was as if their first meeting had never occurred.

Will inwardly rejoiced that the two people he cared most about were getting along just fine. That night as he held his beloved sleeping bride in his arms he smiled. *Everything is going my way. Life is good.*

Chapter 8

Constance sat at her vanity while Gertrude brushed her hair, and scowled into the mirror. "You have been attending her for more than a week. You haven't found *anything*?"

"Nothing, my lady." Gertrude responded calmly. "The girl has nothing to hide. From all I have learned she is exactly what she seems."

"It isn't possible." She fumed. "No one is that perfect! There must be something. You simply haven't found it yet."

Gertrude was used to her mistress' moods and did not take the scolding to heart. "My lady, in all the time I have served you I have never neglected my duties. I have done everything within my power. If there were anything, I would have found it out quickly. The girl has no secrets."

Constance realized the sense of Gertrude's words, but she was not prepared to resign herself to her son's marriage just yet. "Perhaps she has some weakness that can be used to advantage. You must look carefully for any small thing that I might use to dispose of her."

"And if no such opportunity arises?" Gertrude questioned.

"Then I'll find another way to get rid of her." Constance smiled at her reflection, her gray eyes lit by an evil fire.

Some weeks later Moreen had settled into her new life. She was still uncomfortable with the privileges of wealth, but found herself much more able to help the less fortunate. She insisted on accompanying Geoffrey and Will when they visited their tenants, and made mental lists of everything that each family needed. As the men discussed crops and livestock, she conversed with the women and children. Moreen saw much need in the tenements and she was determined to use her newfound resources to ease burdens where she could.

She was soon venturing to visit the tenants on her own. She knew each child by name, and was greeted with hugs and declarations of affection at each home. Her compassion extended to all she met, in the village and on the surrounding farms.

Moreen had tried unsuccessfully to enlist Gertrude's help. Gertrude considered such work beneath her. So she turned to Agnes, who happily agreed to assist her in obtaining and distributing whatever might be needed. She found Agnes to be a pleasing companion for the visits and a great help in learning more about the keep and it's inhabitants.

Her charitable activities were limited to one day each week. The rest of her time was spent in learning to be a proper noblewoman, which aside from supervising the household, basically consisted in doing nothing all day long. Constance was short with her at times, but tried to be understanding. Moreen was appreciative of her mother-in-law's patience in teaching her, she knew she must seem very ignorant, and she tried her best at all times. God had gifted Moreen with an acute mind, which enabled her to learn quickly and do well at almost everything. Constance found that trait both delightful and irritating—it made her work much simpler, but she was running out of ways with which to find fault.

Moreen found that although little was expected of her with regard to practical activity, she could fill the hours with pastimes that were both enjoyable and useful. Her needlepoint skills were often used to make gifts for the wives or children of the tenants. Reading was an excellent way to learn new things. She was very careful with the precious manuscripts so as not to crease the delicate pages. One afternoon she was happily immersed in one such treasure when Agnes arrived.

"You're wanted in the lord's solar, milady,"

She grimaced. "Agnes, how many times have I asked you to call me Moreen?"

"I'm sorry milady." Agnes half-apologized. "You're wanted in the Lord's solar *Moreen*. Master Will and Lady DeFord too. I hear there's a grand surprise." Her eyes sparkled with excitement as she helped Moreen smooth out the wrinkles in her gown.

By the time she arrived in the solar the others had already assembled. Moreen, Constance, and Will stood silently while Geoffrey stared at the piece of parchment in his hand. After a moment, he seemed to remember his purpose in summoning his family. He cut straight to the matter. "We've been invited to King Gustave's court for a celebration. We leave for Vallenburg within the week."

Various reactions abounded. Constance was thrilled, there would be balls and gaiety such as she had not seen in many years. Moreen was both excited and nervous, afraid of making a mistake and embarrassing her husband. Will seemed not to care much. He kept his expression carefully indecipherable. Geoffrey had smiled, but somewhat distractedly, as he told them the news.

"Come Moreen!" Constance latched onto her. "We've a million things to see to." She was pulled from the room before she had a chance to protest.

After a moment Will spoke. "This celebration is a sham." He observed.

"Very astute, son. A chance for Gustave to examine his subjects at close range, to look for any signs of disloyalty." Geoffrey clarified, then added: "To see how we all interact with him, and with each other. We must be very careful."

"I have nothing to worry about. You are the one with the title." Will crossed his arms and leaned nonchalantly against the large table. At Geoffrey's dark look he continued. "Don't worry, father. I shall be on my best behavior."

"Yes, that is what concerns me. Then again, perhaps you will conduct yourself better this time. After all, you would not wish to shame your lovely bride."

Will did not appreciate that comment, mainly because he hadn't seen it coming. The thought of bringing any shame to Moreen distressed him. He was certain he could not bear to see disappointment in her eyes. Rather than allow Geoffrey the advantage of the moment, he repositioned the pressure in the conversation. "Which side of the war are you planning to take?"

Geoffrey was surprised. "I was unaware that you had any notion of the upcoming hostilities. As you can imagine, I am weighing all factors very carefully." He rose to pour himself a drink of his beloved brandy, then indicated that Will should join him in one of the two chairs near the windows. "It's a dangerous business, war. There is a fine line between revolution and insurrection. We've done well under Gustave's rule. And yet...there could be a great deal of wealth, and power, to be gained by supporting another."

"There is also a great deal to lose." Will observed.

"I am well aware of the risks, but I am far too clever to be caught. Gustave's growing distrust of everyone is a nuisance. So much time spent easing his anxieties leaves substantially less for business. Our income has dropped in the last year." The decline was hardly noticeable given the exorbitant riches the DeFord family had amassed throughout the centuries and their increasing solvency, but Geoffrey had learned greed at an early age and was certain there could never be such a thing as too much money. "What would you do, William?"

Will was astonished. In twenty-five years Geoffrey had never asked his opinion on anything. He rather doubted that his thoughts would count for much. Although Geoffrey did not yet know it, he had already made up his mind. Still Will was the slightest bit flattered by the compliment. "I haven't given it much thought. It would make sense to remain allied with the king under whom we have gained so much, and it would alleviate the burden of secrecy necessary to supporting Phillip's cause. Loyalties are fleeting these days. Those who remain steadfast in their allegiance to the king will be rewarded when it's all done with. Since I rather like rewards, I would maintain fealty to Gustave. For our time at court, at the very least, that would be my course of action."

Geoffrey nodded in agreement and sipped his brandy thoughtfully. Just then Moreen called from the doorway.

"Will? Are you still here?"

"Yes. What is it?" The men stood as she entered the room.

"Forgive me for interrupting. Lady DeFord is in a great state and I cannot keep pace with her." She looked pleadingly at her husband and father-in-law. "Is it certain that Will and I must go?"

"My dear, don't you wish to see the royal court of Frandia?" Geoffrey could not imagine anyone of such formerly limited means turning down an invitation to one of the most extravagant and opulent courts in all of the world. He had thought Moreen's rustic ways quaint and charming, but now he was beginning to doubt her intelligence.

"Of course. Until recently I never would have thought I'd have the opportunity. But I won't know anyone there."

"You know me. I'll be there." Will teased her gently.

"You know what I mean Will."

She looked genuinely concerned. It had never occurred to Will that Moreen might be a shy creature. She always seemed to speak her mind easily with him. Now he saw a timid side to his fiery angel, and it only endeared her to him even more. "Stanley will be there." Moreen brightened some upon hearing this.

"I don't trust that boy." Geoffrey remarked.

Will continued. "You will meet all of the important people in the kingdom and every one of them will love you. So do not fret, my love."

Moreen didn't look convinced, but she happily accepted his kiss.

"Moreen?" Agnes called from the doorway.

Will responded angrily "You dare to presume upon such intimacy with my lady wife?"

"Will, do not scold Agnes." Moreen pleaded with her eyes. "I'm unused to being called 'milady' all the time. I asked her to call me by name."

Will could not remain angry when Moreen looked that way. He spoke gently but firmly. "It simply isn't proper. You are my wife and I will not permit anyone to address you in a manner less than you deserve."

Agnes remained frozen in the doorway as Will and Moreen silently argued with one another. Finally Geoffrey spoke. "Perhaps a compromise? Moreen is unaccustomed to being addressed formally, and we do not wish to make her uncomfortable. The title of Lady DeFord is, at the moment, being used. Moreen, I agree with William that it is improper for the servants to address you by your Christian name. Perhaps...Lady Moreen? That is somewhat informal, yet I believe it to be an acceptable alternative. What do you think William? Moreen?" He waited for their nods of approval. "And you Agnes, what do you think?"

She looked around tentatively. "I think you've found just the thing my lord. Lady Moreen sounds all right to me."

"Excellent! It's settled then." Geoffrey congratulated himself on another moment of brilliance. "Now, what was it that brought you here Agnes?"

"Oh!" Agnes remembered. "Lady Moreen, Lady DeFord wants you in her solar. I'm afraid there's no escaping her." Agnes instantly realized she had spoken the last aloud. "Oh, I'm sorry my lord. I meant no disrespect."

"Of course you did. And I don't blame you. My wife can be rather... overpowering at times. Think nothing of it." He gave her a genuine smile.

"Thank you my lord." Agnes fled quickly, before he had a chance to change his mind. Moreen followed her.

Will made as if to leave. "If there'll be nothing else, father..."

"There is one thing more." He paused to be sure Will would stay long enough to hear him. "You'd best keep a watchful eye on St. Robert around your wife."

"Stanley? He would never! He's my best friend." Will was shocked that his father would make such an accusation.

"Friends cannot always be trusted." Geoffrey looked at his son with a cynic's pity.

Will was beginning to get angry. "Moreen would never betray me!"

"Not willingly, no. Moreen would not betray anyone. But your "friend" does have a history of imposing his own will on young ladies he fancies, does he not? Don't get upset. I'm merely trying to protect you, and Moreen. You needn't obsess about it. Just keep your eyes open, Will. You may go."

Will left the room extremely troubled. *Don't get upset? How does one not get upset about something like that?* His fury at the thought of his friend betraying him was mixed with his fury at his father even thinking such a thing. In addition he was puzzled by Geoffrey's seeming concern. *When has he ever tried to protect me, or anyone else for that matter?* But he had called him Will. He had never called him that before. Even knowing his preference for the nickname, both his parents had always called him William. Something was out of place, but he couldn't decide what. He was no longer sure of whom to distrust. Stan was a good sort, but not good enough. Geoffrey on the other hand, he had never trusted. This fatherly advice was out of the ordinary. Will wanted to believe that his father actually cared about him, but he had to be careful not to allow his judgement to be swayed by the way he wanted things to be. *Every time I think I have things figured out something else changes.*

In a week's time they were on their way to the royal court in Vallenburg. It was a miserable journey in the summer heat. It rained the full three days. Geoffrey, Constance, William, and Moreen all rode in the same carriage.

Constance bemoaned Moreen's lack of wardrobe, but turned more positive on the second day when she remembered that Queen Lavinia had a history of generosity toward her guests. She would drop a subtle hint to Her Majesty about her daughter-in-law's lack of appropriate attire, and Lavinia would see to a complete wardrobe for Moreen. None of the other ladies at court would know anything other than that William DeFord's bride was receiving the Queen's particular attention. Her son's stature would be raised and his wife decently appareled with no cost or inconvenience to the family. Once she had worked out her plan she became almost pleasant company.

Geoffrey spent much of the first day attempting to start conversations. He found that no one particularly cared to converse. By the time Constance became more animated, he had given up the attempts and was silently amusing himself with his thoughts and observations. In spite of his uneasiness regarding the true purpose of the occasion, he was looking forward to the festive mood of the royal court and all that went with it—the food, the wine, and the women.

Will spent most of the journey trying to think of a way to ease Moreen's anxieties. She was unusually quiet and he sometimes saw her pulling upon her bottom lip with her teeth, a habit she was not aware she possessed. She was adorable when she was nervous, but even adorable has it's limits. He did not enjoy his feeling of helplessness. He had no doubt that once at the court his Moreen would out-shine any woman there. But he could not seem to convince her of that. In his opinion she was far too modest. He finally stopped trying to cajole her out of her fears, and settled for offering what comfort he could.

Moreen herself was more worried than anyone realized. She had never traveled beyond the village and knew nothing about court life other than the stories she had heard over the years and the tales Constance had thrown about while preparing for the trip. She was not generally concerned with the things of this earth, being more focused on matters that concerned the soul. But it became apparent to her that despite her own feelings about the social class to which she now belonged; she would have to behave as if she were one of them. Will would be judged by her. Moreen did not mind if others thought her backward or odd, but the thought that the man she loved so much might be humiliated by having her as his wife tortured her. She mentally reviewed all that she had learned in the past weeks and prayed for strength and guidance. She desperately wanted the celebration to be over-with, and at the same time wished the journey to the capital city would take longer.

By the third day everyone was weary of sitting in the carriage. Constance was irritated by Moreen's trepidation and unable to refrain from becoming the slightest bit snappish. Geoffrey was tired of all three of his companions and was ready to leap from the carriage at the first sight of the palace. Will too was impatient to arrive. He spent his time considering how best to ingratiate himself to the crown. Moreen leaned into Will and silently pleaded with God for his intervention.

Midway through the afternoon several rays of sunshine struck through the clouds, illuminating Vallenburg in the distance. The downpour continued long enough to create a brilliant rainbow that arched perfectly above the palace. Moreen took it as a sign, and began to feel much better about the weeks to come. Constance fairly beamed at the sight of the palace she had once so frequently visited, and even offered Moreen her seat for a better view. Geoffrey's mood also visibly brightened. Will had not seen the palace in many years, and tried to act as if the sight did not affect him in the least, but even he was impressed by the vision of Frandia's royal residence bathed in golden sunlight and framed by a rainbow.

Carriages were converging on the palace from all directions. Luckily Geoffrey had one of the best drivers in the kingdom; he succeeded in positioning them in front of all but three carriages. As they waited for their turn Will squeezed Moreen's hand and was pleasantly surprised when she smiled in return. A calm had settled over her and she glowed with an otherworldly serenity. *I knew she'd be fine,* he thought.

Their carriage pulled up to the grand entrance of the royal palace and each alighted to be welcomed by servants who were better dressed than most of the people in their home village. They were conducted to their respective suites of rooms, and were informed that Their Majesties would be receiving guests in the Throne Room in three hours' time. The first priority was to bathe after their miserable journey, and don fresh apparel. Constance chose to rest for the remaining time. Will and Geoffrey headed for the great hall to see who else had arrived and try to gauge the other lords' intentions.

Moreen wandered off in the direction of the gardens. She was overwhelmed by the sheer luxury of the palace. Everywhere she looked she saw marble, ivory, gold, silver, precious stones and silks in all colors. She thought the gardens would bring her back down to earth, but in the royal palace even the gardens sang of riches. The blooms were the largest she had ever seen, and in every color imaginable. In the sky there lingered a hint of the rainbow she had seen from the distance.

The sweetest birdsong she had ever heard was interrupted by the laughter of a child running amongst the rows of carefully trimmed hedges. A small boy ran into the clearing where Moreen was and slipped on the wet grass, falling right into an urn full of geraniums. Moreen rushed to him and gathered him in her arms. "Oh, you poor dear! Are you hurt?"

The boy tried to put on his bravest face and said "No."

Moreen gently wiped his tears away as she carried him to a nearby bench and settled him in her lap. "My name is Moreen. What is yours?"

"Andrew." He replied, sniffling a bit.

"Well Andrew, I am very pleased to meet you." She smiled at him.

He gave her a small smile and replied. "I'm very pleased to meet you too."

Just then a woman's voice called "Andrew! Where are you?"

"That's my nurse." he explained as he scooted off her lap and scampered off in the direction from which he had appeared.

Moreen decided she had best return to the palace. She did not want to be late for the reception.

Chapter 9

At ten minutes to six in the evening all the guests were assembled in the Throne Room. There were at least 1,000 people in the colossal room, which was part great hall and part royal display case. Fires burned in hearths all around the room's perimeter, for the heat of mid-summer could not penetrate the thick stone walls. The ceiling was decorated ornately with pressed tin plates that had been gilded and adorned with jewels. The twelve-foot walls were festooned with lavish tapestries depicting Frandian history in brilliant hues. The floor was exquisitely tiled—the best materials and workmen had been brought from all over Europe for the project and the result was a design of superior beauty and durability. Although the royal family had come from an austere line of Englishmen and Germans, over time they had developed a taste for the opulence of the Byzantine court— an influence that was readily apparent in every detail of the splendid throne room, as well as the rest of the palace.

The assembled guests were similarly resplendent. Lords and their ladies wore every color under the sun and simple jewels; as the festivities continued they would adorn themselves more ostentatiously. Even the children present were arrayed in the finest apparel.

A constant hum of voices filled the air. Everyone was whispering as loudly as they could. There was speculation as to who was in attendance, what would be worn to the balls, which members of the royal family would be present, and every other topic that the anticipation afforded. It was a gathering of persons not given to waiting for anything, yet they had no choice but to await His Majesty's pleasure, so they filled the minutes with talk that they could pretend held some import.

The trumpets sounded and the chatter ceased. It was an eerie and unnatural thing to have so many people silenced instantaneously. There was no sound as the king and queen entered the room. All present held their breath—some from awe, some from fear; many from a combination of the two.

King Gustave's flowing purple robes were trimmed in ermine. Around his neck he wore a chain on which hung a golden emblem emblazoned with the arms of his family, the only family that had ever ruled Frandia. The crown upon his head had been fashioned centuries before. A handsome man with noble features, Gustave was the image of his late father and embodied all of King Magnus' charm, if none of his abilities. This striking similarity between father and son, in both appearance and manner, was a source of confidence for those who were blind to Gustave's deficiencies, and sadness to many who were not so fortunate as to be ignorant; yet supporters and detractors alike were struck by his regal presence. Even knowing his shortcomings as they did, his subjects recognized the imposing and venerable figure he presented.

Queen Lavinia was equally stunning. Her gown matched her husband's robes and a smaller version of the crown jewels rested atop her honey-brown tresses. Her subtle beauty was untouched by years of being a sovereign's wife. Her violet eyes were clear and vibrant. She moved with all the grace one would expect of a queen. While her husband had many critics, all the citizens of Frandia respected their queen. Lavinia was quiet and gentle, but strong-minded. She wore a simple silver cross around her neck, a symbol of her deep faith; it was a stark contrast to the rich jewels in her crown.

The king and queen seated themselves in the elaborate thrones, and Gustave signaled for the reception to begin. Servants passed through the hall with drinks as the guests were herded into lines. Contrary to tradition, persons of higher importance were not given preference of position in the lines. This angered some, and amused others. Several lords could barely contain their fury while others had to stifle laughter and the angrier the slighted lords became, the harder it was for the others not to laugh.

Moreen stood quietly next to Will and tried to take in as much as she could. There was so much to see. She was glad that they would have to wait for some time before being presented to the king and queen. The talking had resumed and she heard snippets of conversations, but none of it made sense to her. She focused on the tapestries, trying to remember everything she had learned from her father about the history of their country. She saw the battles come to life in her mind. The great King Leland, mighty and victorious, seemed to smile down at her. Other scenes burst forth in her mind as well, scenes that were not so pleasant. The plague had taken nearly half of Frandia's population. A severe drought and famine a century before had caused the starvation of nearly as many.

"What is the matter?" Will's voice interrupted her thoughts.

"I was just looking at the tapestries, and thinking about all the pain and suffering in our history. I'm glad Frandia is peaceful now. I hope things stay the way they are."

Will pressed a discreet kiss to her forehead and squeezed her hand, but said nothing. She'd had to deal with so much recently. He would not upset her with rumors of war. There was, after all, a chance that it wouldn't happen. There was no need to worry her. He pointed out the chandeliers hanging from the ceiling, and told her everything he could remember about them. It was a pleasant distraction for both of them. He amused her with similar tales until they were nearly in front of Their Majesties.

Finally Geoffrey and Constance stepped forward and bowed to the royal couple. Gustave nodded appropriately and glanced behind them to where Will and Moreen stood. Geoffrey immediately introduced them. "Your Majesties, may I present my son William and his bride Moreen." They stepped forward and bowed humbly.

Gustave stood and crossed the few feet to Moreen. He took her hand and bade her rise. "You are most welcome to my court. May I ask, what was your father's name?"

"Of course, your Majesty. My father was Hugh Kelly, a farmer." She replied meekly.

"And a scholar before that. I remember him." Gustave smiled.

Moreen was stunned. "You knew my father?"

"Yes, my dear. We studied together at the monastery in Lefvelt. We were good friends, he and I. How is he?"

The now familiar pain clouded her face. "He has gone to join our Lord, your Majesty. He and my mother both."

"Forgive me child." The king was truly saddened by the news of his friend's death. "I am sorry. Your father was the best of men. And surely the best of fathers as well. Have you any brothers or sisters?"

"None your Majesty." Moreen blinked back tears. Will put a gentle hand on her arm and she managed a small smile.

King Gustave did not particularly care for the DeFords, but he saw in Moreen and William a chance for redemption in the family's future generations. The scene was not lost on Queen Lavinia. Moreen looked up straight into her eyes and saw a great deal of compassion. The silver cross had caught her attention before. Something passed between the two women, an understanding of sorts, a kinship that Moreen did not comprehend but welcomed nonetheless.

"The only child of Hugh Kelly is certainly an honored guest at my court. I hope we will see you often in the future, Moreen." With that Gustave resumed his place upon the throne.

The DeFords bowed and moved on as the next family in line stepped forward.

Constance was bubbling with pleasure, true that Moreen's favor with Gustave was an irritation, but it would make her plan that much easier. Her son had married the only child of a dear friend of the king. Certainly the queen would do everything within her power to see the girl comfortable, and bestow ample gifts upon her. And William would profit by connection.

Geoffrey was seething inside. He was infuriated to find that Hugh Kelly had bested him again, this time from beyond the grave. He had made up his mind to support Gustave fully when the revolution began, but now all bets were off. He could not stomach the idea of protecting a man who held a life-long adversary of his near and dear. He glanced at Moreen. Though calmer, her pain was still evident. She looked very much like her father, but her temper was her mother's. She reminded him so much of Mary. His fury remained but he could not bring himself to take it out on Moreen.

Will and Moreen were instantly surrounded by people eager to introduce themselves. William DeFord's mystery bride had been the subject of much speculation at court. Now in addition to making her acquaintance, people wished to benefit from her favor with His Majesty. *It is going to be a long evening,* she thought. As a group of ladies started to sweep her away, she reached for Will's arm. She was certain she would drown in a sea of expectations without him there to give her confidence. He merely gave her a smile and returned his attention to the noblemen who surrounded him.

"Oh what a darling creature you are." A petite blond gushed over Moreen. "I do see why Will was taken with you." Moreen felt her stomach clench. How many of these ladies had her husband dallied with? She was so upset she couldn't even remember their names.

Her thoughts were interrupted by a raven-haired beauty. "Everyone is wondering...however did you manage to catch him?"

"I didn't really catch him. He caught me." Moreen knew what they were asking but she didn't have the answer they wanted. She had employed no tricks to gain either his attentions or his affections.

"Oh, you're too modest."

"Please!"

"We're all dying to know."

How to answer? She thought for a moment. "I simply said no. I don't believe he'd ever heard the word before."

The blond chimed in. "Isn't that just the way with all noblemen? Anything they want."

"So you refused him. Of course, that's one of the oldest tricks. Tell a man he can't have you and he can't get enough of you. Then what happened?" Came the query from a girl with rather plain brown hair. At Moreen's questioning look she added "Oh you know, did he take you in his arms and kiss you wildly?" Moreen nodded. "Oh how romantic! And you threw your arms around him and begged him not to stop." The girl looked as if she were lost in a dream.

Moreen almost hated to shatter the girl's illusions. "No. I struck him." Everyone was stunned.

"Struck him?"

"William DeFord?"

Moreen nodded. "Yes, and I threw him out of my home. It's been so very nice talking with you but I'm afraid I must get some air."

She quickly slipped out through the first doorway she could find and wandered the halls until she discovered a gallery filled with paintings and artifacts of all kinds. Chairs and tables were grouped around the room on fine silken rugs. The room was perfectly lit and appeared to be empty—an excellent place to hide.

Moreen let her eyes roam over the portraits of Frandia's royal family throughout the generations. As she ambled around a chair she bumped into something. "Oh! I'm terribly sorry! I didn't know anyone was in here. I mean I didn't think I would be disturbing anyone. Please forgive me." Moreen was terribly embarrassed.

"Of course. Escaping the throng were you?" A lovely young girl around Moreen's age replied. Her hair shone black and wavy in the light of the numerous sconces. Moreen nodded. "Me too. I'm Allyn."

"Princess Allyn?!" Moreen dropped into a curtsey. *Wonderful, I've nearly tripped over the crown princess!*

"Yes. You're William DeFord's wife aren't you?" The princess inquired.

"Do you know my husband?" *Please say no!*

"I don't believe I've ever met him. Mother pointed you out to me earlier."

"Oh. But you weren't there for the presentation." Moreen was the slightest bit confused.

"No. I'm not to be introduced until tomorrow night." Allyn clarified. "But mother and I were in the Throne Room before. I couldn't wait. I've been away at school for so long."

"A girl in school?" Moreen was amazed. "I thought my father was the only one who believed in educating girls."

Allyn smiled. "Then we have something in common. There aren't many fathers who bother to educate their daughters. Won't you sit down? I would like some company."

Moreen took the chair opposite the princess. "I really don't know what to talk to a princess about."

"Anything. Everything!" Allyn laughed. "I don't know much about real life. Outside palaces, I mean. In my opinion my parents are much too protective of me."

"I used to think that too. I'm sure it's only because they love you." Moreen looked up at the portrait frowning above them.

"That's great-uncle Reginald." Allyn supplied. "Father tells me he was quite a prankster, though you wouldn't know it from that painting. One time when he was young he replaced the goose on the table with a live one that had been injured and was unconscious."

Moreen was confused. "How is it that no one noticed the feathers?"

"Oh! Sorry. Well in the court, and some of the very rich households, there is a custom of decorating a cooked bird with it's own feathers so that it appears to be alive. I never saw the point of it. You have to take them off again to eat it. It seems a terrible waste of time to me. Anyway, when grandfather went to carve the goose, it started squawking and flying about the hall. It would have been wonderful to have been there! Nothing ever happens here."

"Nothing?" Moreen was surprised. "Aren't there balls and ceremonies all the time?"

Allyn thought for a moment. "I suppose it does seem rather exciting to others, but when it's been your whole life it's rather dull. I know I should be grateful for all that God has blessed me with, but I can't help wishing I could do something that matters. Do you think that's wicked?" She looked truly troubled by the idea.

"Of course not. It couldn't be wicked to want your life to have purpose. But you are in a position to help so many people! Do you not see all that you could do?"

"No. I do not see it. Mother and father keep me so busy, and I'm hardly ever home. Then when I am home they hardly let me out of their sight. Every time I've suggested doing something new or different they tell me how important it is that things remain the same. I do not understand why they are so concerned." Allyn was one of those merry individuals who could not stand to be troubled for very long. "Please let's talk about something else. Tell me of your family."

"My family is gone." Moreen saw sympathy creep into her companion's eyes. "Please don't apologize. I hear too much of that. I have no brothers or sisters. There is a family I know who are like my own blood, but I have not seen them since my wedding. Will is my family now."

"I know how it is to be lonely." Allyn reached out to take Moreen's hand. "I always wanted a brother or a sister. I would have been happy with either, but I suppose God had other plans." Once again the subject had turned serious, and that was not to her highness' liking. "Tell me, how do you like my father's court?"

"It's very overwhelming. I've never seen anything like it. Of course, this is the first time I've been out of my village at all. I suppose I shall get used to it after a while." Moreen looked doubtful, but Allyn smiled and patted her hand before releasing it.

"Of course you shall. And I will help you. First we must see to your wardrobe."

"Is something wrong with my gown?"

Allyn was already planning gowns for Moreen in her mind, choosing the styles and colors. "Oh no. It's just not in fashion. At court everyone must keep up with the latest in fashion; it's an unwritten rule. I've never had to worry about it, but I wouldn't want to give any of the vipers a chance to disparage my new friend."

Moreen smiled. "Are we truly friends?"

"Well of course we are. You need not fear. They may not like me much but they wouldn't dare go against me." At Moreen's questioning look she explained. "The vipers are the women at court; not all of them of course, just the deceitful ones. I'm sure you've met some of them. They're always sweet to your face, but as soon as you turn your back they strike."

"But you're the king's daughter. Surely they wouldn't cross their own princess."

"Being the king's daughter guarantees everyone will pretend to like you but it doesn't mean they do. I can never be too careful." Allyn frowned thoughtfully.

"Is that why the king and queen protect you so?"

"No. I've always been perfectly able to handle myself. So that couldn't be it. Sometimes it feels like they are keeping something from me, but I know they wouldn't do that. It puzzles me so." She sighed. It seemed that solemn topics just wouldn't stay away.

A voice called from the doorway. "Allyn? Are you in there?"

"Yes mother." She called back.

The two girls stood as the Lavinia entered the room. She was surprised to find that her daughter was not alone. "Moreen. I did not know you were here."

Moreen curtsied while Allyn explained. "She was escaping the mob, mother."

"Allyn." Lavinia sighed. "How many times have I asked you not to refer to our subjects that way?"

"I'm sorry mother. I am trying, I just forget."

"Yes, I know dear." Lavinia was weary; not from the evening's festivities, she was accustomed to ceremonies and celebrations. Tonight she had other things on her mind. "How are your rooms Moreen? Is everything to your liking?"

"Yes your Majesty. It is beautiful."

"Splendid. I did not have a chance before to tell you how sorry I am for the loss of your mother and father. The king is greatly saddened to know of it."

"Thank you, your Majesty." Moreen bowed her head slightly.

Allyn quickly changed the subject, earning Moreen's undying thankfulness. "Mother, we were just talking about a new wardrobe for Moreen. We must put our best seamstress to work on it." She smiled at Moreen. "We'll make sure you have the latest styles in every color on God's earth. The vipers will be so jealous!"

"Allyn!" The queen reprimanded her.

Allyn had the grace to look humbled. "I'm sorry mother, but it's true. They are, only worse for real vipers have the decency to kill their prey."

Just then the door opened and Will stepped through. The door was set into an alcove so that only part of the room was visible. He bowed "Your Majesty. Have you by any chance seen my wife? I seem to have lost her."

"I'm here." Moreen and Allyn stepped into view.

"Thank goodness. I've been looking for you everywhere."

"I'm sorry Will. I had to get away. Have you met the princess?"

Allyn stepped forward. "I don't believe we have met before. I'm Allyn."

Will looked stunned. He was certain he had never seen Princess Allyn before, yet there was something about her that seemed familiar. He bowed. "Your Highness. It is an honor to meet you. I'm terribly sorry but I must steal my wife away from you. It was a very long journey and she must have her rest."

"Of course." Lavinia looked a bit relieved. "Goodnight Moreen. I look forward to seeing you tomorrow."

Moreen curtsied and Will bowed once again, then they left immediately. Will nearly pulled Moreen into the hallway.

"Will, is something the matter?" He looked odd. She didn't know what to make of his mood.

He loosened his grip on her arm and relaxed some. "No dearest. I'm just worried about you. You've had a long journey and a tiring evening. Besides, I've been waiting all night to get you alone, and I will not wait another minute." He pulled her into a passionate, searing kiss.

"How far is it to our chambers?" Her usual patience was diminishing by the second.

"Too far." He nibbled on her ear and she giggled.

"Will! You must stop that before my knees give out or you'll have to carry me the whole way."

"That can be arranged." He scooped her up in his arms and started in the direction of their chambers.

Chapter 10

A sumptuous breakfast of eggs, fried pork, berries, and honey cakes with fresh cream was served to the guests the next morning.

Moreen sat by a window enjoying her meal when there was a knock on her chamber door. "Come in please." She called.

A lady-in-waiting came through the door; her arms loaded with clothing. "Forgive me milady. I meant to be here earlier. Princess Allyn sent these things for you. I am Marguerite. I will be your lady-in-waiting during your stay." Marguerite was tall and slim, with chestnut hair and dove gray eyes; her voice held a soft French accent. She laid the pile of garments on the bed and began to separate them.

"Are you certain these are for me?" Moreen looked over the brilliantly colored gowns in awe. She had never worn anything so fine, except for her wedding gown.

"Yes. The princess said you should wear these while more suitable attire is prepared for you. May I suggest this one for today milady?" She held up a gown the color of the sky at midday.

"It's beautiful." Moreen breathed.

Marguerite helped her dress and styled her hair. In addition to the gowns Allyn had sent ribbons and jewelry to match. Moreen was the very image of a courtier but she didn't feel any less trepidation about the day to come.

"Milady?"

"Yes Marguerite?"

"When I knocked on the door earlier, you asked me to come in." Marguerite hesitated a moment before continuing. "You must not do so again. You must always see who is there before you invite them into your chambers. Most of the time

I will be here to do that for you, but when I am not…you must be careful." Moreen didn't seem to understand so she continued. "You have never been to court milady. You do not yet know who can be trusted."

Moreen knew the sense of Marguerite's words, but it saddened her to have to be cynical when she wanted to believe the best of everyone. And it added one more anxiety to her mind. "You are right of course. Thank you Marguerite."

A knock sounded at the door and Marguerite answered it.

"There's my beautiful wife!"

"Will!" She rushed into his arms. Marguerite busied herself putting away the remaining gowns and accessories.

"I thought I'd better come before the queen and princess call for you. Otherwise I wouldn't see you all day. I hear you've made an excellent impression on them. You look exquisite in that gown. Why haven't you worn it for me before?"

"I didn't have it before. Princess Allyn sent it this morning, and several others. I'm so glad you like it, Will." Her beautiful eyes beamed up at him, leaving him no choice but to kiss her.

"Well, I must go now." At Moreen's slightly petulant look he added, "The king has planned a hunting party for all the noblemen today. I shall see you again this evening, my love." One last kiss upon her forehead and he was gone.

No sooner had he left than a page arrived with a summons from the queen. Moreen followed the young boy to the queen's private solar. She thought of a dozen questions but soon found that this page was new to his duties and knew little more than she did. So she spent the rest of the walk in prayer. *Please Lord; don't let me humiliate my husband, or myself.* As soon as she entered the room she dropped into a curtsey. "Your Majesty. Your Highness."

"Oh you needn't bother with that when it is just us. Isn't that right mother?" Allyn was all smiles and didn't even wait for an answer from Lavinia. "When we are alone you shall call me Allyn, and I'll not hear one word of protestation. You look just lovely in that gown. I knew you would, it complements your eyes beautifully. Come along, we'd best get to work." She led Moreen over to the windows, which took up nearly half of an entire wall, and filled the room with sunshine. Fabric of all sorts, colors, and weights was piled high on a table. "Do you see anything you like?" Moreen stood still and looked at all the material. "I know it's a bit much, but I wasn't sure what you would want, so I just had them bring everything. You're not cross with me, are you?"

"Of course not. I'm just overwhelmed. No one has ever done anything like this for me." She was touched by Allyn's consideration. "I don't know where to begin. Up until a few weeks ago I was a farmer's daughter, and now I'm a future noblewoman."

"Future?" Allyn shook her head. "That will never do Moreen. You *are* a noblewoman now, even if your husband has yet to inherit his title. I will help you. We shall start with the basics. You must have at least 12 everyday gowns."

"So many?" Moreen wasn't certain she was up to this. "Are you certain? After all I won't need nearly as many gowns when I'm back at Thornhill. It seems a bit excessive to have you go to all that trouble for me when I'll only be here for a few weeks."

"It's no trouble at all." Allyn took her hand. "This is my personal gift to you so you must accept it without complaint, however loathsome it will be to be dressed in the finest gowns and the latest styles." Moreen smiled. "There! You see? It won't be so bad. You'll learn quickly, I am certain."

With that the three women started working slowly through piles of fabric. Moreen mostly let Lavinia and Allyn debate colors and fabrics, but she listened attentively. It was discovered that she could wear nearly any color well, and that was a great relief to her benefactors.

Lavinia excused herself graciously. "If you will pardon me girls, I must see to my guests. I shall send my personal seamstress up directly."

Allyn giggled. "Moreen, you look like a frightened bird. There is no need to worry. Madame Sonja is perfectly amiable, and a wonder with a needle and thread. You shall have the perfect gowns for every season and every occasion." She picked up a piece of dark blue fabric. "You see this wool? It's made of fine threads woven very tightly together so it's lighter than coarser wool but just as warm." She handed it to Moreen and began looking through a selection of silks.

Moreen stroked the wool and examined it thoroughly. There was a softness to it that her she had never felt before. Her mother had made all of their clothing, and coarse wool was all they could afford. Such a difference between her birth and her position now, and all of that could be told by a thread.

There was a sudden bustling outside the door and a moment later Madame Sonja breezed into the room followed by a flock of assistants. "Ah Princess Allyn, you are beautiful as ever. You vill be an angel dhis evening in your presentation gown. And dhis must be dhe lovely young lady I hear so much of. I am Sonja. Vhat is your name dear child?" She gave Moreen a motherly smile.

"Moreen Kel—DeFord. Moreen DeFord." She dropped into a curtsey.

"Oh my goodness!" Sonja was astonished. "No vun ever does dis for me. Dhank you child. But ve must get to verk or ve vill be all year about dhis. Moreen, I vill do my very best verk for you. Only de queen and de dear princess vill have finer gowns. Isn't dhat right girls?" The ladies behind her murmured their agreement.

What followed was hour after hour of measuring, debating, sketching, and conversing. Moreen found that Madame Sonja's friendly manner, combined with Allyn's high spirits, made the experience much more enjoyable than she had anticipated. Perhaps being showered with attention at a royal court would not be so intolerable after all.

Will was beginning to tire of the day's events. Hunting is only good for so long before it becomes tedious. This group made too much noise to keep from alerting their intended prey as to their approach. *Why bother?* He thought. Thus far only his father, Lord Boyd and Count DuClerque had managed kills.

The sound of galloping hooves had the entire party turning to look behind them, as Stanley rode up on his magnificent Andalusian stallion.

"Lord St. Robert." Gustave called out. "Late as usual."

Stanley dismounted and bowed with a flourish. "Your Majesty, I offer my humblest apologies. And to my esteemed peers as well." He indicated the party with a sweep of his hand.

"And what is your excuse this time?" Gustave replied impatiently. Stanley had a habit of telling spectacular stories to explain his tardiness. One was never quite certain whether he led a most adventurous life or was simply possessed of an unparalleled imagination.

"My dear mother, your Majesty, has taken leave of this world." There was no mockery in his tone or demeanor.

Gustave had the grace to look slightly embarrassed but recovered. "My sympathies Lord Stanley. You are forgiven...again. You may return to the palace to refresh yourself."

"My liege." Stanley bowed.

The men started on through the woods. Will stayed behind. "Is it true Stan?"

"Yes it's true." Stanley was studying his boot intently.

"Congratulations."

"Don't." He looked serious for a change.

"What? You're not celebrating?" Will was puzzled.

"She's been different these last weeks." He ceased contemplating his footwear. "Like an other person altogether. She was talking about God, and atonement, and correcting past mistakes. Told me to live a life of honor. As if I have any idea how to do that."

"Illness can do strange things to a person." Will did not know what else to say. As far back as he could remember Lady St. Robert had been much like his own mother. He knew Stan would be glad to be rid of that woman, but the woman who had emerged for a few weeks prior to her death seemed to have made a change in his friend. "Come along on the hunt. It will take your mind off it."

Stan shook his head. "I'm afraid I have other hunting to do." He smiled and for a moment the old Stan was back. "Who else is there to keep the ladies of the court entertained while all the men are out in the woods?" He mounted his stallion and rode for the palace, leaving Will to the futility of hunting with the over-privileged and under-witted.

The palace was quiet with the men at hunt. Stanley washed the dust of the roads from his face and neck, and changed quickly. He had inquired from one of the many pages where the young ladies might be found. Brimming with purpose he strode confidently toward the princess' solar and entered without a sound. He positioned himself behind a large plant so as not to attract attention as he surveyed the room, examining each young lady carefully. *Oh no! I've been spotted.*

What on earth is he doing here? Lavinia was well aware that guard duty would have to be commenced with Stanley roaming the palace. "Lord St. Robert."

Stan bowed gallantly, relieved that she had chosen not to announce his presence to her guests. "Your Majesty. You look radiant as usual." She merely raised her eyebrows in response. "I do apologize for my tardiness, your Majesty. I am certain you know that my dear mother has been ailing for some time. She passed on to the next world three nights before."

"I am truly sorry." She knew better than to trust Stanley with the young ladies at court, but she felt genuine sympathy for his loss. "The king and the others have formed a hunting party, I expect you'll wish to join them."

"I reported to His Majesty when I first arrived. After my journey I must admit that an afternoon of hunting does not appeal to me. Your Majesty, might I beg your assistance with regard to a task of the utmost import?"

"Lord Stanley I would be happy to assist you in any way that I am able, but as you can see I have a keep full of guests. Perhaps after the celebration has ended?" He looked dismayed. "Of course if it truly cannot wait I can find someone else to assist you."

"Thank you Your Majesty." Stanley scanned the room briefly. "Have you, by any chance, seen Lady Moreen DeFord?"

"Yes. Wonderful girl. My daughter has taken a liking to her. I believe you will find them in my solar." He bowed and turned to go. "Lord Stanley! Knock before you enter next time."

Stanley hurried toward the queen's solar. He silently congratulated himself on having been a curious youth and learned his way around the royal palace at a young age. He paused to knock on the door. One of Madame Sonja's assistants opened it. "Good day. Might Lady Moreen DeFord be within?"

"Yes milord. A moment please." She closed the door and hurried over to Moreen and Allyn. "Lord Stanley St. Robert is here Your Highness."

An expression of annoyance crossed Allyn's face. "What could he want?"

"He's asking for Lady Moreen." She stood waiting for instructions.

"It must be important." Moreen was curious.

"Certainly." Allyn replied. "He must need advice on which tunic to wear to feast this evening."

"Please Allyn?" Moreen implored. "What if something has happened to Will?"

Allyn thought a moment then nodded her assent to the young seamstress.

Stanley strolled in and bowed yet again. *Why does anyone live at court? It's a pain in the back.* "Your Highness. Lady Moreen. I am here on most urgent business and beg your help in the matter."

"Of course Stanley. I'd be pleased to help you, but wouldn't Will be better suited for your business affairs than I am?"

"Not this time." He took a deep breath and plunged ahead, before he had a chance to talk himself out of what he was about to request. "My sainted mother has passed on to be with God." Allyn rolled her eyes at the word "sainted."

Moreen's heart swelled with compassion. "Oh Stanley, I'm terribly sorry."

"She had suffered for so long that it was a relief to see her go." He paused. *Just do it Stan! The sooner it begins the sooner it will end.* "It was her dying wish that I might take a wife. Yet I find myself ill-equipped to choose."

"Stanley, marriage is sacred—to share your life with another, day in and day out. I could not possibly choose a wife for you. It must be your decision."

"Yes, of course. But that is not what I meant to propose." He hesitated once more.

Allyn mocked him. "Go on. We are expiring with inquisitiveness."

"I know very little about female hearts. And I confess I have not been acquainted with the kind of ladies I should wish to marry. I would ask you to assist me only by informing me of what to look for in a bride." She was about to protest again. "I realize that I must use my own conscience as a guide, but I wish to have another conscience on my side, as my own is not wholly reliable." There was silence so he continued. "For instance: if I point out a specific lady, you might tell me a bit about her, to give me an overall...understanding of her character and inclinations."

It seemed like an eternity before she responded. "Very well Stanley. I will help you. But I must make one thing perfectly clear. I will go forward with this only if you are entirely sincere."

"I assure you I am."

"Then let us begin now." Moreen headed out of the room and asked Allyn to lead the way to her solar.

Allyn flung a warning back over her shoulder. "Stay with us Lord St. Robert. I won't have you off somewhere seducing innocents in my palace."

Chapter 11

Stanley, Allyn, and Moreen had been mobbed as soon as they had entered the solar, but the commotion had calmed down after thirty minutes or so. Allyn took the lead in steering everyone away from Stanley. Moreen had met many of the ladies the previous evening and that morning between sessions with Madame Sonja.

"I really do not know what you are looking for in a bride Stanley."

"Someone kind and gentle and good. A bit like you, only less likely to scold me."

"You should rule out every lady you've dallied with in the past."

"Well that's half the court right there." Stan joked. "What about her? The one in the purple gown."

"That's Madelyn La Fontaine. She is a lovely girl, but a bit more outspoken than you might prefer."

"The red-head in green?" He suggested.

"Arabella Spencer. She would be an excellent choice. Sweet, but spirited, loves to ride. Very amiable, and her father is one of the king's advisors."

"Baron Frederick Spencer?" At Moreen's nod he continued. "No thank you. I have had dealings with him. This is useless. Every girl here is either lacking in virtue, too outspoken, or possessed of a disagreeable sire." He leaned back against the wall with a sigh of discouragement. Just then something caught his attention. His gaze was drawn to an elegant statuesque beauty. "Moreen? Who is that?"

"Who? Which one?" She asked, trying to determine which lady had piqued his interest.

"The one in the blue gown, by the windows." He was transfixed. He could not take his eyes away from her. She had separated herself from the group surrounding the princess and was quietly studying the harp standing in a corner of the room. Her golden hair fell in gentle cascades down her back, waves of sunshine in the dim chamber.

"You would not be interested in her." Moreen stated simply.

"Why is that?" He continued to watch her.

"She's not like the other ladies here. Isabelle is very religious." She explained.

"Isabelle." He breathed. "She's exquisite."

"Stanley. Did you hear what I said?"

"I heard you. She's not like the other girls. I don't mind if my bride is extraordinary, in fact I'd prefer it." He continued gazing at Isabelle as if she would disappear if he took his eyes from her. "And she is very religious. I have no objection to religion. So why would I not be interested?"

"Perhaps I should have said it differently. *She* would not be interested in *you*." Moreen clarified.

"What?" He finally looked at Moreen. "Why not?"

"Stanley, I know that you could be a fine man. But you have a reputation here, and elsewhere. A lifetime of habits such as yours is not changed overnight. Drinking, carousing, lying, cheating—those are not things that a lady desires in a husband and a father for her children."

"Children? I'm not even married yet. I'm not thinking about children."

"*You* aren't, but that is something that a lady considers when deciding her future. Your entire existence is the opposite of what Isabelle would want, and need."

"I'll have to change that." She looked at him askance. "I know, I know. It's not that simple. But she's the one I want.

What can I do to make her see that I am not the man she's heard about?"

"Stanley, you are the man she's heard about! If you cannot win her with the truth, then do not try to win her at all."

"Very well." He seemed to acquiesce. "I'll use the truth. Tell me about her." Moreen sighed. "I swear I'll not say a false word to her."

"She is quite fond of music, and dancing; a truly gentle soul; she has a quick wit and is of a serious nature, but not sullen. She is compassionate and desirous of helping others. I hold her in the highest esteem."

Stan thought that might be a threat, though intimidation did not seem Moreen's style. "And who is her father?"

"Count DuClerque." She provided.

"I know very little about the Count. I hope he knows as little about me. Thank you Moreen. You have been a great help to me. You shall have a place of honor at our wedding feast." With that he began to ease his way toward Isabelle.

Moreen watched from across the room. Isabelle looked up at his approach, her face serene. Stanley was apparently well practiced in the art of setting people at ease. Within minutes he had Isabelle laughing and gazing up at him in adoration. There was nothing left to do but leave the situation to God and Count DuClerque.

When evening came everyone gathered once again in the throne room to await the official presentation of their princess. Moreen was wearing one of the gowns Allyn had sent her, a green satin with silver flowers embroidered about the hem and neckline. She felt almost like a princess herself.

She was comfortably surrounded by several new friends and was actually enjoying herself.

Will was proudly watching his bride when he heard his name being called and turned to see who was trying to gain his attention. "Stan! I wondered when you would turn up. Where have you been all day?"

"You'll find out soon enough. But first—tell me Will, what do you know about Count DuClerque?"

"Honoré DuClerque? Not much really. Why?" He had a feeling his friend was up to something.

"I would consider any information you could give me to be most helpful."

"Alright." He thought for a moment. "Vast holdings. Seems an honest man; no-nonsense sort. Damn good shot. Why do you want to know about DuClerque, Stan?"

Stan was still thinking about the "damn good shot" part. "What? Oh. I have decided to marry his daughter."

Will started laughing. "You? Marry? DuClerque's daughter?"

"Yes. What is so amusing about that?" He demanded.

"I'm sorry Stan." Will attempted to be sober. "I can't picture you marrying anyone, let alone Isabelle DuClerque."

"How do you know her name?"

"Isabelle is the youngest child of the Count and Countess. I once tried to seduce her sister Mariette. I do not imagine DuClerque will look kindly upon your suit, and if he refuses...well, you might consider choosing another girl just in case. She is not your type anyway."

"Why does everyone keep saying that? I find her utterly charming. My admiration for her grows every minute." Stanley was getting a tad irritated.

"Of course Stan. Isabelle is beautiful, and I am certain that she is amiable as well, but she would never choose you for a husband." Will could sympathize, but he wanted to save Stanley the disquietude of disappointment.

"That is ridiculous. One could just as easily say that Moreen would never have chosen to wed you."

Will sighed. "Stan this is different. I didn't have to contend with her father. Unless there is an accident or a sudden illness in the Count's future I'm afraid all your efforts will come to naught. Best to choose someone else and forget about it." He could see that Stanley was discouraged by his words. "Look, here comes Jeanette Raivaux. Why not have a little 'chat' with her? You'll feel better for it."

Stan was not enthusiastic about the idea, but the sight of the buxom brunette was sufficiently distracting to give him a sudden case of amnesia. Jeanette had led him out of the hall and halfway to her chambers before he remembered his intended betrothed.

Moreen was looking everywhere but could not find her friend, who had been laughing one moment and gone the next. She thought perhaps Isabelle had needed some air and gone to the gardens. Moreen was nearing the bench where she had sat with young Andrew when she heard a sound of soft tears. She rounded a shrub and found Isabelle crying quietly in the moonlight. "Whatever is the matter?"

Isabelle turned. "I came out here because I didn't want anyone to see me. It's foolish really." She wiped her tears away, only to have more take their place streaming down her cheeks. "I should have known better than to think he cared for me."

"Stanley?"

"Yes." She pretended to study the roses in front of her. "This afternoon he was so attentive to me. But tonight…"

Moreen stepped closer and put a sympathetic hand on her friend's arm. "I feel that I am partly to blame."

"Oh don't say that." Isabelle insisted. "It's not your fault Moreen. It's just the way he is. How simple I am to have been thinking of marriage—and children—when he was just wooing me to pass the time."

"Why do you say that?"

"You didn't see, did you? He left the throne room with Jeanette Raivaux."

"I'm sorry. Who is Jeanette Raivaux?" Moreen searched her mind, trying to remember if they had been introduced.

"Only one of the biggest whores at court!" Isabelle was surprised at her angry outburst. Everyone at court knew what Jeanette was but it was not talked of, especially by young ladies of good breeding who were not supposed to know of such things, or at least were expected to pretend not to know. She took a deep breath of the cooling night air. "Moreen, please don't think I'm cross with you, I'm not. But if you would not mind, I would like to be alone for a while."

"Of course. I'm so sorry Isabelle." Moreen went back inside the palace looking for Stanley. He was nowhere to be seen so she went to her husband instead.

"Moreen my love, have I told you how stunning you look in that gown? What's wrong?"

"Have you seen Stanley?"

"Yes. But you need not worry, I sent him off with a sympathetic lady who will soon ease his pain." As soon as he had spoken he knew he was in trouble, and he was certain he was about to learn why.

"You?! You sent him off with *that woman*? Will how could you? You had no right to interfere with Stanley and Isabelle!"

"There is no 'Stanley and Isabelle.' Her father would never allow it. It's better this way, so that no one gets hurt."

"No one gets hurt?" She was truly furious now. "*No one gets hurt*? Why don't you tell that to the girl weeping her heart out in the gardens?" She lifted her chin the slightest bit, and stormed gracefully away from him.

"Moreen! Come back." It did no good. Whenever she raised her chin that way it was a sure sign that she was unwilling to back down. He would face better odds unarmed on a battlefield.

Jeanette stood pouting in the hallway. *The nerve of that Stanley St. Robert!* She fumed silently. *How dare he spurn me?* She would have to think of another plan. All the other lords of importance were married. She continued her musings as she strolled the corridors of the palace. Although she could not marry a powerful lord, there was no reason she could not benefit from an association with one. But most of them were old and fat. She looked up in time to see Geoffrey DeFord round the corner.

"Lord DeFord, how fortunate!" She smiled sweetly. "I was just looking for you."

"Were you?" He eyed her skeptically.

"Of course. I am in need of counsel, and only a man as clever as you are could help me." She looked up at him from beneath her lowered lashes and ran a hand up his arm.

"Certainly. What might be the problem, my dear?" Whatever her game was he was willing to play along.

"I find myself quite listless of late. Nothing at court entices me anymore. I must confess to being quite bored with such limited society." She ran the tip of her tongue slowly along her lower lip. "Surely you could help me find something exhilarating to fill my dark, lonely hours."

Geoffrey smiled, appreciative of her offer and her tactics. She was young, but she knew how to manipulate a man's baser nature. As she pressed her body against him he simply said, "Miss Raivaux, I'm old enough to be your father."

"But you aren't, are you?" She closed her eyes and waited for his kiss.

His smile widened as he gazed at her seemingly sweet face. Slowly, with one finger, he traced the curve of her mouth, then lifted her chin as he dipped his head so that their lips almost touched. "Perhaps we can come to some arrangement, you and I." He barely touched his lips to hers before stepping away. "My sweet, I'm afraid this will have to wait." His eyes held her captive as he lifted her hand and pressed a burning kiss to her palm. "I trust I will see you later?"

She nodded breathlessly as he disappeared into the shadows.

Stanley had left Jeanette and headed straight back to the throne room. Not finding Isabelle there, he began to search some of the chambers nearby. He heard footsteps behind him and turned, hoping his lady would be there. "Oh, Moreen. Have you seen Isabelle? Ow! What was that for?"

For the second time in as many months Moreen had slapped a man. "What was that for? What do you think it was for? How dare you spend all day courting Isabelle and then go off with Jeanette Raivaux?"

"Nothing happened with Jeanette." Stan insisted.

"You expect me to believe that? When I think that you enlisted my help and then go and do something like this...I ought to strike you again, you knave!"

Stanley held up his arms to ward off any further blows as he avowed his innocence. "Moreen, I swear nothing happened. I left Jeanette fuming in a corridor and came to find Isabelle. Do you know where she is?"

"Yes." She was still angry but she believed Stanley's claim of guiltlessness. "She is in the gardens, crying."

He put his arms down. "Crying? What happened?"

She threw the words at him like daggers. "She saw you leave with Jeanette. That's what happened!"

"Then she cares for me." Stanley swung Moreen around, then planted her back on the ground. "Thank you Moreen. Where? Where in the gardens?"

"By the roses." She responded.

He hurried off, praying that he would find her there still. *God, you and I haven't always agreed on things, but if you would please help me find Isabelle, I promise I'll change. Wait, make that if you help me marry Isabelle I'll change. Please let her be there!* He was walking so quickly that he came upon her rather noisily.

Her eyes were red. "Go away Stanley. I want nothing to do with you!" Ignoring her request he put his arms around her, and she pushed him away. "Leave me alone. Go back to Jeanette, I'm sure she's waiting for you."

"I don't want Jeanette."

"Then why did you leave with her?"

"Because I thought I couldn't have you. I'm not good enough for you Isabelle. But I don't want anyone else. I swear to you on my life, nothing happened!" He stepped carefully toward her. "I looked at her and I saw your face, so I left her. I've been looking for you ever since. I had to tell you..."

"Tell me what?" She stood calmly, afraid to hope.

He stood arguing with himself, wondering if he could say it, wondering if it was true. He remembered his bargain with God and suddenly he realized that he had given no thought to what Isabelle might want. He didn't want her to marry him because God made her do it. He wanted her to marry him because she wanted to. He reached out his hand to her but she stood motionless and he let it drop.

She did not repeat the question. She stood surrounded by fragrant roses. Her pale hair glowed in the moonlight. It was a picturesque scene, she was a beautiful girl, but it was something else—something in her eyes that finally moved him to speak. There was no hesitation, no uncertainty in his voice, only the urgency of a desperate truth. "I love you, Isabelle. As long as I live I'll never love another." She said nothing, just stood there. He turned to leave.

"Stanley!" She ran into his arms, crying again. "I love you!"

He held her as tightly as he dared. "Don't cry. Please don't cry. I can't bear it. I promise I'll never make you cry again."

She laughed softly. "These are good tears Stanley. I'm so happy!"

"Isabelle? Will you marry me? I know your father might not like the idea, but I'll find a way to convince him..."

She put a finger to his lips. "Don't worry about father. I will marry you Stanley St. Robert. Now kiss me."

Chapter 12

Everyone waited in a state of quiet impatience. Except for Stanley, William, and the king, none of the men had seen the princess in some years. Likewise the older ladies had not seen her that afternoon as they had spent those hours in the gardens. The young ladies who had met her already were eager to see her gown. The children were all terribly excited, though the little ones did not know why.

Stanley and Isabelle had decided to keep their betrothal secret for a time. They were able to stand near one another by virtue of their friendships with Will and Moreen. Moreen was happy to see Isabelle smiling again, but she was still angry with her husband. The four of them stood with Geoffrey and Constance in the middle of the crowd.

Constance was irked by their position, amidst so many of lower rank. Once they had been regularly invited to court and treated with greater deference. She had never been able to determine what had happened, but she was certain it was Geoffrey's fault. Her thoughts were interrupted by a blast from the trumpets.

A low murmur worked its way through the crowd. As the sea of guests slowly parted everyone was craning their necks to try to get the first glimpse of the princess. Allyn stood nervously at one end of the hall, her parents were seated at the other end. *All I need do is walk up there.* She closed here eyes for a moment, said a silent prayer, and started to move slowly toward the thrones. She kept her eyes rooted to the floor in front of her. To everyone else she looked sweetly humble. Confident though she was, she could not bring herself to look at the people who were bowing to her as she walked. She knew that every person there was taking her measure.

The men were struck by her beauty; the women by the beauty of her white gown, exquisitely embroidered with golden flowers. The children were in awe of the lady they thought surely must be an angel.

Two more steps, only two more steps. She curtsied low before the king and queen until she felt her father's hand upon her shoulder. Finally she was able to look up as she rose and turned to face her people. The multitude erupted with their approval. Princess Allyn was their hope for the future, their light in the present, and a living symbol of their past.

As the crowd continued to applaud, one of the king's advisors excitedly brought him news. Gustave stood and motioned for silence. "Good people of Frandia, on this night you have been honored to receive your princess." At this the crowd exploded again. Once more the king held up his hands for silence. "I have just received word that an honored guest has arrived at our court. Shall we welcome him?" The people, already intoxicated by the festive atmosphere, cheered enthusiastically. Gustave signaled for the herald to announce the mysterious guest.

"Your Majesties, Comte Stephan Chevalier, and Comtesse Chevalier of the kingdom of France!"

A murmur went through the crowd. Will tried desperately to get a look at the couple advancing toward the king and queen. He wound his way through the throng of guests; his wife and parents followed him to the very edge of the crowd. He stood frozen in disbelief for a moment as the Comte and Comtesse neared. Just as they passed, Will suddenly lunged at the Comte, pointing his dagger at the man's throat. The Comtesse turned and screamed in horror.

"Will!" Moreen started toward him, but Geoffrey held her back.

"Don't Moreen, you'll be hurt."

The entire court stared in shock at William DeFord holding the Comte Chevalier at dagger's point. "Where is my sister?" He demanded.

"What are you talking about?" Stephan replied bewilderedly.

Gustave angrily shouted. "Guards! Seize him!"

"No!" Moreen cried, trying to break Geoffrey's hold on her.

Will stood menacingly, barely containing his fury. "I will ask you once more. Where is my sister?"

Stephan looked at Will in disbelief. "She died in childbirth...three years ago."

"You lie!" Will's anguished cry sounded throughout the hall.

"William." Geoffrey handed Moreen over to Constance and stepped slowly toward his son. "It's true."

"No!" Will insisted. "It can't be! Why did you not send word?" He glared accusingly at Stephan.

Geoffrey answered "He did. He sent word that very night."

Silence reigned for a moment before Will rounded on his father, his eyes filled with pain and hatred. "You knew? For three years you knew? And you said *nothing*? Damn you!" The guards reached them just in time to save Geoffrey from the dagger's blade.

Allyn had hurried through the crowd, against her father's orders. "Release him." She commanded the guards. She could sense the depth of his pain and believed that it would soon overcome his wrath, rendering him more prone to drowning in ale than to harming anyone. They stared at her blankly. "You have his dagger, now let him go."

"Geoffrey! How could you have kept such a thing from us?" Constance added her voice to the mix. Geoffrey shot her a dark look. She had known of Emmergene's death the whole time, but she would take this opportunity for everything it might profit her.

Moreen suddenly fainted. Allyn and Isabelle rushed to her, and Will struggled against the arms that still held him despite the princess' orders. "Moreen!"

Allyn looked up. "For God's sake let him go!" She shouted angrily. The captain of the guard looked to Gustave. The king nodded his permission, and they released him.

As Will and the others tried to revive Moreen, Constance took the lead in playing to the crowd. "What of the child, Stephan?"

"A girl. She lives." He responded dazedly as he comforted his wife. Comtesse Vivienne had run to his side as soon as the guards had taken hold of his assailant, and had not let go of her husband.

Moreen had regained consciousness, and insisted that she was perfectly alright. But Allyn and Isabelle insisted that she retire at once. Will urged her to heed their pleas.

Constance made a great show of displaying her contempt for Geoffrey, and thanked the princess for her kindness to "dear Moreen." Turning to Stephan she asked, "May I see my grandchild?"

Stephan did not hesitate. "Of course. I will take you to her myself."

"I am going with you." Vivienne asserted. And after asking leave of Their Majesties they exited the throne room behind Moreen, Allyn, and Isabelle.

Knowing that Moreen was safe, and his weapon gone, Will stood face to face with his father and did the next best thing to exacting his preferred revenge: public denouncement. "As long as I live I will never forgive you. *Never!*" As Geoffrey made to protest, Will turned his back to his father and walked away.

Slowly the people began to recover from their shock and started the quickly turning wheels of speculation. Geoffrey still stood looking after his son when Stanley came up to him. "Well played my lord. A word of advice, if I may. This might not be the best time to tell him the dog didn't really move to England."

"Really, I'm fine." Moreen lay safely in bed and continued to protest her friends' concern. Allyn and Isabelle kindly ignored her wishes and, with Marguerite's assistance, ministered to her as they would a sick child. "If you won't let me get out of bed would you at least find Will for me?"

"I'll go." Said Allyn. "But on one condition: that you stay here and rest." Moreen nodded meekly and Allyn left to go in search of Will, pausing with one final and half-teasing thought for Isabelle and Marguerite. "If she even thinks of getting up you have my permission and royal command to tie her to the bedposts."

Allyn tried to think. *If I were in such a state where would I go?* But then she remembered that she had spent the first several years of her life in the palace, whereas William didn't know his way around nearly as well. She searched the great hall, the gardens, she finally found him in the room where she had first met Moreen. "There you are! I've been looking everywhere for you."

"Moreen?"

"No need to worry. I believe this evening's events were simply too much for her. All she needs is rest." Allyn sat down in her favorite chair and watched Will pacing back and forth in front of the fire. "You won't get anywhere traveling this rug you know."

"I can't be still." He said without emotion.

"I have the same problem. I am always up and about. Even when I'm sitting or standing still, in my mind I'm flying about doing everything at once." She wanted to help him but she did not know how. She did not want to intrude, but her good heart and curiosity got the better of her after a full minute of silence. "Were you very close to your sister?"

"I once was—when we were very young. After she married it was as if she'd never even existed. I suppose I didn't miss her much." He was trying very hard to hide his pain. He didn't mind the princess asking, but he didn't know how to react to it either. The only people who'd ever cared about him were his youngest sister and Moreen.

He remembered the last time he saw Emmergene. She was dressed in the finest gown and she seemed happy. She did not know the man she had wed, but Will had known that she was glad to be leaving Thornhill and it's cold familial shackles. One time that day she had looked at him with something like sorrow, but had said nothing. In truth he had envied her, for she was escaping the life to which he was doomed. That feeling haunted him now, and it sickened him to remember how angry he had been with her. What he would give to have a chance to tell her he was sorry!

"I am sorry for your sister." Allyn had become serious, which was unlike her. Will did not know her well enough to fully appreciate that, but her solemnity did console him a little.

"You remind me of her somehow." The realization startled him. "Not your manner. She was always quiet and gentle."

"Goodness milord, I am unused to such flattery." She replied, good-naturedly sarcastic.

"I don't know what it is. Something..." He was thoroughly perplexed by it.

"Well I will take it as a compliment and say thank you. You'd best be on your way to your wife's side. I am sure she will wish to see you before she sleeps."

"Yes." He walked away still confused by why he sensed any resemblance between Allyn and Emmergene; they were as different as night and day.

Marguerite went to the door, while Isabelle watched over Moreen.

"Is my daughter here?"

"Yes your Excellency." Marguerite allowed him into the sitting room and fetched Isabelle.

"Papa. Whatever are you doing here?"

"Is your friend alright?"

"Yes, only tired." She was pleased that her father had inquired after Moreen.

"Please, let us sit." Honoré DuClerque was a good man, and a fair man. He always did what he thought best, and he was not looking forward to his daughter's reaction to what he was going to say. "Isabelle, you are a sweet and good young lady. It is one of the things that make me so proud of you. I would hate to see anyone take advantage of that sweetness."

"I know what you're saying Papa, but Moreen isn't like that. She is not a DeFord. Her father was a friend of the king's." Isabelle had a bad feeling about this conversation already.

"Yes, I know she is not a DeFord, but she is married to one. As for her father, well...our king is not always the best judge of character. I did not know Hugh Kelly, so I will not presume anything good or bad about him. But William DeFord is a wild man, likely he will end up just like his father. I do not want you spending time with people of that sort." He reached to take his daughter's hand.

She sat in bewilderment, her mind racing. She opened her mouth several times, but no words came out. If her father would not let her see Moreen, there was very little likelihood that he would allow her to see Stanley. "What do you mean? Am I supposed to shun Moreen altogether? She would be so hurt! I couldn't!"

He patted her hand soothingly. "Now, now, calm down. I would not ask you to hurt anyone. Of course you can talk to her while we remain at court. After we leave you will have no contact with her. Doubtless her husband will wish the same." Honoré looked at his daughter's wounded expression. "There are things you do not know Isabelle. What I ask is for the best."

"But Papa..." She began to protest only to see the door closing behind him as he left. *This cannot be!* She was so wrapped up in her own thoughts that she didn't hear Will come in and walk straight to Moreen's bedchamber. She was still sitting there ten minutes later when Stanley arrived.

He knocked but there was no answer so he invited himself in and found his intended frozen in a chair, looking distressed. "What is it? Is it Moreen?"

"Oh no. Moreen is alright." She was still desperately trying to think of a way to maintain her friendship with Moreen, and her betrothal to Stanley. She threw herself at Stanley, trusting him to catch her up in his strong embrace. "Oh Stanley, I can't bear to think of living without you! Let's run away."

"Tonight?" *What's going on?*

"Right now. We can be gone in half an hour. We can ride far away and we can be wed as soon as possible." She had a fevered, half-fearful look in her eyes.

"Are you serious? This isn't like you Isabelle." *At least I think it's not.* "We are not running away. Why would we? We have everything we could possibly want here, and the king is paying for all of it. Be patient darling, and I promise you will have a proper wedding as soon as I receive your father's blessing."

"But he'll never give us his blessing. I'm sure of it! Just this evening he told me I can have no contact with Moreen and William after we go back home. He said he does not want me to be around people of that sort. He'll never let me wed you Stanley!"

"Darling calm down. I'll convince him, you'll see." He kissed her hands softly.

She shook her head. "You can't. He won't listen. He doesn't see you as I do."

"Well I should hope not!" He joked. "Now I want you to pretend this whole thing with your father never happened. Leave it to me, and I'll win him over."

"Stanley, you're not listening! He'll take me home and I'll never see you again!"

"Don't worry sweetheart. I won't let that happen. I promise you I won't." Her beautiful eyes were brimming with tears and Stan saw that she was only becoming more agitated. He gently rocked her in his arms. "I must try. I have to talk to him. Isabelle, I want you to have everything in the world that your heart desires. I want to give you a monstrous wedding with the finest of everything."

"I don't care about any of that! All I want is to be with you!" She started sobbing.

"Darling please trust me. Let me try. I'll see him first thing tomorrow. And then we'll decide what to do. Alright?"

She nodded and buried her face in his shoulder. She knew what would happen tomorrow. Her tortured mind began planning. She would pack tonight. Only what was absolutely necessary. Stanley was looking at her. Desperate to keep him from seeing her mind at work, she kissed him hotly. As he caressed her back, she yearned to feel his hands against her skin. "Lie with me tonight." she said breathlessly.

Her eyes were lit with a fire he desperately wanted to feed. "No darling."

She was dazed. "You don't want me?"

"Of course I want you! But how could I face your father tomorrow? No. We'll wait 'til we are married. There will be plenty of talk about me; I don't want anyone talking about you. I will not risk your honor." He kissed her one more time. "Good night my sweet Isabelle. You must go now." He steered her toward the door.

"Will you walk me to my chambers?"

"I don't believe that would be a good idea. Besides which I need to talk to Will."

She looked back at him through the closing door. "Goodnight Stanley, my love."

Stan leaned against the door and stared into the empty room.

"Dreaming, Stan? How goes the war?"

He pushed himself off of the door. "That would depend on one's perspective. Phillip is massing an army in southern France."

"That was not the war I meant, but how did you come by that bit of information?"

Stan merely smiled. "You know Will, this is an exciting time to be alive. We have a chance to change our nation's history."

"Or be executed for trying to. Does that mean you will be siding with the rebels?"

"I have considered it. You know how I love to cause trouble, and I have far more to gain than you have. Though it would pain me to have to kill you. You are siding with the king, are you not?"

"Father will. I haven't yet decided." Will sat down and stared at the fire. "With father on Gustave's side and mother on Phillip's, I've a notion to renounce both and claim the crown for myself. Of course I could side with mother and Phillip just to vex father."

"Don't you ever tire of toying with your parents?"

"Oh it's great fun." Will turned to Stan. "But who *will* you support, Stan?" Stanley shrugged. "Honoré DuClerque is with Phillip."

"Really? That is encouraging. Perhaps I can blackmail him into giving me his daughter."

"A lovely thought but it will not work. He would likely rather burn at the stake for treason than give Isabelle to you." Will was using a tone of mock sympathy.

"Ah well...I must be going. I have an early appointment with the stake tomorrow."

As Stanley opened the door Will called out "Good luck, my friend.

Chapter 13

"Dearest, you must rest. I will not have you wearing yourself out to please a gaggle of ladies you don't even know." Will was trying to persuade Moreen to remain abed.

"I know Isabelle, and Allyn." She protested.

"And I am certain they will happily come here to see you." He kissed her forehead. "I will be back soon."

Will left, hoping Moreen would heed his request, and went to find someone who could direct him to Comte Chevalier's chambers. He was surprised to find that Stephan welcomed him with very little hesitation. Comtesse Vivienne seemed apprehensive about his presence, and excused herself. The men stood somewhat awkwardly for a few moments.

"Would you care to sit?" Stephan offered.

"Your Excellency, I must beg your pardon for my behavior last night."

Stephan waved him to silence. "Please. I had no idea that Geoffrey had not told you. If I had been in your place I would have done the same thing. She spoke of you, you know. She always said we must invite you to visit after the babe. Of course we did not know..." He let his words trail off and Will thought he glimpsed sadness in Stephan's eyes.

"You said the child is alright?" Stephan nodded, so Will continued. "May I...may I please see her?"

"Of course."

"I know French, but I haven't spoken it in years."

"You need not worry. She speaks Frandian as well."

Will followed Stephan through three rooms, into his niece's chamber. A small bundle of ebony curls rushed up to Stephan. "Papa, Papa!"

He scooped his daughter up in his arms and kissed her as she giggled. "Are you behaving yourself this morn?" She nodded, beaming at her father. "Good. Here is someone I wish you to meet. This is your Uncle William." The little girl looked at Will cautiously. "It is alright Jacqueline. He is your mother's brother."

He put her down and she crept toward her uncle shyly. She looked up at him, then tugged on the hem of his tunic. He kneeled so they were almost face to face as she continued to study him with her bright blue eyes. Finally she spoke. "Hello. I am Jacqueline."

He wasn't sure what to say, but he had to try—for Emmergene. "I am honored to meet you Jacqueline. My name is William, but you may call me Uncle Will. That way you will not confuse me with your other uncles."

She sighed. "I don't have other uncles. Just you." Then she smiled Emmergene's smile, hugged him, and ran off to play.

Stephan smiled after his daughter. "She is the image of her mother. I'm afraid I spoil her too much."

Will stood watching Jacqueline, thinking how proud Emmergene would be of her daughter. "You will see that she has every comfort."

"I believe I can be trusted to provide for my own child." Stephan replied.

"I meant...of course you will. Will you bring her to Thornhill?"

"Not as long as those two vultures live. I made a promise to your sister never to let them near Jacqueline. I only agreed to your mother seeing her last night because I knew she would be sleeping. Of course Constance did not really want to see Jacqueline."

"No. That was for effect. I'm sure she knew. She never cared for Emmergene." The two men returned to the Comte's chambers. "I have to ask...I must know. Was she happy?"

Stephan thought back to the one year he had with Emmergene, remembering her smiles, her laughter, her joy. They were a stark contrast to the pain in her eyes the few times she had talked about her childhood. "Yes, I believe she was. At the end, when anyone else might have been frightened, she was happy, and...peaceful." He was standing a few feet from Will, but in his mind he was in France, three years before. "She said God had given her everything she had asked for. I promised I would keep our child safe, see that she has a happy life. She smiled that sweet smile of hers, then she was gone. God rest her soul." He finished softly.

"Thank you." Will had found out all he needed to know, his sister had been happy for a time before she died. If there was a God, if there was any justice, she would be at peace now. It eased his mind to know that Stephan was a better man than Geoffrey, and that he had cared for Emmergene. From his behavior with Jacqueline, he was a good father as well. That sweet little girl would never suffer as her mother had of cruelty and neglect. "I will go now."

"William, you and your bride may visit us in France any time you wish. If you survive the revolution."

Will stared at Stephan in astonishment "How do you know about that?"

"Did you not know that Phillip has been to Avignon to see His Holiness? And he is building his armies in France. Surely you do not think me ignorant of such happenings in my own country."

"He's been to Avignon? Was that before or after he went to Rome?"

"So he is playing both sides. Taking no chances with his claim, is he? Sound thinking, as long as neither side finds out." Stephan caught Will's questioning gaze and anticipated the question. "I am for neither man. This is not my war, nor do I wish to make it so. I am here at the king's pleasure. Yours and mine. Though I, at least, am certain of who my king shall be when I return to my home. If we do not speak again before I depart, fare you well brother."

Will nodded before letting himself out.

Brother. Why would a man such as Stephan Chevalier admit to any connection with him? He was as baffled by that comment as he had been by Stephan's ready acceptance of him when he appeared at the door. Pleased, but baffled. He continued to consider the entire exchange as he headed back to Moreen's chambers.

Stanley nervously awaited Count DuClerque. He had been told that the Count would be returning any moment. That had been thirty minutes ago. He paced the length of the room several times.

"What are you doing here?" Stan turned to see the Count watching him. He was almost as tall as Stanley, rather grayed, and had a look of displeasure on his face at finding Stanley in his chambers.

"Your Excellency. I am Lord Stanley St. Robert."

"I know who you are. What business do you have with me?" The morning was not off to a good start with his horse gone lame and his daughter still upset with him from the night before. Honoré was irritated by the mere presence of the celebrated profligate, and he had a suspicion that this encounter would be yet another deterrent to recovering the good mood he had possessed only 12 hours before. "Well? Speak up man. I have things to do this day, and wasting time is not one of them."

"Very well, Your Excellency. I will come right to the purpose of my visit." Stan paused for a breath before plunging in. "I am here with the sole intention of requesting your daughter's hand."

Honoré stared at him incredulously. "Do you jest?"

"No, your Excellency. I am in earnest. I wish to make her my bride, and I have come to ask your blessing."

"Why?"

Stan thought he must have heard wrong. "Why?"

"Why marriage? Why my Isabelle? And why on earth would I consent to such a union? What have you to offer my child other than a bad name and a lifetime of pain? I have heard of your exploits Lord St. Robert. You are not worthy of her."

Stanley had expected to hear all of those things, but not all at once. "I have made some..." At a pointed look from the Count he amended, "*many* mistakes in the past. I know I am not worthy of her. I will not insult you by pretending to be other than I am. I only ask you to judge me for yourself, not by what others have said. I have every hope of redeeming myself."

"I commend you for it. Every man deserves a chance to make recompense for his sins. I wish you success. But I'll not wager my daughter's happiness and security on your 'hope.'"

"If you believe that every man deserves the chance to transform himself, would you then deny me that chance? Without hope of Isabelle's love what reason would I have for change?"

"The state of your soul is your own affair. If you wish to take your chances with God's good nature, it is not my place to say otherwise. If you see no reason for amendment beyond obtaining my daughter's hand, there is little hope for you. A life is not changed in an instant. If you wish to change for yourself, do so. You will gain nothing from me for it."

Stanley found himself at a loss. He could not charm DuClerque into acquiescence. He had no flowery arguments to make. "I love her."

"Love? What do you know of love? How many young ladies have you lured to ruination and heartache by speaking of love?" The Count's face turned red. "If you have shamed my daughter..."

"I have done no such thing! If that was what I wanted I would not be talking to you." The count was visibly relieved, but Stanley was angry now. "Do you think so little of Isabelle that you believe she would do such a thing? For shame milord! Your daughter is the sweetest and purest lady that ever lived and she does not deserve to be insulted thus by her own blood."

Honoré was surprised by Stanley's vehement defense of Isabelle's honor. It was a step in the right direction, but it did not erase the truth, or the shame, of his past. Honoré thought better of his previous direction in dealing with the young man. He began again, quietly. "You may love her. Certainly she inspires such devotion where ever she goes." He paused for a moment. "Lord St. Robert, imagine for a moment that you have a daughter, whom you have watched grow from a gurgling infant to a young woman of grace and beauty; your pride and joy, the light of your life; a comfort to you; absolute proof that you have done something right in this world. What would you do if a man whose sinful exploits have become legendary came to you and asked you to hand your precious child over to him? Could you sacrifice your daughter's future for the hope that the man would change? And what if he does not change? Could you bear to see your child's life destroyed, and her dreams dashed? I put it to you milord, what would you do if you were in my situation?"

Stanley remained silent as he mulled over the Count's words. He imagined a miniature of Isabelle, laughing and dancing. He knew very well what he would do. "I must say that I would do the same as you have done, or perhaps worse." At that moment Stanley realized that Honoré DuClerque was a man among men; someone worth looking up to, someone he wished he could be more like. He continued humbly. "My lord, I understand your position. I respect you as my superior, not in rank, but in life. I can only add that I do love Isabelle, and I want to make her happy. I would never wish to cause her pain. Thank you for speaking with me Your Excellency. Good day."

Stanley left without a backward glance.

Honoré was stunned by what he had just heard. *Perhaps there is hope for the boy after all. I shall have to observe him for a time. And we shall see if he means what he says.*

"Your Majesty. May I be permitted to apologize for the scene my husband caused last evening?" Constance spoke from a deep curtsey.

Lavinia had not wanted to see her, but there was little choice. She had known that Constance would play this card. "'Twas your son I believe who caused the scene, Lady DeFord."

"Of course, Your Majesty—but only because of his father's unforgivable actions. William is terribly protective of those he holds dear. And when his sister's husband appeared with a new wife... Naturally William and I were concerned. I'm afraid his heart overpowered his reason. When I think of all the pain that Geoffrey has caused! And poor Moreen is still so weak this morn." Constance made a show of blinking back tears that, in reality, didn't exist.

"I do hope Moreen will recover." Lavinia knew very well the pain that Geoffrey had caused in his lifetime thus far.

"Mother? I must speak with you about the...oh! Forgive me, I did not know anyone else was here." Allyn gave a small curtsey and looked at Constance.

"Princess Allyn." Constance curtseyed appropriately and looked up into Allyn's bright blue eyes. She gasped. "Forgive me, Your Majesty. I have just...remembered... something. I... Forgive me." She hurried from the room.

"Allyn fetch your father at once! Then go to your chambers and stay there until he or I send for you!"

"Mother you look pale. What is the matter?"

"Go!" Lavinia commanded.

Allyn did as she was told, but she did not understand what was happening. Why would her mother be so upset? What could have happened?

The warm morning sun coaxed the flowers' perfume from them. Their scents, mixed with the smells of earth and sunshine, drifted on the breeze to fill Moreen's senses. She was convinced that she needed fresh air more than rest, and had gone in search of a comfortable spot in which she might have both. She strolled slowly along, enjoying the day that was blossoming around her. Eyes closed, she listened to the birds' songs, and walked right into someone.

"Oh, I am so sorry." "Forgive me, I did not see you." They said at once.

The stranger turned around and Moreen called out. "Wait. Won't you stay? I would be glad of some company. This is too beautiful a day not to be shared."

The lady smiled. "Very well. I shall stay if you wish. Are you not...young Lady DeFord?"

"Oh please, do not call me that. Lady DeFord is my husband's mother. I am simply Moreen, or Lady Moreen, though I am not yet accustomed to hearing myself called so. May I ask, what is your name?"

"Jocelyn. My husband is a nobleman but, like you, I am of more humble birth. Do you wish to sit, or shall we walk?"

"Oh let us walk. There is such beauty here! I could not bear to miss any of it. God's creation is so peaceful. So soothing." Moreen observed.

"It is." Jocelyn agreed. "But I pray you do not express such sentiments to the groundskeeper here, as he thinks he alone should have the credit for this splendor."

Moreen swooned, but Jocelyn caught hold of her in time to help her to a bench. "Thank you. I...I do not know what is the matter with me."

"You had quite a shock last evening."

"Could that truly be the cause? It seems my life has become quite a shock. Only two months ago I was at home on my father's farm. Now I am at the royal palace."

"It must be difficult for you. But I can assure you, after a time you will be comfortable in your new life." Jocelyn smiled. "Lady Moreen, I think we should go back inside. You may lean on me. I shall be happy to help you."

"Very well. Thank you." Moreen stood and took Jocelyn's arm. They walked slowly toward the palace and presently ran into Will, who was looking for his escaped wife.

"There you are." He noticed how Moreen leaned upon her companion. "I told you that you would tire yourself. You are going straight back to bed."

As Will lifted Moreen in his arms, Jocelyn spoke. "You are right, milord. She needs rest. I feel certain that she will be all right in time."

Moreen had not realized how very tired she was. She laid her head on Will's shoulder and closed her eyes. Will turned to address Jocelyn. "My thanks for your assistance to my wife. I shall see that she does rest now."

The door to Geoffrey's bedchamber slammed open and Constance stormed through it. "You snake! You bastard! You... Get rid of your slut!"

Jeanette gasped indignantly and would have responded but Geoffrey stopped her. "Perhaps you should go, my dear. Better that you should not have to endure my wife's tirades." Jeanette picked up her clothing, and Geoffrey handed her a pouch full of jewels. "A gift, my sweet. For your... enthusiasm." She plastered herself against Geoffrey and demonstrated her thanks with a smoldering kiss. Her eyes glinted with triumph as she swept past Constance.

Geoffrey watched her leave; delighted by the sight she made wrapped in the scarlet coverlet. When the door closed behind her he turned his attention back to the shrew to which he was eternally bound. "Now my pet." He looked around for his clothing. "I trust you slept well."

"I trust you slept very little." She snapped.

He grinned as he began to dress. "Why would that suddenly bother you after so many years of indifference? I have never taken you to task over your lovers." In truth he had never found any evidence that Constance had been unfaithful, but he goaded her occasionally, hoping she would give some indication.

"You are the lowest creature ever to have slithered upon this earth." She was desperately trying to maintain her control. "I suppose you thought I would never find out. This explains why we have not been invited to court in so long. Tell me, Geoffrey, does the king know, or have the two of you fooled him all this time?"

"Constance, what on earth are you talking about?"

"How dare you!" She slapped him with all of her strength. He sat on the bed, stunned. In all of their years of feuding, of wounding each other, she had never struck him. "How dare you pretend ignorance? I know Geoffrey! I saw for myself. Why she's the very image of Christiana!"

"Christiana? What has she to do with anything?" Their eldest daughter had long since married and had been living in Rome for more than ten years.

"It will not work. I know everything. Our 'virtuous' queen, whom all adore—what will everyone think of her when I tell them that she bore you a bastard?" Constance was alight with her anger and the evil triumph of revenge forming in her mind. "I shall tell Gustave. He will see you dead for this."

She ran out of the room in search of the king. Geoffrey slowly pulled his boots on as he thought over everything Constance had said. He had never bedded Lavinia that he could remember. He supposed the best thing to do, would be to see the queen and ask her what nonsense his wife was spouting. She could be downright joyous when she thought she had him cornered, and that could never happen. For if she ever succeeded in her quest to see him fall, he would be dead. That was certain. Constance left nothing to chance.

Chapter 14

As Geoffrey approached the door to Lavinia's solar, he saw Constance and Gustave coming from the other direction.

"You see! Did I not tell you he would come here?" Constance's voice rang with pseudo-righteous indignation.

"Did *I* not tell *you* madam that I will not heed your ranting?" Gustave rarely raised his voice, but Constance had a way of bringing out the worst in people. He turned to Geoffrey. "What do you know of this matter?"

For once Geoffrey was able to truthfully deny any knowledge of wrongdoing. "I know nothing other than my wife's accusations, and they are absurd to me."

At that moment Lavinia opened the door. She was not entirely surprised to see them all standing there. Geoffrey bowed, but Constance offered no such show of respect. Lavinia merely stepped aside to allow them to enter. Silence reigned for a moment as everyone was deciding what to say.

Constance began. "Your Majesty, I beg you to examine the evidence. If you merely look at Geoffrey you will see the proof of your queen's infidelity."

"I have never lain with that man! Nor would I choose to!" Lavinia replied angrily.

"Forgive me if I believe otherwise. How else would it be possible that *your* daughter has my husband's eyes? The princess is the very image of my eldest child. You cannot barter away the truth any longer."

"She is right Lavinia." Gustave said softly. Constance took it as a sign of victory.

Geoffrey took a step forward. "What do you mean?" He looked to Lavinia. "My lady queen, was there a time that due to the effects of wine I have forgotten?"

"You villain!" she cried. "As if I would have let you touch me! You who have ruined more lives than you know!"

Gustave tried to comfort her with an embrace. "Shall I tell them, my dear?"

"No!" Lavinia stepped away from the protection of his arms. "I must be the one. For I made the promise."

Neither Constance nor Geoffrey had any idea what to expect.

"Lord DeFord some years ago, though I doubt you remember it, you were a guest at court in our palace at Niezagh. One of my ladies in waiting became enamored of you. Her name was Anne—Anne Beauville. I tried to tell her what you were. She did not heed my warnings. You seduced her, and she believed every word you said to her. I tried to tell her that you would leave her, but she would not hear me. She was in love with you.

"When you left she begged to go with you. You laughed at her as if she were a child. When you had gone she came to me, weeping for her foolishness, begging my forgiveness. Nine months later she died giving birth to a child. I promised her that I would raise her daughter as my own. And when our infant son died we buried him beside her, as her child. I promised her that I would do everything within my power to keep you from knowing the truth. For seventeen years I have been silent, and I would gladly have remained so until my death." She turned and stared out a window.

Geoffrey spoke thoughtfully and quietly. "Anne. I remember her. Then...Allyn is my daughter?"

Lavinia rounded on him. "She must never know. No one must ever know. You have caused enough pain. You destroyed Anne. I won't let you destroy Allyn!"

Gustave pinned a gaze of iron on Geoffrey. "I will have your word sir. You will tell no one."

Geoffrey was not about to cross Gustave now. "You have it...my word and my loyalty, my king."

Constance was furious. "No! You may wish to hide behind the throne but I will tell all of Frandia what you've done."

In a flash Geoffrey had her backed against the wall, his jeweled dagger at her throat. "You will keep your silence madam, or you will lose your life." His eyes stared hard into hers.

For the first time in her life Constance was afraid. She saw murder in his gaze. He would not hesitate to end her. Her eyes faltered under his glare, and he knew he had won. He lowered his weapon and she snapped "This is not finished. I will triumph! I will see you dead."

"Perhaps, but not today." He sheathed his dagger and watched her as she fled the room.

"You must leave Geoffrey." He turned at Gustave's words. "As soon as possible."

Geoffrey nodded his agreement. "If you will give me leave Sire, I will see to it at once."

He did not even see the corridors of the palace as he strode back to his chambers. He tried to remember seeing the princess. She had long, raven hair. He had not seen her eyes, but surely they must be blue. The DeFord's were known for the distinctive shade of their eyes, among other things. He had come to his chambers without realizing it. He looked up to find himself opening the door. "Pack my things. We are leaving at once. Where is my son?"

Moreen lay sleeping with Will watching over her. He had sent Marguerite out as soon as Moreen had settled into bed. He listened to the soft sound of her breathing. His life would be over if he lost her. She must get better. She must regain her strength. Nothing less would do. She would be fine. He repeated these things to himself again and again 'til he was nearly going mad.

"Lord William? May we come in?" Isabelle and Allyn were standing just outside, their hands filled with offerings. He motioned them in and they set down their loot. "Fresh fruit, bread, tea, and a few honey cakes I stole from the kitchen." Allyn explained. "I do hope they help. I am sorry I could not come sooner. Mother had me locked up."

"You are all so sweet to stay with me." Moreen was gratified to see Will and her friends. "Are those honey cakes?"

Isabelle handed one to her. "We thought you might like them. You really must rest Moreen, or you will not be able to attend the ball tonight."

"We will not be attending the ball." Geoffrey's frame filled the doorway. "We are leaving." He looked at Allyn, who had looked up at the sound of his voice—her hair, the unmistakable blue of her eyes. Yes, she was his child.

"Why are we leaving?" Will demanded. "Moreen is ill. She should not be moved."

"I am fine." She insisted.

"You may be ill Moreen." Geoffrey agreed with his son. "But in three days time you will be at home. One always mends more quickly when breathing one's native air. The king has entrusted me with an important task which will be best completed at Thornhill." It wasn't quite the truth, but truth had never been one of Geoffrey's priorities. "I shall have Marguerite begin packing your things. We leave in two hours' time." His eyes rested once more upon Allyn before he exited.

"Oh Moreen! I shall miss you so!" Allyn threw her arms around her friend.

"And I." Isabelle blinked back tears, remembering her father's words.

"I shall miss you both terribly. But we will see each other again soon. I am sure of it." Moreen smiled at them. "Now I must get ready. Allyn, the gowns you lent me..."

"Keep them. I don't need them—truly I don't. And when the new gowns are finished you must come back for them."

Two hours later the DeFords were settled into their carriage for the three days' journey back to Thornhill.

"I am glad to be home." Thornhill, in comparison with the palace, seemed drab to the others, but for Moreen the comfort of familiarity was more important than ostentatious luxury. She stretched her aching body. She was nearly numb from sitting for so long. Will wanted her to go straight to bed, but she softly refused. She wished to visit their villeins. Will would not hear of it. It was much too far from the keep for her to be safe.

Geoffrey took up the argument for his son. He had decided that the best way to further enrage his wife was to concern himself with Moreen's well being and happiness. He knew that Constance was still looking for anything she could use to rid herself of their daughter-in-law. By making himself Moreen's unofficial protector he could once again put a stop to Constance. His hope was that she would become so incensed as to commit an error so grievous that he could finally be rid of her.

Moreen agreed to retire early after the meal. Will, of course, retired as well. Constance had been silent all during the journey, and had disappeared quickly once inside the keep.

So Geoffrey retreated to his beloved solar, and his best brandy. It was a time to reflect, to plan, to celebrate. It was almost midnight when he heard the door opening. *This used to be such a quiet, peaceful room. Oh how I miss those times!*

"In all of our years together you have rarely set foot in my little sanctuary. I believe this to be your third apparition in two months. If I did not know you as well as I do, I would think you were pursuing me. What say you, Constance? Have you come to fight for me? Beg me to cast my paramours aside and sate you with my ardor?"

"In twenty five years I have not desired your company. I do not believe I shall change that course. I am a creature of habit." She stood half in the room, half out of it.

"Then state your purpose, my pet." He took a large draught of his brandy. He could no longer enjoy the drink with her nearby.

"I have come to discuss terms of surrender with you. Your surrender, of course." He snickered at her. Unaffected, she continued. "If you wish to hold on to your son, you will do as I say. What are you laughing about?"

"You, my dear. Do you think I care if you have your claws in the future lord of this estate? My daughter is the princess. Her son—my grandson—shall be king one day."

"Phillip shall be king. And you and your bastard will be executed. Then *my* son will be exalted for his service to the crown. Yes, he will side with Phillip and your downfall shall be his glory."

"A charming delusion, but Gustave will not be overthrown. William is strong, but he is young. He could not match me any day. That is the way with revolution, the youth rebel and the men of the country crush them. Then it is your son who will die."

"You would not allow your heir to be put to death." She argued.

"What is one heir? He can be replaced."

"You are mad. I could not give you another son if I wanted to."

"Did I say anything to that effect? You see my dear, after this little revolt is put down Gustave will persuade His Holiness that our marriage was never valid." He paused to sip his brandy again. "I know a lady or two who would be more than willing to assist me in producing an heir. Lady Jeanette DeFord has a pleasing sound to it. Don't you agree? Hmm. Better perhaps that I keep Jeanette as a lover. Then after William is beheaded for treason I can wed Moreen."

"Never! I will not be cast aside! I have not spent thirty years of my life to be replaced by some child!" She was angrier than he had ever seen her.

"And that is why you hate Moreen so, isn't it?" Emboldened by his plan to dispose of Constance, Geoffrey no longer felt any hesitance about pushing her beyond whatever limits she might possess. Thirty years of tolerating her venom was enough. "You see her lithe young body, her soft smooth skin, the light in her eyes. It drives you mad with jealousy. Even thirty years ago you were not so tempting as that sweet morsel. Every move she makes, every word she speaks makes a man hunger for her. The only man who ever worshipped you was your son, and he too has fallen under Moreen's seductive spell. Tell me Constance, do you lie awake at night imagining them together, and wishing you were in her place?"

"You disgust me! There are no words to describe the filth of your mind! You are no better than a dog." She inched back toward the door, tears of rage filling her eyes. "I swear before I leave this earth I shall see you pay for all you have done!"

As she ran from the solar, Geoffrey settled back into his chair and his brandy with a smile on his face. He felt like a new man—a man who would get everything he deserved.

Chapter 15

"Oh, you are awake!" Agnes was just peering in to check on Lady Moreen. "One moment milady. I shall fetch a tray."

Moreen felt as if she had slept for days. She was very much restored to her usual energy. By the time Agnes returned with her breakfast, she had already dressed and braided her hair.

"Milady you look beautiful in that gown!" Agnes set the tray on the table by the window.

"Thank you Agnes. It was a gift from Princess Allyn." As Agnes walked toward the door Moreen asked "Won't you sit with me? I have missed your company."

Agnes flushed slightly. "Lady Moreen you are very kind. How could you miss me when you were among so many fine people?"

Moreen smiled. "You are a fine person Agnes, and many who may look fine are not. Most of the people there were rather like empty chests—they look rich enough, but there is nothing inside of them. I did meet some very nice ladies, but no one I can talk to as I do with you." She looked out the window to see the sun climbing the sky. "Have I slept so late? Why did someone not wake me?"

"My lord gave orders that you were not to be disturbed. He was most insistent."

"Isn't he wonderful? I have the most thoughtful husband." Moreen smiled to herself.

"Oh no, not Lord William, Lord DeFord." Agnes corrected. Moreen looked disappointed. "Oh Lord William said that you were to rest as well."

That brightened her somewhat. Agnes told her the news of the keep and the village as she finished breaking her fast.

"All right Agnes. We must visit everyone, starting this very morning."

"But Lady Moreen, are you sure? Lord William said that you should rest."

"Agnes, you can see that I am perfectly well. I have rested, and now I must get back to my duties. I cannot wait to see everyone!"

"Milady, please. If you do too much you will take ill." Agnes was truly concerned. Lady Moreen looked different somehow.

Moreen thought about her weakness of late. Though she felt back to normal, she could not callously discount the fears of those who cared for her. "Very well. We shall start in the village, and only visit a few families. In a few days' time everyone shall see that I am well, and everything will be as it was before."

Agnes readied the necessary supplies and led Moreen to the stables; she had already sent a message with a page. "Lord DeFord said that if you insisted on going to the village we should take horses, so you would not tire yourself with walking."

"That was very kind of him." Moreen remarked.

A boy with soft brown hair, and kind hazel eyes led two horses out. He smiled at Agnes.

"I have never ridden by myself." Moreen lamented.

"Not to worry milady. Maida here is gentle as a kitten." The boy helped her onto Maida and turned to Agnes shyly. "I've chosen Nealie for you Agnes. She's one of the best in the stables."

She beamed at him as he helped her onto her mount. Then they were on their way.

"Agnes, you didn't tell me about your friend in the stables." Moreen teased.

Agnes blushed. "There is nothing to tell milady."

"I saw the way you two looked at each other. Come now. Tell me everything."

"Well we've known each other since we were children, in the village. But I hadn't seen him in so long. I didn't even know he was at Thornhill. Then one day I was bold enough to think about going riding. I couldn't even go in the stables I was so frightened. I'd decided to go back to the keep, and I just turned the corner when a hand grabbed me—it was him. Since then we've seen each other every day. Oh Lady Moreen, he's wonderful. Hardworking and kind, he is too." She was glowing.

"Agnes, it is good to see you so happy." Of course she had never seen Agnes unhappy, but this was the first time she had seen her practically flying with joy. "And what is the young man's name?"

"Chauncy." Agnes sighed happily. "I know it does sound odd at first. He was born in the west. But once you get used to it, Chauncy is a lovely name."

"And his family?" Moreen inquired.

"He has none. His parents died when he was a wee babe. A cousin of his mother's lived in the village here and 'twas she that raised him. But now she's gone on as well. So he has no one."

"Except you."

Agnes blushed. "Well, yes. But he hasn't asked me anything yet. I hope he will soon. I can't wait to be married and settled with wee babes of my very own."

Moreen had not thought much about children. She wanted them, she always had, but the swirl of recent events pushed the thoughts, and the longing, from her mind. Now she envisioned a child of her own and felt her heart ache with yearning. All throughout the morning she visited families with young children, some with babes that had been born while she was at court. With every child she held she could not help hoping that one day she would be holding her own babe in her arms. She so wanted to give William a son, but she would be happy with any child God gave her.

Back at the keep for the noon meal, she was preoccupied with her thoughts about children and tripped over a loose stone in the floor. Luckily Geoffrey was there to catch her. "Moreen, are you all right?"

"Yes my lord. Forgive me, I should have a care where I step." She pulled away from him and straightened her gown.

"Are you certain? You look weary. I fear you have taken on too much too soon."

"Not at all. I was merely occupied with my thoughts and paid no heed to the dangers of stone floors. I shall be more careful in the future." Will came towards them as she began to thank Geoffrey for his thoughtfulness. "I must thank you my lord, for allowing me the use of your horses. 'Twas very kind of you."

"Yes, very kind indeed." Will added. He had heard about his father's concerns for Moreen and was displeased.

"'Twas nothing. Any man would do the same for his family." Geoffrey smiled warmly at Moreen, earning him a dark scowl from his son.

"As if you know anything of family!"

"William please. I am trying to atone for my mistakes." He assumed what he thought would pass for an expression of humble contrition.

"Atone some other way. I will take care of my wife. She does not need your 'kindness.'" Will sneered over the word.

After Geoffrey had left them Moreen asked. "Why did you do that Will? He is trying to change."

"He is not capable of changing, nor does he wish to do so." He was not about to give his father the benefit of the doubt.

"How can you be so heartless? Your father has been kindness itself to me since we've returned. Does that mean nothing?"

"It means he has no scruples about using you to get to me. I've known him all my life Moreen. He is not to be trusted— ever! I want you to stay away from him as much as you can. I won't have him manipulating you." His tone was overbearing and brusque.

Moreen did not respond well to such curtly expressed sentiments. It seemed to her that her husband was more interested in a battle of wills with his father than he was in her welfare. "I won't seek him out. I would not do so anyway. But I will not be rude to any man in his own keep. If he approaches me I shall be as courteous as I would be to anyone."

She lifted her chin in that adorable, maddening way and left William standing there wondering why she could not comprehend the depths of his father's treachery.

The meal passed uneventfully, but silently. There was a feeling of eerie calm in the great hall. Something was building but not everyone agreed as to what. Some thought it must be the talk of war. Others insisted that the lord and lady of the keep were about to come to blows. Still others claimed the stirring in the atmosphere foretold the coming of an early winter. Whatever the storm brewing, everyone was keenly aware that something was about to happen.

Moreen believed the cause of the tension to be the feud between William and Geoffrey. Surely that must be why Constance was so unusually quiet. It must distress her a great deal to see her husband and son so at odds. Moreen determined that it was up to her to heal the breach between father and son. She had promised she would not seek Geoffrey out, so she simply waited until he happened by.

"Lord DeFord!" She called from the stairs as he strode through the entry hall. He turned in time to see her lose her balance and cling to the railing.

"What are you doing up and about? Are you trying to make yourself ill again?" He looked around for someone to help her and as the hall was empty, he took her up in his arms and started toward her chambers.

"Forgive me, my lord. I wish to speak with you." She spoke weakly and laid her head against his shoulder.

"You should be abed. You must take better care of yourself my dear. The future of the DeFord family depends on you." He spoke firmly but gently.

Moreen, feeling very weak and having no clue as to his intentions for her, thought he was referring to the grandchildren she might produce. "Of course." She murmured.

Gertrude was in Moreen's chambers and was surprised at seeing her being carried in by Lord Geoffrey. "Lady Moreen! What has happened milord?"

"Help me get her into bed." He said as he carefully maneuvered through the narrow doorways. He laid her gently atop the coverlet and turned to leave her to Gertrude's attentions.

Moreen reached out and took hold of his hand. "Please, don't go. I must speak with you."

He looked down at her pale face. "Later my dear. You must rest now. I do not want to see you out of this room."

"You will come back then, won't you?" She asked sleepily.

Geoffrey smiled. "Yes. I will come back. I promise." He kissed her hand and softly added, "Rest now my sweet."

Gertrude, who had been tending to the fire, heard the entire exchange. She played it back through her mind several times to be certain she would remember it correctly when she relayed it to Constance.

It was some hours later that William entered the keep after a long afternoon of avoiding his father. That had been easy enough. Knowing Geoffrey's preference for the interior of the keep Will had simply remained outdoors. He had missed the evening meal, but he was hoping to evade his sire yet again, thereby gaining several hours thought for dealing with the snake. He was just removing his sword belt when he heard the scream. Everyone in the hall froze. "Moreen." He half-whispered. He ran to her chambers and burst through the door. Nothing could have prepared him for the site that met his eyes.

Moreen was lying on the bed crying, her chemise torn. Geoffrey lay beside her, holding her wrists captive.

The point of Will's sword easily found it's way to the back of his father's neck. "On your feet, sir."

Geoffrey stood tentatively. "Are you planning to kill me?"

"If you insist." Came the reply. William showed no signs of his legendary temper. He was deadly calm. "A sword!" He called out to the crowd that had gathered in the corridor.

Moreen still lay on the bed, crying and clutching the coverlet to her. She was vaguely aware of her surroundings, but unable to speak.

One of the elder pages brought the requested sword to William. He kept his eyes fixed upon the villain before him. "Give it to him."

"Are you certain that you want to challenge me, William?" Geoffrey had an evil gleam in his eyes. There was no need of waiting for a revolution. He would end this insolent pup right now.

"Your time is past, old man."

"Will you allow me to don my tunic?" Geoffrey asked in a tone of indifferent boredom. He was playing for effect, much as a cat teases and tortures its prey.

"You chose this battle. Fight as you are." Will was perfectly calm as they began to circle each other.

Steel clanged against steel as each taunted the other with slight, testing blows. Geoffrey struck first and advanced upon his son, driving him through the adjoining room and into the hallway. The crowd of servants followed them. Gertrude sent one of the girls to find Constance.

It was an even match in strength. William had the advantage of youthful stamina; Geoffrey, of deadly experience. Blow after blow rang out with an eerie sound of warriors groans and the ring of a collision of steel, each clamor reverberated off the stone walls and drifted into the distance like a frightened specter. First Geoffrey had the advantage, then William. They reached a corner and Will backed into the wall. Geoffrey charged, only to have his target slip behind him. Will used the element of surprise to full advantage, driving his father back several feet. In a moment they were nearing the staircase in the entrance hall.

Constance watched in horror from below, terrified for her son. She cried out. "Stop this madness!"

At the sound of his mother's voice Will turned slightly and Geoffrey's blade caught his left arm. Constance screamed at the sight of her son's blood. Geoffrey had known how to exploit Will's momentary distraction. He charged again, only to be blocked by Will's blade. Face to face they glared at each other.

"I *will* kill you!" Will growled.

"Before you do, you should know that your wife's screams were screams of pleasure. She begged me to ravish her."

His words had their intended effect. As a red-faced Will uttered a guttural sound of pure rage, Geoffrey slammed the hilt of his sword into Will's abdomen. Will responded by ramming his head into his father's chest. They wrestled for long moments, and were dangerously close to the stairs when Geoffrey brought his hilt down on Will's back.

"No!" Constance could not stand to watch, yet could not look away as William fell from her view and Geoffrey backed up several paces.

Heaving, Geoffrey lifted his sword with a look of triumph. "You see? I always win." He began his final charge to end his only son.

William lay prone, watching as if in a dream. He could see Geoffrey's boots and blade approaching. Acting on instinct, and a burst of desperation, he began to rise and thrust his sword upward to block the deathblow. The tip of William's blade caught Geoffrey in the stomach and in twisting away he was thrown over the railing by the force of the impact when William's body rose as his own fell forward.

He fell soundlessly to the floor, and landed with a ghastly thud.

The world froze.

Constance stood looking at what remained of her husband, unable to believe his reign of terror was finally at an end. Now she would carry out her plans. Her reverie was shattered by a voice from above.

Gertrude had taken it upon herself to act on her mistress' behalf. "Milord, your lady wife should be punished. I saw with my own eyes how she encouraged his advances."

Will's bloodstained blade was instantly at her throat. He shouted loud enough for all to hear. "I will not hear any of your poisonous slander against my wife! One thing I know — that she is innocent of any wrong, and I will take her word above all others! You will leave my keep at once and you will never return. The next time a man or woman dares to impugn Lady Moreen DeFord's honor I will not be so forgiving."

Constance listened in stunned silence. A single tear coursed down her face.

"You there." Will addressed Agnes. "See to my lady. You shall attend her from now on."

"Yes milord." She hurried off to take care of her mistress.

Will disappeared down a hallway and the servants dispersed. Constance alone remained in the hall.

She circled her deceased husband slowly, and then strode purposefully away. Shoulders squared, chin lifted high, she walked directly to her chambers. Her time was over. She had outlived Geoffrey, but she no longer held any power. Her dreams of discrediting Moreen would never reach fruition. Gertrude, her only friend in the world, was lost to her. She reached into her writing desk and grasped a familiar object. The ornate dagger was a Richelieu family heirloom. Its cold weight in her hand had a soothing, almost hypnotic effect. She had dreamed of driving it into Geoffrey's black heart. Now she sat and plunged it into her own.

Chapter 16

The sky was gray, but no rain fell and no wind broke the stillness as the people of the village shuffled past the body of their dead lord—paying their respects to a man they had feared, even hated, but never respected.

At William's request the funeral mass was held graveside. Geoffrey had never in his life set foot in the village church, so Will saw no reason he should now that his life was over.

There was some disagreement as to the cause of death. The local gossips had twisted the reports several different ways. One story held that William had killed his father; no one was bothered by this possibility, to the contrary they thought it likely given the family's history and William's infamous temper. Another version claimed that William had intended to spare Geoffrey's life, and it was the accidental fall that killed him. Yet another tale had Gertrude pushing Geoffrey to his death and being banished rather than slain because Geoffrey DeFord's death was more a blessing than a wrong to be avenged, and so his son saw no reason to press for the lady-in-waiting to be punished.

Constance's demise was less interesting. It was known by all that she had taken her own life, as such there could be no funeral mass for her. Constance had been a mystery to the villagers. She had rarely set foot outside of Thornhill. Despite the lack of familiarity with her ways, she was not particularly liked within the village. Not knowing any of the details of her life, the people assumed she had killed herself as a result of being driven mad with grief at the loss of her husband, though many had believed her to be mad beforehand as no sane woman would have wed Geoffrey DeFord.

Thomas Sinclair took Will aside. "How is Moreen? I heard what that bastard did to her."

"How?" Will demanded.

"Your servants. A word of advice your lordship, do not punish them for it. It is love of Moreen that led them to repeat what happened. And no one in this village will ever speak of it openly—none of us would wish to remind her of such an event."

"Very well. I shall heed your advice." Will acquiesced. "I wonder that so many have come. I was fairly certain that no one liked him any better than I did."

"Well I can't speak for the rest of them, but I came to make certain he's dead. It's always best to see with your own eyes." Thomas glanced briefly toward Geoffrey's corpse, his face smashed from the impact of hitting the stone floor. "He's never looked better to me."

They talked a moment longer and then it was time for William to toss the first handful of earth onto his father's body. He stepped toward the grave, spat upon the deceased, and walked away. The priest stared at Will's retreating back in shock, and quickly began to intone in Latin for the soul of the deceased as well as the souls of the surviving family, for it seemed they certainly needed the prayers.

Moreen had not been herself since the attack. Will had immediately ordered their things moved to his father's chambers, and all of Geoffrey's possessions burned. That night she had wept bitterly in her husband's arms and begged him to forgive her for not heeding his warnings. He had tried to soothe her, but he had little comfort to give. He did not blame her, but he could not keep her from blaming herself.

Since that night she had not cried, but neither had she smiled. Her appetite suffered and she could not be teased out of her bleak mood. In spite of her forgiving nature, Moreen could not bring herself to attend the funeral mass. She had not even set foot out of doors. Will did not push her for fear of causing more harm, but he was quickly exhausting his supply of ideas.

As the sun sank below the horizon on the night of the burial two travelers arrived on horseback.

"Stan! What are you doing here? And…Isabelle?" Will's shock was evident.

Isabelle laughed as Stanley helped her down. "We thought we'd pay you and Moreen a visit. You don't mind do you?"

Will stood speechless.

"Where is Moreen? I must speak with her."

"She keeps mostly above stairs of late. I'm afraid you will find her much changed." Will proceeded to explain the events of the previous days.

"Oh poor, dear Moreen!" Isabelle's tender heart ached for her friend, but then she brightened. "Perhaps we can jolt her out of this dark humor. Do you think she might be willing to help me with my wedding?"

"Do you mean to tell me that you two have traveled all this way without a chaperone, and you are not even wed?" Will's tone was one of mock astonishment. "I daresay a wedding is as good a reason as any to rally the spirits. I am glad you have come."

"That was Isabelle's idea. I wanted to take her straight to Kenleigh, but she insisted we could not be wed without the two of you present. Isn't that right, darling?"

She beamed at him. "Yes it is, though I confess I had another reason for suggesting Thornhill as our destination. Stanley's home will be the first place my father will look for us." The men stared at her with surprise and she grinned. "Someone must think of these things while my handsome warrior is busy being besotted with me. I shall go find Moreen and leave you two to speak of fighting and horses and such."

They watched her depart for a moment, then Stanley spoke. "Isn't she wonderful?"

"If you say so." Will signaled for Chauncy to take the horses. Steering his friend toward the keep he asked, "Stan, how would you like some brandy?"

Meanwhile Isabelle ran into Agnes on her way to Moreen's chambers. After introducing herself, she convinced Agnes to let her take the tray with its tea in to Moreen. Isabelle pasted a large smile on her face and stepped through the door. "Your tea, my lady."

"Isabelle? What are you doing here?" Moreen was so surprised that she jumped out of bed and had to grab the bedpost to steady herself.

Isabelle quickly set the tray down. "Are you yet ill?"

"No, only tired. I have not slept well these past few nights." Her eyes were shuttered, but Isabelle already knew of the painful events that were plaguing her.

"I'm afraid you must sleep better from now on, else how will you help me plan my wedding?"

Moreen brightened. "Isabelle! Is Stanley here?"

She nodded. "How else would I have gotten here? I'm afraid we must be married soon. I wish to be Lady St. Robert before a week has passed. I'll take no chances. Father will come after us, and when he does there must not be anything he can do to come between us." Moreen looked at her with pity. "It was the only way Moreen. Father would not consent. Stanley insisted upon speaking with him but it did no good. He would not agree, and what's more he said that you and I could not be friends. I could not have that! So you see I had to run away with Stanley." She finished with a saucy grin and they both burst out laughing. "Do say you'll help me."

"Of course I will. The chapel should be opened and scrubbed thoroughly, a feast prepared, oh I don't know what to do!"

She was looking pale and Isabelle was concerned that perhaps her request might cause Moreen to work overmuch.

"You are Lady DeFord now. Simply tell the servants what you want and it will be done."

"I am Lady DeFord. It hardly seems so. I fear I have been spending too much time abed of late. I must start acting like a lady." She had set her mind, and there would be no dissuading her now.

"Wonderful! And while you are acting like a lady let us redecorate this keep. I've never seen a place so forbidding. This is *your* home, and it must look so." Isabelle had taken note of the somber décor on her way to find Moreen. While the wall hangings and furnishings had once been the height of style, the atmosphere of the place was rather dreary. She did not wonder at Moreen's lack of spirits. Who could possibly be joyful in such dismal surroundings?

"I must ask Will first. If he would not approve, I would not dare. It is his home as well and it has been this way all of his life. He might wish things to remain as they are." Moreen rather hoped the contrary was true, for once Isabelle had suggested the project, her mind had rapidly begun planning. Anything they wished to be rid of would be given to the people of the village and surrounding farms. Any new thing that they desired might easily be made by local craftsmen and artisans. For the first time in days she felt content and was looking forward with anticipation to the days, and weeks, to come. "You may stay at Thornhill as long as you like." She enfolded Isabelle in a fond embrace. "Oh, I'm so glad you have come."

"So am I. And I am very grateful that you and William will let us be wed here." Isabelle replied.

"As if we would even have thought of refusing!" Moreen sighed contentedly. "When do you wish to have the wedding?"

"I would be married tomorrow, but Stanley insists that we have a more fitting wedding. He says he will not hear of our being wed without a celebration. So I am resigned to wait. I'm not certain how long."

Moreen rose slowly. "We shall all talk about it on the morrow. Now I must see that rooms are prepared for you both."

"I'll come with you, if you would not mind." Isabelle kept a close eye on Moreen for fear that a weak spell would come upon her. Her concern seemed to prove unnecessary, as Moreen appeared nearly herself again.

William and Stanley were in what had been Geoffrey's solar. Along with the master's chambers, Will had ordered most of the things in the solar burned. He had gone through various scrolls and pieces of parchment to ascertain what was necessary to keep, and the rest had been instantly dispatched. Certain rather sensitive documents he had burned personally. The table and the chair behind it Will kept as a reminder that he had slain the dragon his sire had been, and now occupied the throne. The two chairs by the window remained for lack of suitable replacements.

Stanley savored the brandy merrily. "Damn good to be able to enjoy this without a plan for explaining it's disappearance, eh?"

Will nodded absently and stared into the flames in the hearth.

"Pardon me sir." Stan attempted to gain his host's attention. "My lord, His Royal Stanleyness commands you to pay homage by gifting us with several cases of this blessed ambrosial drink."

"Mmm-hmm." Will nodded again. "What was that?"

"You just agreed to join me in pillaging the local village, then setting fire to Thornhill and riding off to join the brothers of St. Francis." Stan grinned at his own jest as Will began to chuckle. "Shall we be about it then?"

"Certainly. Once I've finished sacking Paris we shall be off upon your noble quest."

"On second thought, perhaps we had better stay here." He raised his drink. "To sloth!"

Will laughed. "To sloth. Now when do you mean to have this wedding?"

"Not until the players arrive." Stan said idly.

"What players?"

"Oh, didn't I tell you? We met a company of them on our way here. They were expected at an estate a few leagues north of here, but happily promised to join us in a fortnight or so when I told them that our generous host would pay them quite handsomely."

Will was mildly irked, but not surprised. "And what expense, if any, shall you bear for this wedding?"

"Dreadful expense! Almost half my wardrobe is at the palace. I shall never be able to go back for it."

"You miserable popinjay." Will laughed. "I suppose I shall keep you as a friend for the considerable amusement you provide."

During the ensuing days the keep was a flurry of activity. The chapel was scrubbed from floor to ceiling and readied for the first mass it had seen in more than two generations. Having gained Will's approval, Moreen and Isabelle were proceeding with the plans to redecorate, and had already given away many things that would be of use to the local populace.

Word of Moreen's plans had spread rapidly and every tradesman for miles had come to offer his talents in service to the new mistress of Thornhill. Generous to a fault,

Moreen gave commissions to all of them. William's only interference was to insist on a portrait of his beloved wife, as soon as she would have time to sit for it. He was pleased with the change in her since their friends' arrival. She took such joy in her efforts, that he could not deny her. Had she asked for the crown jewels he would have agreed.

At last the day of the wedding arrived. Stanley and Isabelle had lovingly argued over details, with Isabelle quickly gaining the advantage. She had convinced him time and again of the insignificance of certain things: they need not have roast suckling pig, goose would do nicely; it was unnecessary to invite the entire country, as they needed no one beyond Moreen and William to witness their vows; the wine in the cellar at Thornhill was excellent, there was no need to send to France for a different vintage.

Isabelle had sneaked her best gown out of the palace for this very occasion. She was radiant in the soft blue silk. Her hair was fashioned in one long braid down her back, and delicate white flowers woven into a crown rested atop the golden tresses.

"You look so beautiful!" Moreen had tears in her eyes.

"Oh, you must not cry, or I shall as well." Isabelle smiled nervously. She was anxious to be wed to her beloved Stanley.

An hour later it was done, and the feasting began. Despite the lack of time to prepare, there was an impressive display of food. Most of the villagers were in attendance for though they knew nothing of the bride, and little of the groom, they had been secretly celebrating since Geoffrey's death and they now reveled in the chance to rejoice openly.

Though they commented appropriately on the food, the wine, and the players—who were extra jovial for the occasion and the price they would receive—Stanley and Isabelle noticed very little of the festivities surrounding them. Intent upon each other, they cared not for the noise or the audience. Stanley whispered something to his bride, who in turn whispered to Moreen. Moreen then sent a message to the musicians. Stanley stood, bowed to Isabelle, and offered his arm to escort her to the space that had been cleared for dancing.

The music began slowly. It was an old Frandian folk dance that everyone knew and nearly everyone took part in. The old, the infirm, and the very young watched as the dance progressed, gradually faster until the music reached a rollicking tempo. The crowd of dancers cheered and laughed so much that no one noticed when the bride and groom disappeared. In truth they were not missed for nearly an hour, at which time many of the guests were departing. Those who remained past sunset were mainly the youth of the area, and many a lass hoped to catch the eye of a handsome lad and be dancing soon at her own wedding feast.

Next morning some revelers awakened to sore bones, having slept off their inebriation in a less than comfortable berth. Moreen was feeling unwell but she insisted upon visiting the tenant farms. Her conscience would not allow her to put off such things any longer. She guiltily realized that she should have made her visits long ago, had she not been preoccupied with her guests. She and Agnes were walking in the warmth of the sunlight when she remembered something.

"Agnes? Did William seem odd to you at all?" Moreen saw that she had confused her companion. "I mean the way he spoke of being worried for our safety. No one here would harm us. I cannot think what is the matter with him."

"Perhaps it's just that he doesn't wish to see you take ill again. A guard would be right helpful if you were to faint, milady. Chauncy said something too, but then he's always like that. Always protecting me." She smiled happily.

The morning passed uneventfully. Every family was pleased to see Moreen again. There had been rumors that she was taken of a fever, and everyone was most happy to see that was not the case.

At noon she told Will of her morning and he listened out of duty rather than genuine interest. The newly wed couple were no where to be seen, and Will was contemplating sending a page to rouse them. Now that the wedding had taken place, he had business to discuss with Stan.

The revolution was now certain to occur and Will needed more information before he could decide for either faction. He had not yet told Moreen for fear of upsetting her. She had been so happy for the last week, how could he worry her when they might end up left out of the whole mess? He was hoping that Phillip would march his armies straight to Vallenburg, bypassing Thornhill altogether. Neutrality would be the best option, if only he could be certain to have that option.

As Will was preoccupied and Isabelle did not require her company, Moreen set out again with Agnes to visit the farms they had not had time to stop at during the morning.

Back at the keep, Stanley had finally appeared and was immediately ushered into William's solar. Stanley played for time to annoy Will, insisting upon eating before talking, and then upon a drink of that beloved brandy. Finally Stan ran out of stalling tactics and began to enlighten his friend.

Even in speaking of war and treason Stan could not be serious for very long and the conversation was interrupted by laughter more than once. Only Stanley could find humor in such a dangerous undertaking. Despite his levity, Stan provided excellent information—beneath his jocular exterior was a keen and able mind.

"But Stan," Will finally asked, "do you really think Phillip stands a chance of winning?"

"Yes. I do. The numbers of Gustave's warriors will not seem so daunting when half of the nobles have joined the rebellion. Then there are all of those who will join once they realize that the revolution will succeed. We have the element of surprise, Will. Gustave has no idea that so many of his men have joined Phillip. He knows some have, but he overestimates his own persuasiveness."

A servant appeared in the doorway. "Milord there are riders approaching! It looks like a whole army!"

"Expecting someone?" Stan raised a quizzical brow.

"No." Will said simply as they both headed to meet whoever was coming.

The riders reached the bailey just as Stanley and William did. Honoré DuClerque was among them. "I believe they're here to see you, Stan."

A rider came up through the ranks of the group and they parted like the sea.

"My lord!" Stanley cried, glad to see a less than murderous face. "What brings you to Thornhill?"

"You do, St. Robert." Phillip had a regal bearing and a commanding voice. "I believe Count DuClerque has a grievance."

"I want my daughter. I know she is here with you." DuClerque glared at Stan and Will.

"My liege," Stan addressed Phillip, "The lady in question *was* the Count's daughter and is now Lady St. Robert."

"I'll kill you!" DuClerque bellowed.

"You will not. He's the best swordsman in my entire army." Phillip was calm in the face of the Count's wrath.

"I demand satisfaction! He stole my daughter away in the night and wed her without my consent."

"So kill him after the revolution. Until then I want the two of you to remember that you fight together, for your king. Any trouble and I will arrest you both."

A commotion from behind startled the horsemen. Agnes came through the crowd in tears, her head bleeding. "My lord, someone has taken Lady Moreen!"

Chapter 17

"I am sorry about this. This is not about you—truly, it's not."

"Then let me go." Moreen was slung over the back of a horse, her hands bound. Silence was her captor's only response. "Will you at least tell me where you are taking me?"

"I cannot do that. But I give you my word that you will not be harmed."

They continued for what seemed to Moreen to be several hours. It was dark now, and they traveled through the forest. She believed his promise not to harm her. But she was frightened nonetheless. She knew that Will would be searching for her, and that he would not rest until she had been safely returned, but she did not know how long that might be.

Her position was not one of comfort, and with the sight of trees moving past she began to feel sick. "Please sir. I believe I shall be ill!"

He stopped at once and helped her down and away from his horse. Her stomach's meager contents quickly landed among the bracken. She straightened and tried to walk, but found herself too weak. Her captor took pity on her and helped her back to the animal. This time he let her sit in front of him, with his arms around her. She was too weak to protest the impropriety, and she was uncertain as to whether a kidnapper would care about such things anyway. She leaned back against him and closed her eyes.

When she opened them again she found that they were approaching a keep, and her fears returned as she realized that she had no notion of her own whereabouts. A groom came out to meet them and greeted her captor warmly. The knowledge that he was welcomed thus comforted Moreen somewhat. He dismounted and helped her down. The groom made no comment as to her hands being bound, only gave his master a look of incredulity and led the horse away.

He led her into the keep. In the torchlight she could see his face. He was rather handsome, but much younger than she had thought him to be. "Come along now." He tugged at her bonds and led her up a staircase.

Moreen followed with some difficulty. She was too weary to match his pace. Her stomach began to protest its state of emptiness, but despite her hunger all she wanted was to be freed from her bonds and to sleep the clock round. They finally seemed to slow down as they neared a door. He knocked and briefly waited to be admitted.

He sauntered into the room with his prize, smiling for all the world like a tournament champion. "Look here, brother!" he proclaimed proudly.

Lord Roger Boyd stared at his younger brother Sebastian in amazement. "What in the name of all that's holy have you done?"

He knew Sebastian to be somewhat daft at times, but until this night he had not suspected him of being truly mad. His gaze shifted to the girl. She looked pale and bedraggled... and vaguely familiar. "My God!" He rushed over to her and immediately untied her wrists. "Lady DeFord! I do apologize!" He briefly regarded his brother, barely containing his rising fury. "Leave us at once and send for my lady wife."

Moreen was rubbing her wrists. "Thank you, milord."

Roger led her to his own chair. "Do sit down milady. I cannot tell you how truly sorry I am at the indignities you have suffered this night. Be assured my brother shall answer for this outrage."

"You wanted to see me husband?" Lady Boyd stood in the doorway and gasped at what she saw. She quickly took in Moreen's disheveled appearance and reddened wrists. She swept gracefully toward her unexpected guest. "Lady Moreen, how lovely to see you again."

"Jocelyn!" Moreen said in surprise.

She smiled. "I am glad that you have remembered me. This is my husband Lord Roger Boyd. Please let me apologize for the...manner...of your...journey. But though your visit is unexpected, it need not be unpleasant. We are honored to have you as our guest, are we not my lord?" She looked to her husband.

"Yes. Quite so." Roger was constantly amazed by his wife's ability to handle any situation with perfect grace. He silently thanked God once again for having led him to such a treasure. A look passed between husband and wife that communicated a great deal. Jocelyn's perceptive nature had quickly led her to believe that Sebastian was behind this turn of events, but she had every confidence that her husband would soon set things right.

"Now then, would you care to join me for a light supper?" Jocelyn smiled reassuringly.

"Yes, thank you." Moreen rose and followed her hostess from the room. She had taken an instant liking to Jocelyn while at court, and was relieved to find herself in that lady's care.

Jocelyn was careful to maintain a rather slow pace. She was very much aware of how pale Moreen looked, and how exhausted she must be. They went straight to the great hall, which was not as large as the one at Thornhill, but far more pleasant. Jocelyn had stopped only to speak briefly to two servant girls about the supper and about readying rooms for her guest. By the time they reached their destination a modest but aromatic repast awaited them.

As they chatted over warm bread and a fragrant stew of lamb Moreen began to relax. Jocelyn had a way of putting her at ease, and the atmosphere of the keep was both cheerful and soothing.

Moreen had many questions, but she grew increasingly drowsy and was sent off to bed before she could ask anything of import. As she closed her eyes she bade herself remember to ask Lady Jocelyn and Lord Boyd about her abduction on the morrow. Her final thought before succumbing to her exhaustion was to thank the Lord that she was spending her captivity in a warm bed rather than a cold dungeon.

Meanwhile at Thornhill Will had spent the evening roaring at everyone.

Agnes had eagerly told them all she could remember about Moreen's abductor. She had not gotten a look at his face as he had grabbed Moreen and started to drag her in the opposite direction of the way the ladies had been walking. Agnes had flung herself onto the man's back and demanded her mistress' release, but had been quickly shaken off and fell to the ground, hitting her head. She sobbed out her distress and apologized repeatedly for failing her mistress until Isabelle wisely removed her from Will's presence. Poor Agnes was inconsolable, for she truly felt that she should have been able to do more, and she was certain that whomever the scoundrel was who had taken Lady Moreen, he meant no good. Even Chauncy's whispered words of solace could not absolve her of the guilt she felt.

Stanley, Isabelle, Phillip, and Honoré watched Will pacing before the hearth in his solar, a dagger clutched in his right hand. He was too upset even to drink, which had Stanley very much concerned. The room was disturbingly silent for having such strong-willed and outspoken occupants.

Isabelle refused to speak to her father after he had refused to address her as Lady St. Robert. She had informed him that she would have nothing to say to him as long as he continued to deny her marriage. Her position, though amusingly reminiscent of Honoré's own stubbornness, increased his ire towards her husband. Stanley's one attempt at smoothing things over between father and daughter met with resentment on both sides, and he had since decided it was best to stay out of the quarrel.

"Will, you look very much like a lion pacing back and forth as you do." Isabelle observed. "If you continue we shall have to stop calling this your solar and refer to it instead as your den." The comment drew smiles from the other men, but Will payed no attention to the remark.

He paced in silence several minutes more before rounding on Phillip. "This is all your fault—you and your blasted war! If it weren't for your damned revolution this never would have happened!"

"I had nothing to do with your wife's disappearance, DeFord." Phillip was surprised at the accusation, but feared nothing, as he was innocent of any possible charge.

"Perhaps not, but with such a flurry of rumors and unrest the people have been stirred up into committing acts of the grossest stupidity. Mark my words Phillip: if she is not returned to me unharmed I hold you responsible, and I will have my revenge." Will pointed his dagger toward Phillip but made no move against him.

Phillip stood and addressed his host once more. "Lord William I will do everything in my power to help you find your wife. I took the liberty of dispatching several of my men to scout the area. They have orders to report directly to you."

Will was irritated at actually feeling grateful. "I suppose if your men prove helpful you will expect my support in this rebellion of yours."

"I would welcome your support, but I do not expect it. True loyalty must be given freely—it cannot be purchased."

Will strode to the window and stared out into the darkness. Somewhere out there Moreen was being held prisoner. He hoped that she was safe and vowed to himself that if she was not he would torture her captors slowly before killing them even more slowly. He would not sleep that night, nor any other until she was in his arms again.

After seeing Moreen settled comfortably, Lady Jocelyn made for her husband's solar. Roger would not wait 'til morning to have it out with Sebastian, and she wished to be present for the safety of all involved. Roger would not begin the confrontation without her, as she could offer an objective point of view that neither man was capable of seeing. And he had another reason—neither man would say or do his worst if she was present, they would restrain themselves as much from the soothing effect of her presence as from the great respect each had for her. She dreaded the conflict to come, but wasted no time for the sooner it was begun the sooner it would end.

She entered the room to find the two men staring at each other. Knowing full well how loud this discussion would become, she immediately closed the solid oaken door.

Roger began at once. "What have you to say for yourself?" But he did not allow his brother to answer. "What could you possibly have been thinking? Kidnap a noblewoman? Drag her here bound hand and foot like an animal?"

"I only bound her hands." Sebastian stated, as if that one assertion would clear him. His brother had finally lapsed into furious silence and glared at him, waiting. "I did this for the rebellion. You said it yourself, that William DeFord was the wild card in this war. This will force him to make a decision."

"And did it not occur to you that he might well decide against our cause?"

Sebastian pouted. "Well at least we will know where he stands so we can start fighting."

Roger grabbed him by the tunic and pushed him up against the wall. "You fool! Don't you know what you've done? You think a war is some glorious thing! We'll see what you think when you look into the eyes of men you played with as a boy as they die of a blow from your sword. If you even live long enough!"

Jocelyn put a gentle hand on her husband's arm. He dropped his baby brother and stalked over to a decanter of port. He was just swallowing a goodly measure when Sebastian spoke again.

"I am not afraid to fight!" He had misunderstood his brother's reasoning. It was not Sebastian's courage that he was questioning.

"Courage to the point of idiocy is vice, not virtue. Will you never consider the consequences of your actions?" Roger ran a hand through his hair in frustration. "I have protected you your entire life Sebastian. But you have gone too far this time. I will not let you destroy everything our family has built—I owe it to our ancestors and to my son. You have signed your own death warrant little brother."

"You won't frighten me with such nonsense."

"Nonsense?" Roger stared at his brother incredulously. "You have abducted a member of the most ruthless, dishonorable and deplorable family in the history of Frandia! To cross a DeFord is deadly. William DeFord killed his own father! Why should he hesitate to kill you?"

Sebastian paled. "I did not think..."

"You never think, you idiot!" Roger fumed.

"Please. Brother! You would not let him kill me?" Gone was the rash man of a moment ago—in his place stood a terrified boy.

"I might save him the trouble." Roger wearily fell into his chair and Jocelyn went to stand behind him, her hand resting on his shoulder.

"Sebastian, surely you know that Roger will do everything he can." Jocelyn said. "But there may be a day when your rashness leads you into a situation that we cannot help you out of."

A sober and thoroughly humbled Sebastian merely asked for leave to go to bed.

Roger waved him away without looking up from his contemplation of the floor. When Sebastian had gone, Roger regarded his wife. "That boy will be the death of me."

She chuckled softly. "What shall you do, my lord?"

He sighed heavily. "Is Lady DeFord settled?"

Jocelyn smiled, knowing that her husband had no doubt of their unexpected guest being well taken care of. He had merely asked to gain time to think of a strategy. "Yes. We had a lovely chat over supper. I am certain she is deep in slumber by now."

"DeFord will have men searching everywhere for her. I'll have to get a message to him somehow. But what can I say that won't arouse suspicion?" He rubbed his eyes wearily.

"You will think of something, my love. You always do."

He grasped her arm gently and pulled her around to sit on his lap. "How is my lady this night?"

"Tired. Content. Very much under your spell my lord." She leaned into him, enjoying his warmth and smiling up at him.

"As I am under yours my lady." He touched his forehead to hers and thus they sat for several moments. "Off to bed with you wife! I have a cryptic message to contrive and I shall make no progress with you in the room."

"As you wish my lord." She strode away, but looked back from behind the door. "Roger? Do not stay up very late. Nothing must be done that cannot wait until the morn."

Next morning Moreen joined Jocelyn in the great hall for breakfast. The men had already eaten, and so the two ladies were able to talk. Moreen was quite at ease and answered affirmatively when her hostess inquired whether she had slept well. Insignificant niceties continued for several minutes.

At last Moreen could wait no longer. "Lady Jocelyn please, I must know, why was I brought here?"

Jocelyn sighed. She had known Moreen would ask, but she found it no less difficult to explain. "You met my husband Lord Roger last evening. It was his brother Sebastian who abducted you."

"Yes, I heard him call Lord Roger his brother. But why did he take me? I do not understand." Moreen had tried several times during the previous day's journey to make sense of the situation.

"Lady Moreen, many men do not share such information with their wives as my husband does with me. And so I must believe that you are unaware of the state of things in Frandia." Moreen looked peacefully ignorant of the turmoil surrounding her, and Jocelyn was sorry to shatter her idyllic world. "There are many who are dissatisfied with King Gustave's rule. And he has a brother—a half brother who would claim the throne. There will be a revolution."

Moreen sat silently for some time. "Is it certain? Is there any way to stop it?"

"I am afraid not." Jocelyn put her hand over Moreen's on the table. "This must be a shock for you to hear. I would not have told you but that you must know it. You see, the reason my brother-in-law abducted you was to try to force your husband to choose which king he would support."

"But would that not make Will more likely to choose whichever man you oppose?" Moreen asked in confusion.

"Yes, well...Sebastian does not think things through very well. He is young, and very foolish, but he meant you no harm Lady Moreen."

Moreen nodded. She had surmised that he was not intent on injuring her, or he would have done so immediately. For that she was thankful. "Will! He must be so worried. He will have scores of men looking for me."

"Do not worry. Roger will get a message to him somehow." Jocelyn rose and walked to a window to take in the view she had come to love so well. "I am truly sorry about all of this. But I am pleased to have you as a guest in my home." She turned and smiled at Moreen.

"Lady Jocelyn, may I ask something of you?" At her nod, Moreen continued. "I would know more of this revolution. Why would anyone wish to replace our king? Is he not a good man?"

"A good man perhaps, but not a good king. Gustave has been weak. He surrounds himself with men who counsel for their own benefit rather than for the benefit of the people. He cannot see through their flattery, and his people have suffered as a result of his reliance on such men."

"And what of the man who would oppose him, his brother?"

Jocelyn reclaimed her seat. "Phillip of Arbandeur is a good man, and a strong one. He will not be led astray by those who would use him to further themselves."

"You support this Phillip?" Jocelyn nodded and Moreen again fell silent, contemplating all she had learned. Her reverie did not last long, as a bundle of bouncing boy entered the room and launched himself into Jocelyn's lap.

"Mama!" the boy cried, then realizing there was someone else at the table he turned. "I remember you."

"Why, I remember you too. You are Andrew." Moreen smiled and he hurled himself into her arms. "How is your knee?"

"It's better. I'm going to go play now." With that he scampered off.

His mother smiled after him. "I did not know you had met my Andrew. It is difficult to imagine, but one day he will be Lord of this keep." That seemed to remind her of something. "Lady Moreen, does your husband know…about the child?"

"What child?" Moreen looked up to see Jocelyn's knowing smile.

Chapter 18

William was still in his solar, though he had ceased pacing some hours before. As the night had worn on he had become more desperate for news of Moreen—news that had not come. He had indulged in one drink, but had refused to imbibe more. He needed his head clear.

The players had stayed on to amuse the newly arrived at no extra charge. Phillip had been effusive in his praise of their talents, and had recruited one of the younger men in the company for his army.

Isabelle still refused to speak to her father, but was everything gracious and charming to the others. She had taken on the role of temporary hostess. Though nearly as worried for Moreen as Will was, Isabelle handled the situation well. Only in the comfort and solitude of Stanley's arms did she give in to her fears and cry. She seemed a center of calm in the storm though she felt anything but calm, and thought surely that she would have crumbled without Stanley there to steady her.

Stanley spent his time alternately with Will and Isabelle. He felt rather in the way at times, but would not think of deserting his friend in time of need. His naturally cheerful demeanor was sorely tested by the circumstances. He did his best to be as positive as possible, and was determined that if any amusement could arise from such a situation he would be the first to find it. Stanley kept his own fears to himself. He would gladly have shared them with his bride, but he did not wish to add to her anxieties. In truth he worried for Moreen as well. She had become very much a sister to him and he dreaded what might have happened to her.

Honoré found himself in the unique position of having nothing to do. The Count was a man used to being in command and engaged in productive activity, but he was not of much use in the situation at hand: he had no experience with abductions; his daughter would not speak to him; he had no wish to speak to Stanley; Phillip's plans were formed, and therefore his counsel was not required at present. Thus it was that Honoré found himself drawn to the stables. He had always found horses superior to people anyway. He was having a most amiable conversation with Chauncy when the sound of a galloping horse drew their attention to the bailey.

The rider was one of Phillip's men, and his haste could only mean that he had some information as to Lady Moreen's whereabouts.

Will heard the hoof beats as well, but after the long night of waiting, he despaired of any news. The sleepless night had left him too tired to get up for every little thing, and so he waited for the report to be brought to him.

Phillip escorted the rider into Will's solar. "Lord William, there is news of your lady."

Will jumped up and snatched the message from the man's hand. He tore it open and his eyes scanned the parchment. "I have news of your wife...come to Glenbrae...Lord Roger Boyd." Will was clearly suspicious.

"It is not a trap. Roger Boyd is one of my men, and as honorable as ever a man I've known. If he says he has news, then he has." Phillip waited as Will thought over his words. "If you wish, I will accompany you to ensure your safety."

Will was not well versed in the behavior of decent men, but he knew the actions and inclinations of dishonorable men and Phillip was not one of them. "Thank you, no. I shall go alone." He left the solar shouting for his fastest horse to be readied and trying to think what news Lord Boyd had that could not have been disclosed in his message. *No matter. I'll soon find out.* Glenbrae was within a day's ride of Thornhill. He would be there by nightfall.

Lady Boyd and her guest had enjoyed a day of conversation and needlework. Moreen had asked many questions of her hostess—particularly concerning Jocelyn's thinking her to be with child. Moreen had attributed her weakness and change of appetite to the recent upheavals in her life. She was pleased to learn that those changes, and others, stemmed from a far more pleasant source.

The rest of the afternoon she had spent learning all she could from Jocelyn about childbearing, and when that subject had run out they had easily moved on to others. In the course of that one day they had become fast friends. A rapport had existed between them when they first met, and the afternoon had served only to strengthen the affinity. The ladies were sharing a light supper with Andrew when a page brought word that Lady Moreen would be wanted in Lord Boyd's solar after the meal.

Will impatiently followed a servant, wondering when they would reach whatever room they were heading toward. Every minute dragged out for an eternity. Will was a jumbled mixture of feelings: hope that Moreen was all right; anger at her being taken; fear that she might have been harmed; puzzlement regarding Lord Boyd's cryptic message. He kept his eyes open. Boyd was wealthy enough—there was ample evidence of a healthy income—but there was something else about Glenbrae that was a marked difference from most of the keeps he had known. He could not decipher what the difference was, but it was not an unpleasant one.

As he entered the room, Will had the advantage of observing his host. Roger was intently studying a map spread on the table. He was a man of around thirty years, of medium height and build, a thatch of relatively short brown hair with matching beard lent him an air of distinction that his appearance would have otherwise lacked.

"Lord Boyd?" Will asked impatiently.

He looked up. "Lord DeFord. Won't you sit down?"

Will accepted the offered seat and waited for his host to speak. He declined a drink and began to think of asking straight out what the man knew when Roger began to speak.

"I must thank you for coming. No doubt you noticed the lack of detail in the message I sent to you. Let me assure you that Lady DeFord is safe and unharmed."

"Thank God." Will whispered. "Where is she?"

"A moment please." Roger took a gulp of his drink. It would be no easy tale to unfold before such a man. "No doubt you know about the war to come. What you may not have heard is that I have chosen to throw my lot in with Phillip." Will was looking both angry and impatient. "I know, you are wondering what this has to do with your wife. I am getting to that. Some of the men in this part of the country have been..." he searched his mind for the word, "anxious, to know which side you would take. It was well known that your father would have favored Gustave, but it is also well known that you did not always agree with your father. You have no brother. You do not know how fortunate you are on that score. My younger brother thought to force your hand in this war...by abducting Lady DeFord."

Will jumped up, sword at the ready. "Where is he? Tell me where he is! I'll kill him!"

"William DeFord, you'll do no such thing!"

"Moreen!" He dropped his sword and crossed the floor to take her in his arms. "Are you all right? Are you hurt?"

"I am perfectly fine." She closed her eyes, content to be held against her Will.

"I will kill the man who dared to touch you." He vowed.

"No you will not!" She insisted. "He is just a boy. He did not hurt me, and I am certain that Lord Boyd will deal with him in a fitting manner. I'll not have more blood shed over me." Her eyes filled with tears.

"Very well." He pulled her close again. "How have you been treated?"

"Oh quite well. Lady Jocelyn is a most gracious hostess. You will remember her from court. She and Lord Roger have been most kind to me." She smiled up at her husband. He had come to her rescue again, as she had known he would, the only difference being that she did not truly need to be rescued this time.

Roger, who was once again intent on his maps, tried his best not to listen to them. But he need not have worried as Lady Jocelyn came up behind Moreen and Will let her go; though he kept her hand in his.

"Lord DeFord, you are most welcome to Glenbrae. I do apologize for the circumstances that have brought you here, and I hope that you will not let that unpleasantness hinder your acceptance of our humble hospitality." All this was said with the sweetest smile that between Jocelyn's affability and Moreen's look of expectancy Will could not refuse the offer.

After seeing Will properly fed, the remainder of the evening passed quite pleasantly for all. Young Andrew was quite entertaining. Will was rather ill at ease at first, but gradually grew accustomed to the boy's antics. Moreen and Jocelyn got on quite well together, and Will found Lord Roger to be a passable partner in conversation.

At last Lord and Lady DeFord retired. Theirs was a joyous reunion. He confided all of his fears for her safety and that he had gone nearly mad over her disappearance. She drank in his words, reveling in yet more evidence that he truly cared for her. She had never felt so happy in all her life. She lay comfortably in the arms of the man she loved, with the happy secret that she was carrying his child. Yet that knowledge was not meant to remain a secret, and Moreen never could keep from sharing her joy with those she loved.

"William? Are you still awake?" She half whispered.

"What's wrong?" He sat up; ready to jump to do her bidding.

"Nothing is wrong." She put her hand on his shoulder and he eased back down.

"Then why did you call me William? You haven't called me that in months." He pulled her close and buried his nose in her hair.

"I don't know. I suppose I thought...I don't know." She took a moment to try to compose her thoughts. She had been so busy being happy all day that she had not even imagined this conversation. *How to tell him?* "I have learned something of late. Something that I think will please you. I mean, I am pleased. And I do so hope that you will be too." She took a breath. "I am with child."

She waited for the response she had thought would be instant. It seemed like an eternity before he spoke. "With child? Are you sure?"

"I am quite certain." She turned to face him, a look of concern on her face. "Oh Will, you are pleased, aren't you?"

"Of course. Of course I am pleased. Just surprised. I did not think it would be so soon." He kissed her gently and she settled back into the comfort of his embrace. Several moments passed as he tried to put his whirling mind in order. He had said that he hadn't thought it would be so soon, in truth he hadn't thought about it at all since they had been wed. *What kind of a father would I be?* He was afraid to find the answer to that question. What if he was just like his own father? What if he was worse? *That's impossible,* he reasoned, *no one could be a worse father than Geoffrey DeFord.*

He simply did not know what to do or think, so he turned his attention to the angel in his arms. She wanted him to be happy. He wanted to be happy, but happiness was not something with which he had much experience. He did not know how he felt about their child yet, but he knew how he felt about his child's mother. He kissed her hair and whispered "I love you."

Her eyes filled with tears as her heart filled with joy. *He loves me.* She fell asleep knowing that no matter what happened on the morrow she would always have this one moment of perfect happiness.

"Why exactly should I join your cause?" Will was once again ensconced in a comfortable seat in Roger Boyd's solar.

"I wish I could offer you a set of figures that would compel you on our behalf. But you are rich enough that you have no need of gain, and quite a bit to lose. What I can tell you is that with or without your support we will win this war. Of course many of us would rather it be with your support. It is a fact that the royal army has become very lax. Gustave's men would rather sit at banquet than sharpen their skills."

"I know all of that. I know all of the facts at present." Will thought for a moment. If he knew all the facts, what else did he need to know to make his decision? "Why did you decide for Phillip?"

Roger was surprised by the question, asked as it was in a respectful tone. "I am weary of the corruption that rules this country. Like you I have no need to build my fortune. And I do not seek glory on the battlefield. But it is time to stand up to the minions who would steal our future. Phillip of Arbandeur will not be swayed by the empty flattery of those buffoons who crowd round Gustave. He will bring true peace back to Frandia. I would rather it be done without fighting. But I will not tell my son that I saw his homeland fall into despair and I sat back and did nothing. My children will know that I did everything in my power to help this great man take his country back from the thieves who would rob us of our very hopes. That is who we answer to on this earth—

not the mighty, nor the powerful, but the little ones who look to us to show them what is right and what is good, and what is worth fighting for."

Will nodded appropriately.

"I wish you a good journey DeFord. I thank you for your temperance in the matter of my brother. He will not go unpunished, I assure you. Please convey my thanks to Lady Moreen as well."

Will made his way to the great hall to collect Moreen. She was bidding Lady Jocelyn and young Andrew goodbye. "Come Moreen. We must be on our way if we wish to reach Thornhill by nightfall."

Moreen was silent during their journey. She was too happy to speak, and weariness soon overtook her. As she slumbered in his arms, Will thought over the events of the past two days. He had a decision to make.

The revolution was no longer something he could avoid. Even having Moreen safe in his arms could not erase the memory of his night of anguish fearing for her. This war had come to stare him in the face, and he could no longer sit idly by. Roger's words echoed in his head as he thought about what he owed to his wife and unborn child. He could die in this war, but he would die someday anyway. Better to die in battle defending something, than to die of some illness that could neither be seen nor fought.

He began to see the sense of joining with Phillip. He would at least be able to fight with Stanley instead of against him. And Lord Boyd did not seem a bad sort. He could stand cold and hunger if it came to that. The worst part of it would be leaving Moreen behind for however long the fighting lasted. But he would be forced to leave her either way—if he did not join Phillip then Gustave would call upon him for assistance. At least he would have the comfort of knowing she would be safe. Phillip was still planning to attack from the west, and once they captured Vallenburg, or were crushed trying, the majority of the war would be over. The fighting would never reach Thornhill.

It was well after dark when he finally woke Moreen. "Dearest, we are home." He dismounted and helped her down. Chauncy took the horse, and Will insisted on carrying his wife into the keep.

"Moreen! Praise God you are safe!" Isabelle rushed to meet them, with Stanley close behind. He had been staying close to his bride, so as to avoid meeting with his father-in-law.

Phillip and his men were still in residence. The would-be king had given orders to his men to steer clear of the master of Thornhill until further notice. Phillip himself was making use of Will's solar, and knew of their arrival but thought it best not to intrude upon what he hoped would be a joyous homecoming.

After a light supper during which the entire tale was recounted, Moreen spoke to Isabelle while the men adjourned to Will's "den" as they were now calling the solar.

"Isabelle, I have the most wonderful news. I am not certain if it is proper to speak of such things, but I know you will not think it amiss. I am with child." She spoke in hushed tones and beamed with happiness.

"Are you certain? Oh Moreen, how marvelous!" Isabelle embraced her friend. She hoped that she would be able to share such news herself one day soon. "When will the babe be born?"

"In the winter. I can hardly believe it! I have wanted a child, yet I can scarce believe I shall be someone's mother." Moreen held a gentle hand to her abdomen. She could not feel any difference. She hoped that her unborn child could sense how much he or she was loved.

"You must retire at once!" Isabelle knew very little about these matters, but she was determined to see that Moreen would not be overtired.

Moreen laughed. "You must not fuss over me like a hen with her chick. I am perfectly well. But I shall retire, as you wish." She looked down. "We need our sleep, don't we little one?" She thanked the Lord for the twentieth time since learning of her child, and she would thank him many more times for the blessings bestowed upon her.

The gentlemen were standing around Will's table, awaiting his pleasure. He rather enjoyed having such men on pins and needles anticipating his words.

Phillip had inquired after Lady DeFord's health, as was both appropriate and natural to him. He had a genuine concern for the lady, as he had no quarrel with her and had heard reports of her goodness and charity. Phillip was a compassionate individual and every man in his army believed him to be a great leader, worth fighting for; some would go so far as to say worth dying for.

Will toyed with his dagger as he regarded his audience. Phillip was impatient to know his decision, yet showed no sign of agitation. DuClerque cared very little what Will would decide, but was there out of respect for Phillip and to stare daggers at his daughter's husband. Stanley fidgeted openly—it grieved him to think of finding himself on the opposite side of a war from his only true friend, and he had no clue what Will was about to say.

Finally the man in question looked up. "My lord king, when do we attack?"

Chapter 19

October 1396

The revolution began in September. Phillip's army had marched peacefully through several villages, but the cities belonged to the king. Any town that held significant trade, and thus significant money was guarded. Gustave had doubled the number of soldiers in what he considered the most important cities in western Frandia. He believed that one decision to be sufficient to put an end to his brother's pathetic uprising. The first city to fall was Niezagh, the center of the wool trade in the nation and a major port on the Lingau River. Niezagh fell in only one day.

Gustave had sent spies to see who was helping his wayward brother in his rebellion, and they had finally returned. "You are certain?"

"Yes my liege. DuClerque is with your brother. St. Robert as well." The man said.

Gustave's face registered disbelief. "DuClerque *and* St. Robert? Damn! That little disagreement over his daughter must have been a ruse. It got them both out of my court just in time." He had heard several other names, but those two surprised him. He had not thought DuClerque would side against the rightful king, and he had not thought St. Robert willing to spoil his clothing in a battle.

The spy looked a bit nervous as he relayed his last bit of information. "My liege, there is one other of the rebels you should know of: Lord DeFord has joined them."

"It is not possible. DeFord is with me." Gustave dismissed the report.

"I am afraid not my king. William DeFord has joined your brother. I am certain of it. I saw him with my own eyes."

There could have been no mistake. Not another nobleman in all of Frandia had bright red hair.

Gustave remained silent and still for a moment before throwing a dagger across the room with an angry shout. He hung his head, trying to think what he could do to compensate for the loss of three of the most valuable men in his acquaintance, as well as all of the men fighting under their banners.

"Your Majesty, may I offer a suggestion?" Another of the spies stepped forward. A stout and unkempt man with a scar running the length of his left cheek.

"Speak." Gustave grunted tersely.

"There may be a way to influence certain members of the rebellion. Lady DeFord and Lady St. Robert are in residence at Thornhill. That's a long way from the battles, and nearly every able man gone off to fight." The man grinned, revealing a missing tooth and grimy dimples.

"How did you come by this information?" Gustave demanded.

"I have a cousin in the village near Thornhill. Does Your Majesty wish me to invite the Ladies to visit? I would be honored to lead the company escorting them."

"They are not to be harmed." Gustave commanded. The man nodded in agreement. "You shall have your company. What is your name?"

"Douglas Andin, my liege." He bowed.

Gustave scribbled quickly on a piece of parchment, signed it and thrust it at Andin. "This is my order for the arrest of Ladies DeFord and St. Robert. Go at once."

Douglas bowed and hurried from the room.

"Do you think that is wise?" Baron Frederick Spencer alone questioned Gustave's reasoning. Kidnapping was beneath a regent. He would essentially be holding the ladies for ransom—such a thing simply was not done by civilized people.

"Wise makes no difference at this point. It is necessary. Once we have them we will find a way to make sure DuClerque, St. Robert, and DeFord learn of it."

"That will only draw Phillip's armies closer to Vallenburg." Baron Spencer was concerned that perhaps the king had gone mad. What leader in his right mind would wish to draw the enemy closer to his capital in the midst of a string of victories? In less than a month Phillip had captured three important western cities. The rebels now controlled wool and wine, the border with France, and a full third of the country's farmland.

"Yes, and the sooner he reaches us the better. I will show him what kind of leader he is: foolish; impulsive; weak. He is not half the man I am. I will cut him off at the knees! I'll grind his army into the very earth they would steal from me! No fool will ever dare to challenge me again when I've done with those traitors." Gustave ranted with a savage combination of bloodlust and lunacy.

Baron Spencer bowed hastily and quit the room. He hurried down the corridor, gripping the wall with one hand as he walked. *Something must be done. He must be stopped! But how?*

Moreen was resting again. She had never felt so tired in all her life. Isabelle stayed with her during these times and quietly talked to her or did needlework. The sickness was not too terrible. She was ill in the mornings, but after her stomach had emptied itself the rest of the day was no trouble.

Agnes brought a tray of tea, which she nearly dropped when young Edward rushed past her to deliver a breathless message. Edward was the newest page at Thornhill and felt much importance in his every task. "My Lady!" he panted. "There are riders, soldiers I think." He stopped briefly to breathe. "They are coming fast and...I forgot the rest!" His little face turned red and he hung his head in shame.

"It is all right Edward. Thank you. You have done very well." Isabelle looked at Moreen's weary face. "I will see what these men are about. You stay here and rest. I am sure it is nothing."

Moreen nodded and closed her eyes.

Isabelle reached the great hall and found it full of servants and soldiers in the king's employ. "Welcome to Thornhill! What is your errand that you have come in such haste?"

Douglas stepped forward. "Be you Lady DeFord?"

"No, but I speak for her. What brings you to Thornhill?" She asked again. He handed her the king's order and waited while she read it. "This cannot be! It is some vile mischief you have contrived. Be gone at once and do not trouble us again!"

"It is no jest milady. I've been given the charge of arresting Lady DeFord and Lady St. Robert. And if you are not one, you must be the other. No mere peasant lady wears a dress so fine. Come along like a good girl."

"I certainly will not! This is preposterous. The king has known me since I was a child. He would never have written such an order." She was frightened and trying desperately not to show it.

"I saw him write it with my own eyes Lady St. Robert. If you will not come willingly, you will be bound." She hung her head down and he knew she was resigned to the situation.

"Very well. But Lady DeFord is ill. She cannot be moved. Could you not stay and keep us under guard? We will give you no trouble, I promise." He shook his head. "Then take me and leave Lady DeFord. She is much too ill to run away."

"My orders are to take you both to the palace." He said firmly. He would not be persuaded.

While this exchange had taken place, Chauncy had slipped into the hall and out again. He had a sword and had practiced using it. He silently crept up the stairs to Lady DeFord's chamber.

"Chauncy!" Agnes was shocked to see him in the keep in the daytime, and with a sword. "What is happening?"

"Some men have come to arrest Lady Moreen and Lady Isabelle."

"Arrest?" Moreen sat up. "We have done nothing wrong."

"They have an order from the king." Chauncy put his hand on Agnes' arm as she fretted.

"I will go with you." Agnes assured her mistress.

"You are not going anywhere, neither of you. Do not fear, milady. I will protect you." At the sound of footsteps he pushed Agnes behind him. "Go to Lady Moreen, and stay with her no matter what happens."

One man burst through the door. Several others had not yet made it up the stairs and down the corridor. "Move aside, boy." He ordered.

Chauncy stood firm. "I will not. You have no business arresting a sickly and innocent lady."

"She looks well enough to me. And it's for the king to decide whether she's innocent. Stand aside or you'll get yourself hurt." He grinned mockingly at the puny youth brandishing his weapon. The lad would likely thrust the blade right into the table and slink off red-faced.

"You must stand aside for I will not. You will not take Lady Moreen." He stared him down rather well, he thought, until he heard the man's laughter.

Suddenly the man drew his own sword and thrust at Chauncy. He was surprised to find the boy knew something of swordplay and blocked the blow quickly. Smiling he tried

194

again, anticipating a bit of fun. Blocked once more. The lad was better than he had thought.

Agnes had gone to Moreen as Chauncy had commanded, but it was Moreen who was the stronger of the two. Agnes clung tightly to her mistress' hand; her face had gone white and she could barely breathe.

Several of the other soldiers had appeared in the room and were shouting comments to the combatants.

On they fought, oblivious to the faces and voices around them. Every clever maneuver by Chauncy angered his opponent more. A trained warrior should have been able to dispatch this weakling easily. Quick though he was, Chauncy was not conditioned to fight and he began to tire. The other man did not let the opening pass and Chauncy fell.

"Chauncy!" Agnes screamed and ran to him, covering his wound with her hand in an attempt to halt the flow of blood. She held him in her lap as best she could and cried over him.

"It's all right Agnes." He whispered. "You know I'll always love you. You must take care of Lady Moreen. I am sorry I failed you."

"No!" Agnes cried. "No Chauncy! You can't die!" Her tears fell on the pale skin of his face.

"I love you." He breathed, and then he was gone.

"No." Agnes cradled his head against her. "No!" She sobbed violently until she felt a gentle hand on her arm. Moreen helped her to her feet and held her for a moment before she twisted away angrily. "You!" she indicated the man with the blood stained sword. "You killed him!" She flew at him, beating as hard as she could with her fists until two others dragged her away.

He stood stunned at her assault, and looked down to where her fists had left the boy's blood on his tunic.

Moreen gathered her strength and tried to sound commanding. "Let her free. She will not harm anyone." She whispered to Agnes. "You musn't do that again. He could have hurt you if he wasn't so shocked."

"I wanted him to. I want him to kill me too." She wailed.

"Is that what Chauncy would want for you?" Moreen stroked her friend's hair and offered her arms. Agnes fell willingly into the embrace, assailed by fresh tears from the agony of an empty heart.

After several moments she straightened and wiped at her tears. "Do not worry for me milady. I shall be fine. I shall go with you to the palace. I've never seen a palace." She failed to sound enthusiastic but she was determined to take care of Lady Moreen as Chauncy had said, and as she would have done anyway. She shut herself away from all emotion. It was the only way she could walk away from her love's body and into the custody of the soldiers. The numbness was a blessing. She felt neither pain nor fear. Her unusual calm was oddly soothing to Moreen, who longed to comfort her but knew not how to do so.

Moreen and Agnes went willingly as far as the bailey. There stood Douglas Andin and his cousin Rupert.

Rupert grabbed for Moreen, and Douglas pulled him roughly back. "None of that now Rupert."

"I told you they were here, now I want my payment." He reached for her again and was again pulled back, this time more harshly.

"They king gave orders. They're not to be harmed." He gave his cousin a warning glance.

"I don't care what the king ordered. I did this for myself." He lunged at Moreen and Douglas caught him round the middle, slamming him to the ground and drawing his sword.

"The king gave orders." Douglas said slowly. "I don't give a damn what you want. I've been given a company of soldiers to command, and I'll not let you ruin my fortunes, runt. Think yourself lucky to be left alive, and take comfort in having done your duty by the king. Get you gone!"

Rupert ran off as if a pack of wolves nipped at his heels, and the company left with their expected prisoners plus one lady-in-waiting. The ladies were allowed to take their horses from the stables. Isabelle had her own mare, which she had brought with her when she left the palace to run away with Stanley. Moreen rode Maida, as she was not comfortable on any other mount. Agnes felt a fresh wave of nauseating pain when she mounted Nealie—the mount Chauncy had chosen specifically for her—but willed herself back to the blessed relief of numbness.

The journey to Vallenburg took four days instead of three, due to the slowness of Lady DeFord's mount, and the inexperience of the rider. They were lucky to have made the journey before the nights turned very cold.

Moreen and Isabelle were not prepared for the shock of entering the palace as prisoners. They were not bound, but neither were they shown anything like the deference they would have expected under different circumstances. The dungeons were not as comfortable by half as the servants' quarters of the palace. They were cold and dank, and had a most unpleasant smell that defied identification. The ladies were put into one cell together, which allowed them some solace. The two noblewomen were rather frightened.

Agnes had cried herself to sleep each night of the journey, when she had been certain no one would hear her. She had wept out enough of her grief to be very much impressed with the city, the palace, and even the solid construction of the cell in which they were to languish. She said she had been in worse places as a girl. Neither of her two companions could imagine anything very much worse, but they were not desirous of an illustration of the possibilities. There was a low stool in the cell that both Agnes and Isabelle insisted Moreen take.

They had been incarcerated for what seemed several hours when Moreen became too tired to sit on the stool and lay down on the cold, bare earth. She was nearly dreaming when a noise startled her back to consciousness.

"I will go through!" It was a feminine voice, followed by a masculine one of less authoritative tone.

"You cannot! I have orders. No one is to see them."

"Gerald, convince him please." The lady ordered. The command was followed by a grunt and a thud, as well as a jingling of metal, and footfalls.

One more moment brought the lady and Gerald into view.

"Princess Allyn! What are you doing here?" Isabelle asked in shock.

"What kind of question is that? I've come to rescue you, of course." She found the necessary key and unlocked the cell's door. Instead of letting them out, she let herself in, handed her torch to Isabelle, and took several bundles from Gerald. Having accomplished that, she pulled the door shut and flung the keys as far away as she could. "There now, Gerald. I went into the cell before you could stop me and threw the keys away."

"Your Highness, I don't know about this. I don't want any trouble." Gerald scratched his chin. He was a rather large man, but Allyn commanded him with ease.

"Nonsense. You will not be in any trouble. I will see to that. And when I am queen I will remember your kindness in assisting me. Do try to rouse poor Rolfe. He seems to have fallen and hit his head." She smiled and turned as Gerald sauntered off. "How nice it is too see you both again." She turned to Agnes. "Hello. I'm Allyn."

Agnes managed to curtsey. "Agnes, Your Highness."

"Agnes, it is a pleasure to meet you. Now see what I have brought." She had packed well for her mission: two blankets; bread; cheese; apples; three honey cakes; and several large candles to brighten the gloom. She busied herself with lighting the candles and placing them where they would not set fire to either the cell or its occupants. She picked up a blanket and turned around to find the other three staring at her. "Well, we will not be here long. Come Agnes, help me spread this on the floor and we shall soon have our refreshment."

Moreen sat up. "I am glad to see you Allyn, but you should not be here."

"Oh, my dear Moreen! You look quite pale." It was then that Allyn noticed bloodstains on Agnes' gown. "Did they hurt you? They shall be punished for this!"

Isabelle took Allyn aside and explained everything that had happened at Thornhill, while Agnes pretended to be very intent on setting out the food.

"I don't understand why you were arrested in the first place. Have you sold cook's secret for roast duck?" Allyn joked.

"It is not us. It is our husbands." Isabelle hesitated to inform the princess of the truth. She did not wish to lose Allyn's assistance, nor did she wish to hurt her friend. "Stanley and William have joined the rebellion against your father."

Before Allyn could respond there was a great commotion of feet and voices. Gustave appeared and stared in disbelief at his daughter. "Allyn! What do you think you are doing?"

"What does it look like, father? I'm having a picnic. I'm sorry but we haven't enough food to go round, or I would invite you to join us."

"Young lady, come out of there at once!" He bellowed.

"I'm afraid I can't father. I've lost the keys." The men with her father were obviously searching for them. "Oh you needn't bother to find them. I will not come out even if you do." She stared her father down.

"I command you as your father and as your king."

"No!" she folded her arms in a most insolent manner, "not until you release my companions."

"Gustave, what is happening?" Lavinia rushed into the light and groaned when she saw Allyn in the cell. "Allyn, please come out of there!"

"You see what this is doing to your mother?" Gustave fumed. *Stubborn, headstrong girl!* "You do not understand Allyn. I cannot release them merely because you wish to invite them to tea."

"They have done nothing wrong! You cannot punish them for the actions of others!"

Moreen shivered and Agnes wrapped the remaining blanket around her. The movement caught Lavinia's eye. "Lady Moreen, are you yet ill?"

"Yes, Your Majesty." She replied weakly.

"She is with child." Allyn supplied.

"Allyn! It is improper for you to speak of such things." Gustave reproved.

"It is true. And if any harm befalls her or the child it will be because of you!" Her blue eyes glittered angrily.

"Gustave please!" Lavinia pleaded. "Let them go. You cannot wish harm to an innocent child."

Gustave considered his wife's words, and his daughter's stubbornness. "Let them out." He ordered. "But they will be confined to your rooms, Allyn." He warned.

She jumped into his arms. "Oh, thank you papa!"

Allyn was very happy to have them confined to her rooms, as she insisted she had more rooms than she could use. Moreen received the best care Allyn could afford her, including a visit from the royal physician. The king was left unaware of his daughter's activities, as he was occupied by the far more pressing problem of his brother's army advancing quickly toward Vallenburg.

Chapter 20

February 1397

And then there was one...one conflict that would decide the future of Frandia. Certainly there would be pockets of resistance for years to come but no matter who won the struggle for the capital, the war would not last long beyond the final blows of this next battle.

Phillip of Arbandeur was within spitting distance of the royal palace. Vallenburg was less than one league from his camp and his men were eager for what all hoped would be their final fight. But first they had to get into the city. When they had conquered just over half of the country Gustave had ordered all of his men back to Vallenburg and let the other cities fall. The result was a rather peaceful march toward the capital by Phillip's army.

He'd had a devil of a time restraining his best fighters one month before when they'd received the news of Lady DeFord and Lady St. Robert's arrest. DeFord and St. Robert had been ready to strike out for the palace. Luckily DuClerque had been able to help Phillip reason with them until they realized the necessity of patience. No doubt Gustave had let that information slip for the very purpose of provoking them. Phillip was glad to have the Count's assistance in the matter. He had easily convinced them that the ladies were safe. *Do you think I would be here yet if I believed my child to be in danger?* DuClerque had argued. Both young men were still eager to storm the palace, but were now willing to wait until the proper time.

"Shall I summon the others?" Baron Landigson asked.

"Not yet. Let them rest for now." Phillip was contemplating his life, fully aware that it could be at an end very soon. "Sundown." He said absently. The baron nodded and left him to his reverie. He gazed in the direction of the palace. *What are you thinking right now brother?*

Damn! Gustave raged inwardly. At last report his brother's army was within a week's journey of Vallenburg. That had been nearly a week ago. "They might well be in the forest right outside the city walls!"

The king's counselors hurried to assure him that the rebels would never enter the city, and that there were provisions enough to withstand a siege of many months. They were as eager to convince themselves as the king. Profuse statements of confidence in the army, as well as of the superior intellect of their sovereign, were the order of the day as each man sought to placate His Majesty. A task in which no one succeeded.

Gustave was furious that Phillip's revolution had lasted this long. In five months Phillip had not given up his foolish notion of ruling Frandia. Gustave had sent word to His Holiness in Rome, requesting his assistance in the matter and had received no reply. Initially he had attributed the lack of reply to be due to interception by Phillip's men, but as time wore on he became convinced that His Holiness had never sent any such correspondence. Without the blessing of the church, and lacking other allies, the outlook grew darker every day.

A page walked in timidly. Delivering messages to His Majesty was becoming dangerous. The poor boy hoped fervently that the message might be a good one. Gustave did not care to be bothered with it, and so Baron Spencer took the note from the boy and read it silently. He signaled the boy to leave, and waited until the lad was well out of hearing range before speaking. "Your Majesty, Phillip is in the forest less than a league from the city walls."

"Damnation! Is there not one man in my kingdom who is capable of procuring information before it is too late to be of use? Why the devil was he allowed to come this close?"

"We could set fire to the forest." One brave soul ventured.

"And burn down the entire city? Tell me, what would be the use of that other than to hand my blackened crown over to my idiot brother? How did this fool gain entrance to my circle of trusted advisors? Take him to the dungeons! I'll not have madmen among my counselors!" Gustave bellowed.

Baron Spencer stood in silence, no longer shocked by Gustave's outbursts, as the man was hauled away by the guards. He had been searching for a way to help the king, but had found none and began instead to seek an opportunity to meet with Phillip. This might be the chance he needed. "Indeed, Your Majesty. The king's service is not a place for the weak-minded. I am appalled at the lack of ability shown by these informants! And so, my liege, I wish to take upon myself the task of spy." He waited to see Gustave's reaction, which was merely an expression of surprise. "I will go into the forest, in disguise of course, and find their camp; learn their numbers, their supplies, in short their weaknesses. If you will give me leave, I shall start at once."

"Baron Spencer, you honor me with your sound thinking, and your steadfast loyalty!" Gustave clasped the other man's shoulder. "I only wish I had more counselors like you!" He eyed the rest of them suspiciously. "You have my leave. I am confident you will succeed!"

"Thank you, my lord king." He bowed and left as quickly as he could. Though his conscience pricked him, he proceeded with his plan to aid the rebel force. He would not have thought himself capable of such deception, but circumstances compelled him to consider the greater good at stake. He knew very well that Gustave's other advisors were lying. The army was incompetent—made up mostly of indolent lords who spent their time feasting and mistreated their serfs to the point where hardly any of the men were fit to fight; the few who were trained were skin and bones. Even though Phillip had allowed trade to continue uninterrupted, the city did not have the provisions needed to survive one month's siege, let alone many months.

As he hurried to his chambers to don the disguise he had ready and waiting, a frantic princess Allyn rushed past him muttering an apology.

Seconds later Allyn burst into her mother's bedchamber. "Mother! You must come at once! Something is wrong with Moreen!"

Lavinia's placid nature did not keep her from concern for both mother and child. She tried to soothe her daughter as they walked to Allyn's solar, but the poor girl was consumed with worry.

Isabelle met them at the door. "Your Majesty," she curtsied, "Thank goodness you have come."

Lavinia calmly floated over to Moreen. "Lady Moreen, what is the matter?"

"Your Majesty..." she began but her words were cut short as she doubled over in pain. "Pain! Terrible pain!"

Agnes bobbed a brief curtsey and addressed the queen. "She's having them every few minutes."

Lavinia smiled. "It seems your babe wishes to join us."

"No, it's too soon!" Moreen cried. The pain was gone, but she was terrified for her child.

"Calm down, child. Babes are born when they are ready, not when we are. There is no reason you should not have a strong and healthy child in your arms by nightfall." Lavinia then began directing everyone. She sent for a midwife and ordered Allyn from the room, but allowed Agnes to stay at Moreen's request.

Ten minutes later Isabelle stepped into the corridor and right into Allyn. "How is Moreen?"

"Allyn, I almost ran over you. Moreen is fine, but it will be a while yet before the babe comes."

"How do you know that?" Allyn demanded.

"The queen said so. Allyn, you cannot stay here all day waiting. You must find something to do." Isabelle reproved her gently.

"I know, but I'm so worried. I had no idea it would be painful for her. She must be so frightened!"

Isabelle nodded. "Yes, but mostly for the babe, not herself. I know she wishes William was here." Neither girl saw the queen step out.

"Well he would be if it weren't for father!" Allyn said angrily.

"Allyn! Do not ever speak of your father in that tone!"

Isabelle wisely went back in with Moreen.

"It is true! If he hadn't dragged Moreen here, or allowed this foolish war, she would be with her husband right now." Allyn protested.

"Husbands do not enter the birth chamber, Allyn. Moreen is fortunate to be here now, if anything should go awry our physician will see to her." Lavinia took a breath. "Do you know why your father ordered Moreen and Isabelle arrested? The real reason?"

Allyn swallowed a sarcastic retort and pondered. "Because he is desperate." She stated simply.

"You are far too intelligent for your own good, but I am glad you came to that conclusion. I did not know how to tell you. Your father is not himself, and has not been for several months. He is consumed by his fear of being deposed. Your uncle's army is in the forest just outside the city."

"So close? What will happen to us if they win this war?"

"Do not think like that! They will not win! They must not." She finished quietly. "I will go back to tending Moreen. Find something to do and the time will pass more quickly."

"Mother?" Allyn's voice halted her. "You will send me word when the babe has come, won't you?"

The queen nodded and re-entered the chamber, and Allyn resumed pacing. *What can I do? Music? No. Reading? No. There must be something.* After half an hour of such contemplation she finally decided on a course of action, but she would have to wait until after sundown. In the meantime, she had another idea *Perhaps I can help after all.* She smiled to herself and went in search of Madame Sonja.

"Your Majesty, someone to see you."

"Send them in." Phillip called. Without looking up he asked "Who are you and what do you want?"

"My lord prince, I am Baron Frederick Spencer. I am here to offer my assistance to you."

Phillip looked up quickly. Spencer was one of Gustave's staunchest supporters. "And why should I accept such an offer from a man who has sworn loyalty to my brother? Do you mean to trap me, or are you merely a traitor to your king?"

"I fear I am the latter. It grieves me to break my oath. Your brother is no longer the man to whom I swore fealty. He is mad, or close to it. He can no longer see through the false men around him, if he ever could. The people of Vallenburg will not survive a siege. I am here to prevent one, if I can."

Phillip was intrigued. "How?"

"I can get you into the city—and the palace."

He tried to gauge this baron. The man looked him in the eye, and spoke simply. "What do you wish in return?"

To his credit, Baron Spencer did not hesitate to answer "Only that as few lives as possible be taken."

"A moment please." Phillip stepped outside and sent one of his guards to summon his advisors. Count DuClerque was the first to arrive, as Phillip had hoped. "There is a Baron Spencer just inside. What do you know of him? Is he trustworthy?"

"Frederick Spencer? Yes, he can be trusted. He is as honest a man as any I've ever known. It must be worse than we imagined or he would not have sought us out. Spencer holds his honor too dear to break an oath under anything less than dire circumstances."

The others had arrived and they all went inside the pavilion. Phillip immediately addressed Baron Spencer. "I accept your offer and your terms. Baron Spencer has offered his assistance to us in gaining entry to both the city and the palace. Gentlemen, we have a strategy to plan."

"I liked the old strategy." Baron Landigson grumbled.

"Course you liked it," countered Lord Carlisle, "you had a leading part in it."

Phillip eyed them both sharply. "If you two wish to renew the feud you pledged to reconcile when you joined me, you may leave this camp and beg my brother's mercy at the gates of the city." Phillip called to a young lord. "Navarre, can you manage as a hostage?"

"A hostage?" Eduard Navarre was a mere twenty years of age, and had been hoping for a more heroic charge.

"A hostage. Spencer, you will go back to the palace and tell them you ran across my scout, Navarre here. You must insist on escorting him to his cell in the dungeon, so that he has no chance to escape, and to ensure that he is not harmed before he can be tortured to obtain information."

"Torture?!" Eduard was quickly losing his desire to serve.

"You must be certain to hand him the key to the cell, and leave him some means to fight his way out if necessary." He turned to address the young lord. "Navarre, you must wait until well after dark. Once you are free you must free all the other prisoners and make your way out of the palace. Keep your eyes down and if anyone stops you tell them you've been sent for firewood. Get to the eastern gate of the city as quickly as you can. We'll have twenty men create a disturbance at the north gate then retreat, drawing the soldiers into the forest. Landigson, that will be your task. Lead them to the camp." He paused at the surprised gasps. "Lead them to the camp, and see that all of our wine and mead are near the main fire."

"Ah, disappear up the trees and watch 'em drink themselves sick. I like it!" Landigson grinned at his task, and the importance of it.

"Carlisle," Phillip continued, "You and your men will beg admittance to the city as Franciscan Brothers. Stay near the east gate and wait for Navarre. You know what to do after that."

Carlisle nodded. "Get the gate open."

"Precisely." Phillip replied. "Boyd, St. Robert, DuClerque, and DeFord, you and your men will come with me to the palace. The rest of you will secure the perimeter and guard the gates so that no soldiers can enter the palace or the city. Understood?"

Everyone nodded except for Navarre. "Just one question, Your Majesty. How will I know when to make my escape?"

Phillip looked round at his advisors, who seemed to have no more idea than he did how to answer that question. "Baron Spencer? How many men guard the dungeons?"

"One, my lord." He answered, rather embarrassed at the folly of having one man guard so many prisoners.

"Is it possible this one guard has a weakness for any certain lady?"

"None in particular, but I do know of one who I'm certain can be most persuasive." Spencer grinned.

"Excellent. Send her down at ten." Phillip turned his head. "Navarre, when you hear the voice of a female seducing the guard, that is when you should escape. I hope you shall not mind being bound."

"Not at all, Your Majesty." Eduard was smiling now that he understood his part to be most vital. With all of the prisoners let loose, the soldiers in the palace would be very distracted.

"Spencer, Navarre, I wish you the Lord's protection." Phillip watched them leave.

Spencer peered back inside. "My lord prince, might I have a few of your foot soldiers? It might be good to have some fighting break out in the taverns. I'll go back to the city through another gate and say they are my men."

"Certainly. See to it Navarre." Phillip called in answer. "Landigson, Carlisle, ready your men."

"Your Majesty, would you like me to have my men set up one or two other fires with spirits and draw out even more of the king's men?"

"No Landigson. More things going on means more things going wrong. Besides, don't you think they might get suspicious after the second group doesn't return?"

"As you wish Majesty." Landigson and Carlisle walked away, the latter grinning at the former's stupidity.

Phillip sent out everyone but the four men who would enter the palace with him. "Now my lords, what shall be our strategy once we are inside?"

William cleared his throat. "Your Majesty?"

"Yes, DeFord?"

"We need some kind of signal." The others looked baffled. "So that everything works with regard to time. If the camp is empty and all of us are at the city walls, how is Landigson to know when to have his men ride?"

"I suppose you have something in mind." Phillip guessed, and William nodded. "See to it, then. Now, back to the question of how to proceed once we are inside."

Stanley began to speak but DuClerque waved him to silence. "I believe I know more about the palace than you do."

Stanley took the insult good-naturedly. "Really? Do you know how to get from the kitchens to the king's bedchamber without alerting the guards?"

Four men stared at him with questioning gazes. "I was seven years old and sneaked to the kitchens in the night. I stumbled against a wall and found a hidden staircase so I followed it. Actually that passage leads a number of places." Stan smiled at the memories of some of his escapades.

Meanwhile Spencer and Navarre, along with four others, were on their way to the western gate of the city.

"Tell me something, Navarre." Baron Spencer's curiosity had gotten the better of him and dissolved his intention to know as little as possible. "How is it possible for Carlisle's men to pretend to be Franciscans?"

Navarre did not mind the question, or even the ropes that bound his hands. "About a month ago we came upon a monastery that had been sacked. All the brothers had been slain, the treasures looted. His Majesty insisted we bury the dead. It seemed that the robes might be useful to us sometime, so we took them with us. His Majesty said he did not think the Lord would mind, as the original wearers had been killed by the very men we are fighting."

"Do you mean to tell me that Gustave's men sacked that monastery?" Spencer stood still, bewildered. "Impossible. Gustave would not tolerate such a thing."

"But where is he when these things happen? You may think your king is a good man, but did he not choose the men who lead his army and kill innocent monks? He might not have given the order, but he allowed such men to come to power under him. Those monks were dead when we arrived there, and no one else in Frandia would have the ability to have done it even if they had the inclination."

"It is no crime to trust the wrong people." Spencer insisted.

"No. It is not." Navarre agreed. "But one who cannot tell truth from lies should not rule a kingdom indefinitely. The fate of so many depends on him, yet he has shown he cannot be the king we need. I would see Phillip rule, but I wish his brother no harm. I do not seek to punish Gustave, only to see that the wrongs done in his reign are righted. He has not the abilities that Phillip has. His only claims to the crown are birth and divine right. If it is truly God's will that Gustave continue as king of Frandia, then the revolution will fail."

Baron Spencer did not speak for the rest of their journey.

Chapter 21

Lavinia swabbed Moreen's face with a cool wet cloth. "It is almost over now."

The screams were unnerving to the young ladies. Agnes stood firm despite her terror. She stayed by Lady Moreen's bedside and did everything asked of her. Isabelle had defected to the corridor with Allyn, who had returned from her visit to Madame Sonja, and both prayed it would stop soon. Suddenly the screaming ended and a new cry sounded—a fragile yet demanding cry.

The midwife crowed triumphantly. "A boy!" She handed the infant to the queen, who swaddled him carefully and took him to his mother.

"Well Lady Moreen, what do you think of your son?" Tears shimmered in Lavinia's eyes—tears of joy for a new life, and tears of painful remembrance of her own babe.

Moreen gazed at the tiny boy lying next to her. "He's so small." She touched his hand, and his little fingers curled around one of hers. She leaned down to kiss his head. "You are so beautiful! Agnes, look at him."

Agnes beamed at her new young master. "You've a fine healthy babe milady, and a handsome one he is too."

Allyn and Isabelle burst into the room as soon as they were allowed entry. "Oh look how tiny he is! May I hold him, Moreen?"

"Of course you may." She leaned back, exhausted but happy.

Allyn carefully picked up the wriggling bundle. "Was I really this small once?"

"Yes, you were. I've never seen a more beautiful child than you were." Lavinia smiled at her daughter.

"Until today, of course." Allyn corrected. "Such beautiful eyes you have little one. They look just like your mother's."

"May I hold him too, Moreen?" Isabelle requested. "Moreen?"

"Shh," said the queen, "Let her sleep. She has earned it." And taking the babe from Allyn she instructed Isabelle how best to hold him. "Here you are."

"Oh my!" She smiled down at his little face. "I hope I have a son like you someday. Then the two of you shall play together like your fathers did when they were boys. Oh look! He yawned. I must be tiring him."

"Babes sleep quite a bit for the first few days." The midwife informed her before taking the queen aside. "She had a rough time of it." At Lavinia's worried look the woman continued. "Oh she'll be good as new in no time. What she most needs is to rest. Brought some herbs with me to make a tea that'll help her sleep tonight.

Allyn slipped out unnoticed just as Moreen began to wake. "Where is my son?"

"Here Moreen. Right here." Isabelle placed him beside his mother again. "He is beautiful—and strong; wouldn't let go of my finger."

A young lady stood in the doorway and knocked tentatively. "I'm here to nurse the babe." She said shyly. *So this is the palace. I do hope I'll be with a good family!*

"Come in." Lavinia escorted her to the bedside. "Moreen this is..."

"Berta, Your Majesty." The girl supplied.

"Berta. She is here to help you and your son." The queen finished the introduction and the nurse took up the child. Moreen saw that Berta was at ease with her charge, and said a silent prayer of thanks to God for sending her someone who knew something about newborn babes.

"He is a handsome child, milady." Berta said. "Have you thought of what you want to call him?"

"Chauncy."

Allyn slipped through the woods as well as she could in her borrowed shoes. It was a cold night. She was glad she had worn the thick woolen cloak, unattractive though it was. *They must be here somewhere! I'm sure I've gone more than a mile.* She tripped and fell in the snow, breaking a twig in the process.

"Who's there?" A gruff voice called out.

"Will you help me please? I think I've hurt my ankle!" She called back.

The man crept forward slowly, making certain she was alone. The moon was hidden, but the clouds held that faint light peculiar to snowy nights. They would be in for a storm before the morn.

"All right miss." He helped her to her feet and watched as she shook the snow from her cloak. "What are you doing out on a night like this?"

Allyn knew she couldn't tell him the truth. She thought quickly. "My betrothed is with the rebellion. I haven't seen him in months. I just want to know if he's alive. Could you take me to the camp?" She decided to add a little something for effect. "You...you aren't one of the king's men are you? Please don't hurt me! Please!"

"Quiet, woman! No, I'm not one of the king's men and I won't hurt you." He looked toward the city and then back into the forest, trying to decide. He knew he should turn the little baggage back. But if he did, she'd likely start crying and screaming and then the soldiers would come running.

"I'll take you to the camp, but you must keep quiet." She nodded and they set off.

She had to hurry to match the man's stride, and it took all of her concentration to keep from falling down again.

"Who does your man fight under?" He asked.

She almost said DeFord, but thought better of it. "Lord St. Robert."

Not another word was spoken until they reached their destination. "Lord St. Robert, this lady says she has business with you." He stalked off rather than remain to answer the questions he knew would be coming.

"Who are you and what business could be so important that you'd risk your neck to come here?" Stanley had no interest in entertaining foolish ladies who had no sense. The only thoughts he had were of battle and of Isabelle.

"St. Robert. Where is Lord DeFord?"

He knew that voice. "Princess Allyn! Are you mad? Don't you know how dangerous it was for you to come here?"

"Of course I know. That's why I must get back as quickly as I can. Now where is he?" She answered.

"Here." He called as he stepped from the shadows. "Your Highness, how lovely to see you again. Pleasant night for a stroll, is it not?"

"Most amusing, my lord. I've come to tell you," she looked at Stanley, "both of you, that your wives are safe. They have been under my care, and I swear to you no harm has come to them."

"That is good to know, but you need not have put yourself to such trouble." Will replied. "We would have found out soon enough anyway."

"There is more. You have a son, William—a fine, strong, healthy son."

"A son. When...?"

"Just this evening. I do not know what Moreen has called him. I came right away to tell you."

Will sat on a downed tree. "Moreen. Is she...?"

"She is well. Weary, but well. I had to come and tell you. Now I must go." She took three steps, then turned back. "God keep you safe—both of you."

She carefully retraced her steps through the camp and into the forest. She was so intent on the ground before her that she nearly ran into a solid object in her path. She started and the hood of her cloak fell backward as the moonlight broke through the clouds.

"Allyn! What are you doing here?"

"Phillip!" She threw herself into his arms. "Phillip! I thought I would never see you again."

Phillip disentangled himself from her embrace. "You must go. Don't you know there is a war going on?"

"Don't I know? How could I not? Phillip, why are you here?" Allyn's expression of adoration changed instantly to one of incredulity. "No. You can't be! Tell me you are not leading this rebellion!"

There was no way around hurting her now. "I am."

Her anger was instantaneous. "How could you? All that time in Paris! How could you lie to me like that? I can't believe I trusted you!"

"I did not lie to you." He protested.

"No you just let me believe you cared for me." She flung the accusation in his face. She tried to walk past him but he blocked her path.

"I do care for you. Why do you think I left when I did?"

"Because you had gotten all the information you needed from me!" Her eyes snapped with fire and hatred.

"I did not use you for information. I enjoyed your company." Her hand was as quick as her mind and he reeled from the blow.

"How dare you? Don't ever touch me again you scoundrel! How could I have been so stupid? I should have known to be suspicious. The way you followed me; lavished me with your attentions. You even spoke French so I wouldn't know you were a Frandian!"

"I spoke French because we were in France! I am sorry to hurt you, Allyn."

"Ha!" She tried to get past him again and he restrained her. She struggled to get free and her cloak fell to the ground. Bloodstains caught Phillip's eye. The stains had not come out of the gown, but Agnes had refused to part with it. Allyn had not remembered the stains when she took it.

"What is this? Who hurt you?" His voice was savage.

"No one save yourself. I borrowed this gown."

He pulled her close in his relief. "Allyn." When he would have released her she threw her arms around his neck and kissed him. For the briefest moment he surrendered to the warmth of her lips, and returned the kiss full measure. Then just as quickly he broke away and turned his back to her.

He could hear the tears in her voice when she spoke. "Why did you not tell me?"

He exhaled sharply. "I thought it would be best if you did not know. I never meant to deceive you. I only wanted to meet my brother's daughter, to see if he was a better father than king. I did not intend to feel anything more than an uncle's affection. I had already known I would fight this war."

"You knew that I loved you." She cried. "How could you not tell me who you were? Did you think I would not learn the truth?"

"Yes. If Gustave was half the father and husband I had thought him to be, you and your mother would be safely out of Frandia. Go back Allyn. Find some place to wait out the battle safely."

"Do not do this, Phillip." She pleaded. "If you stop this we could be together."

He turned to face her. "No Allyn. It is too late to stop it. By morning I will either be king or be dead." She was sobbing openly and his heart ached for her. "I wish there were some other way. I will not let anyone hurt you, or your mother."

She wiped at her eyes. "What about father?"

"He will be exiled, or kept prisoner. It is the only way to ensure his safety. He has allowed too many crimes against our people."

Once more she threw herself into his arms. "Please tell me I can stay with you!"

"I can't do that." He held her while she cried, wishing to the heavens that things were different. But no amount of wishing changes truth. "Allyn, look at me. I do care for you."

"Say that you love me!" She begged through her tears.

"No."

Allyn instantly pulled away from him and retrieved her borrowed cloak. She shook the snow from it, and threw it around her shoulders before walking away. After a few minutes she turned back for one last glimpse of him. He still stood in that same spot, his head hung down. She resumed her course with as much speed as she could muster, trying to outstrip the pain in her heart.

Her tears continued for some time and obscured her vision. She walked as quickly as she dared toward the vague destination of the city walls. She did not care where she was. She did not care if she never gained the protection of the city. William had said they would have soon known that their ladies were safe, and Phillip himself had said he would be king or dead by morning. At the times, neither remark had registered its significance in her mind. Now everything clicked into place. Suddenly she knew that she must get back to the palace to warn everyone. But she had not considered how difficult it might be to enter Vallenburg after sundown.

She was saved from lengthy scheming by a group of Franciscan Brothers at the east gate. She quickly made her way to their group, hoping to slip through the gate unnoticed. All was going well until one of the guards observed that she was not wearing a monk's robe. He grabbed her and stopped one of the Brothers. "Is this woman with you?"

"No ladies travel with us." He replied.

"What are you about then woman?" The guard's hand bit into her arm as she tried to twist free.

"I lost my way in the woods, else I would have been at the gate before dark." She continued to squirm as the vice-like grip on her arm grew tighter.

"And what were you doing in the woods? Plotting with those rebels?" He called for his captain. "Eh! We've got a traitor over here. Just returned from meeting with those scum."

The captain relieved his underling of the prisoner. He steered her away from the gate. "To the palace with you. His Majesty will be pleased to have another rebel in the dungeon."

"I will not be treated like a common criminal! Release me this instant!"

His mouth gaped open at the voice coming from the prisoner. "Your Highness! What...? I apologize Princess."

"It will be forgotten if you release me and word of this never reaches my father."

"I am sorry Princess Allyn. I have very strict orders to arrest anyone who tries to enter the city after dark. That guard who spotted you will tell the entire company the tale of his intercepting a rebel at the gate. I must take you to His Majesty."

Allyn quailed inwardly, but she had been taught from an early age not to show her fear. She squared her shoulders and tried to sound unconcerned. "Very well. My father shall sort this out quickly and there will be an end of it." *Or of me.*

She marched bravely into her father's solar, head held high.

Gustave looked up from the map he had been studying. "What is this?" He was irritated already at the interruption.

"Papa, I can assure you it is..."

He cut her off. "Not you. Captain what has my daughter done now?" Allyn fumed at the humiliation of both being interrupted and being already considered as in the wrong before the facts were known.

The captain was visibly uncomfortable. "Your Majesty, Princess Allyn was apprehended sneaking into the city just moments ago."

Gustave's disbelief quickly turned to rage. He had no doubt of the report's truth. One look at her angrily defiant face confirmed it. "You have gone too far this time! Consorting with my enemies? How long have you been part of this plot to overthrow me?" He shouted. "Answer me!"

"I am not part of any plot!" She buried the pain of her father's willingness to believe the worst of her, and focused on the truth of her motivations.

"Then why were you out in a forest filled with traitors?" His face was fully red and fierce.

"I did go to their camp." She admitted, but continued while Gustave's fury rendered him incapable of speaking. "To tell Lords St. Robert and DeFord that Moreen and

Isabelle are safe, and that Lord DeFord has a new son. I am not part of any treason."

"Not part of any treason? What do you think secretly meeting with an enemy is?" He yelled. "You will tell me where their camp is."

"So you can slaughter them like sheep?" Allyn shouted back. "I will not! Execute me if you will." Her own death no longer frightened her, for nothing could be worse than the pain she had experienced this night. Much though Phillip had hurt her, she would not betray him; she could not. No punishment on the earth could move her to send the man she loved to his death.

Gustave shook with rage. He said nothing as he grabbed Allyn's arm and dragged her out into the corridor. His grip was more painful than that of the guard who had accosted her. She cried out in anguish and begged him to let her go, but he would not hear her pleading. He ignored the open stares of people they passed as he pulled her to her chambers. Marguerite gaped in shock and ran at once to find the queen.

Gustave opened the door and flung Allyn through it. He slammed the door shut and turned to the guards who had followed him. "No one enters or leaves these rooms! I want all the doors guarded!"

"Yes, Your Majesty." They all nodded. No one would cross the king when he looked ready to murder his own child.

Lavinia came running to meet him as he stood, still red-faced. "What have you done?"

"Better to ask what your daughter has done!"

Lavinia moved toward the door, but Gustave blocked it. "You will not go in there. No one goes in!"

She could not believe what she was seeing and hearing. Gone was the man she had spent her life with; in his place stood a mad tyrant. "What has she done to merit this?"

"Consorting with the enemy."

"I do not believe it!" She cried, torn between love for her child and fear of her husband.

"It is true! Of her own admission. And she will pay for it as soon as I've done with this war." He stalked off toward his solar and Lavinia followed him.

"You cannot believe that Allyn would plot against you. She is headstrong but not treasonous. She would never have done such a thing, Gustave."

"Ha! I have her confession. She went to meet with them in secret to pass on information. Is that not the very definition of treason?" He ranted. The walk between Allyn's chambers and his solar went much more quickly when not dragging a disobedient princess in his wake.

"Gustave think!" Lavinia pleaded with him. "You cannot do this to your own child!"

"But she is not my child, is she? She is a traitor, just like her brother and all of her friends! And I will have no traitors in my court!" He shouted. None of the guards had followed the king and queen, but Gustave was too incensed to care if anyone heard the truth. "And you, madam, will stay away from her. Do not let me hear that you tried to see her, or the consequences for you will be dire."

There was an evil gleam to his eyes that had not been there before. His weakness had allowed him to slip into madness. The fear of losing his power had driven him to this desperate insanity. Lavinia slowly backed away from him then turned and fled, tears streaming down her face. Her heart broke for Allyn, and for Gustave, but also for herself. She could not bear to lose both her husband and her daughter. In her soul she knew that Allyn had not betrayed Gustave. But there was no way to make him see that now. He was lost.

Chapter 22

Everything went according to plan. Carlisle's men waited near the east gate. Landigson's men readied themselves to ride to the north gate. The four men who had entered the city with Spencer and Navarre were in taverns as near the palace as possible, starting massive brawls that would take many soldiers to break up. Spencer stood in the window of a room at the top of a tower, ready to signal Landigson. Phillip, DuClerque, DeFord, Boyd, and St. Robert along with the others, crept silently toward the eastern gate.

It was ten o' clock. Spencer paced to the hearth to light the torch he held. He strode to the window and waved the torch back and forth. Landigson's men let out a yell and galloped into action. The Baron nodded to the girl waiting near the door and she started for the dungeons.

Gustave was meeting once again with his counselors. Baron Spencer kept his expression carefully guarded. "I will interrogate your brother's spy on the morrow my liege. He seems a rather fearful type. A night in the dungeons should loosen his tongue. I believe he will prove very useful to us."

The captain of the guard came in to report.

"What news, captain?" Gustave asked uninterestedly.

"Nothing much of note to report, Your Majesty. Some disturbances in the taverns. A party of rebels rode up to the northern gate of the city, but we were quicker. I sent a company of soldiers out and the traitors retreated at once. We will know their camp's position by dawn."

"Excellent! Did I not tell you my brother was a weakling? What kind of leader would let any of his men attempt to attack a city without a strategy?"

Everyone laughed, and many of the men congratulated Gustave on his victory. He turned back to the captain. "Has anyone tried to see my daughter?

"No, my king."

Gustave smiled. "Excellent. Thank you captain, you may return to your duties. And captain: do not bother me with trifles this night. I need not hear of every tavern brawl. I will be celebrating my victory."

A chorus of cheers went up among the king's advisors as the wine was produced, and they all joined in a toast to a noble victory for the rightful king.

Agnes strolled the corridors aimlessly. She had gone back to the princess' chamber only to be informed by guards that no one could pass through the door, but she had no other place to go. She thought of going to the queen, but could not work up the courage. Instead she found herself wandering the ground floor of the palace. She was looking up at a tapestry when a man walked into her.

"Oh, I'm sorry miss. Are you hurt?"

"No. Thank you."

"What are you doing in here?" He seemed anxious to leave; yet his curiosity got the better of him.

Agnes had not thought this room would be forbidden to visitors. "I'm sorry. I didn't mean to...it's just that I cannot attend my mistress."

The man's head snapped up. "Who is your mistress?"

"Lady Moreen, I mean Lady DeFord."

"Why can you not attend her?" He quizzed her.

"I don't know. I stepped out for a few minutes and when I got back to the princess' chambers there were guards there who told me on the king's orders no one can go in or out." For some reason she felt she could confide in this man. "I am worried for my mistress. She is so wearied now that her babe has come. Why would the king lock up his own daughter?"

At that moment Baron Spencer entered the room. "What are you still...Oh, forgive me madam I did not know you were here." He looked pointedly at the other man.

The man straightened and spoke. "My lord, could you tell this good lady why the princess, Lady DeFord, and Lady St. Robert are restricted to the princess' chambers by the king's order?"

"Lady Moreen is my mistress and I am worried for her. She was very weak when I left her."

The Baron looked behind him and closed the door, then took Agnes by the arm and sat her in a chair. "You are Lady DeFord's lady-in-waiting?" She nodded and he continued. "The princess has been arrested for treason after meeting with the rebels outside the city." Agnes seemed to understand, so he continued. "The rebels will be in control of the city, and the palace, by morning. You must stay here until I come for you. Your mistress will not be harmed. I will see to it. But you must promise to stay until I come back."

Agnes nodded. "Of course I will."

"And do not repeat a word of what I have said, or all our lives will be in danger."

From outside the room came shouts of disorder and panic. Spencer rose. "Navarre, you'd best be going."

"Yes, thank you Your Excellency." The two men left, and Agnes sat very still as she prayed that the rebels would truly win so that Lady Moreen would not be in danger. Of course she wanted Lady Isabelle and Princess Allyn to be safe as well. They had been very kind to her. The noises increased and Agnes decided it might be best to hide in the shadows of the room. She settled comfortably on the floor and watched the fire in the hearth, trying not to be bothered by the sounds of chaos in the corridors of the palace.

Navarre slipped out of the palace and ran to the east gate shouting. "Guards! Guards! To the palace! The prisoners have escaped!" At once the soldiers rushed to the palace, leaving only two guarding the gate. Those two were easily dispatched and the gate opened to let Phillip's army pour into the city.

Phillip and his party slowly eased toward the palace, waiting for their opportunity.

"Soldiers! More soldiers!" One of the king's guards cried as he ordered the portcullis lifted. In his confusion, the man did not see his mistake until it was too late. Phillip's men charged into the palace and secured the safe entry of those behind them. Stanley made for the kitchens with the others following closely behind him.

He burst in upon the kitchen servants noisily. Startled, one boy dropped a pot on his foot and howled with the pain. "Do not be alarmed!" Stanley shouted. "Your pies are excellent! We would not harm those who will feed us. Let us through and roast several joints of beef. We shall want nourishment before this night is through!" With that he hurried to find the secret passage and disappeared inside it.

The servants watched silently as the line of men steadily disappeared into the wall. When the last man had gone, the cook addressed his staff. "Well, you heard 'im: get to work! We have a new king to impress. You lot there: start cutting apples. We shall give them some of our excellent pies, as well." The cook was a practical man. He had been looking forward to retiring for the night, but he would not pass on the chance to ingratiate himself to his new master. A night of fighting would make them hungry enough to eat earth, but there would be no shirking in *his* kitchen. They would create a meal fit for their new sovereign, despite the hour.

Phillip followed Stanley carefully. It was clear that the passage had not been used in some time. Stanley had sent one of the younger soldiers ahead to clear the cobwebs. Phillip mulled over Stanley's words to the kitchen staff. *Only St. Robert would order supper in the middle of an invasion!* Still, he supposed he would be grateful to have something to eat when it was done. As they carefully made their way up narrow stairways and through dusty corridors, his thoughts drifted to Allyn. Her tears had cut him deeply, but there had been nothing he could do or say to change the situation. She hated him, and rightly so. He should have told her that he was her uncle, told her he was wed, told her anything that might have kept her from feeling something for him.

The worst of the situation was that he had fallen in love with her as well. He had stayed in Paris much longer than he had intended in order to be near her. Knowing there was no future in it, he had allowed himself to fall deeper under the spell she unknowingly cast, and involved them both in a web of betrayal and pain. He would not have done so had he had any hope of her returning his affections. Every small thing that spoke to his heart he convinced himself he had imagined. Then one night she had confessed her love for him.

She had stood so bravely, almost daring him to reject her, but clearly frightened by the thought that he would. He had been unable to resist the impulse to take her in his arms. He had known at the time that it was wrong, but he could not send her away when she had risked her heart and her pride in coming to him. Her kiss had shaken him to his very being, and he had told her that they must not be caught in an embrace. He had mumbled something about her honor that had made her eyes shine with love for him, and bid her goodnight before he lost his senses entirely. He left that night, knowing he should have done so long before, and half hoping never to see her again.

The movement of the line of men stopped. Stanley beckoned to Phillip. They had reached the king's bedchamber. Slowly and silently Stanley opened the wall and peered into the room. He turned back to signal that all was well and stepped into the room. Phillip came through next and was momentarily struck by the grandeur of the chamber. As a son of a king he had lived rather well, but not nearly this well.

The men continued to fill the room, which was large for a bedchamber. The silence, which was so crucial to their mission, was broken when one of the men stumbled, and the man behind him fell over him. Fifty pairs of eyes glared at the two men and they shrugged in apology. It seemed no one had heard the noise.

William and Stanley were eager to lead their men into the rest of the palace. Phillip, knowing that leaving them together would be a mistake, motioned William to him. He then sent DuClerque over with Stanley, to the utter annoyance of both. Boyd, St. Robert, and DuClerque were to secure the surrounding areas, so that Gustave and his advisors would have no chance of escape. DeFord and Phillip would go after the king. Stanley and Honoré led their men quietly out of one door; Roger led his men out of another.

Phillip and William waited to hear the sounds of swords clashing in the corridors before moving toward Gustave's solar. They reached the solar only to find it empty. They had not long to wait before soldiers greeted them with weapons drawn.

The palace was in chaos. The queen heard the sounds of steel against steel and knew that Phillip had succeeded. She held little hope that Gustave would remain king, but she was determined to see his life spared if she could. She argued with herself over the folly of running out into corridors filled with battling men. Her fears for Gustave and Allyn finally overcame her sense and she rushed out into the midst of the fray. The air was filled with the sounds of fighting and the smell of blood. She could not get to Allyn so she ran instead to Gustave's solar.

"The queen!" One of the men cried at the sight of her.

Phillip called out "She is not to be harmed! Where is Allyn?" He shouted.

"In her chambers, with guards at her doors." She called back. "Please do not hurt her!"

Phillip reached Lavinia, panting from exertion. "I would never harm her." He assured her. His men had gained the advantage and he called one of them over to guard Lavinia. "When the fighting is over, escort the queen to the throne room." With that he rushed out into the thick of battle in the corridors.

The fighting lasted three hours before the last of the royal army surrendered. Phillip's men had secured the palace, and Stanley went to find Isabelle. Honoré eagerly followed, ready to take his daughter home and see that Stanley was punished for taking her in the first place.

Baron Spencer stood at the door arguing with one lone guard who was young enough to think he alone could turn the tide of revolution. Honoré pointed his bloodied blade at the stubborn fool and he took off running. Stanley rushed through the door to an empty room.

"Isabelle? Isabelle!" He called, frantic to see her. At the sound of his voice, she came running from another room.

"Stanley! Thank God you are safe!" She cried tears of relief as he caught her up in his arms.

Honoré stood back and watched his daughter with her husband. She truly loved him. Her tears of joy at the reunion touched her father more deeply than any words she might have used. In the months he had been stuck fighting with Stanley he had seen that his daughter could have chosen worse. He still would not have agreed to the match, but they were already wed. He left them to their elation. He would not seek Stanley's ruin. Isabelle's happiness was more important than his need for vengeance.

Allyn hurried to the throne room, where she had been told the king and queen were being held. She entered the room cautiously, and managed to slip through the crowds unnoticed. She still wore the borrowed gown, and but for her unbound hair she looked like any servant.

Phillip's men were everywhere, and all in residence at court had gathered to watch whatever might take place. The king's hands were bound and he was flanked by guards on each side. The queen stood nearby, stoically resigned to the situation but flinching with each insult to her husband.

"Leave him alone!" Phillip's voice sounded in the room. The men parted to let their leader pass.

Gustave paled at the sight of his brother. He had little doubt what was in store for him. He knew what he would do were he in Phillip's place.

The men began to call for Gustave's execution, but Phillip silenced them. "No! He shall live. I will not kill my own brother."

Baron Landigson stepped from the crowd. "He ordered my father killed. I will have my revenge!" Landigson lunged at Gustave.

"No!" Phillip rushed between them.

Allyn screamed.

Three men grabbed Landigson as Gustave fell. The blade had passed under Phillip's arm.

"Papa!" Allyn cried as she and Lavinia rushed to him.

"Take him to the dungeon!" Phillip ordered the men who held Landigson. He turned and looked down at his brother's body and the weeping queen and princess. "I am sorry, so very sorry." He knew not what else to say, so he fled the room.

Some minutes later he stood in what was now his solar and stared into the flames.

"It was not your fault." Lavinia spoke. She and Allyn stood in the doorway. "May we come in, Your Majesty?"

"Of course." He was bewildered. He had not expected Lavinia to seek him out, but what truly baffled him was that Allyn was not flying at him with fists and insults.

"What will happen to me now?" Lavinia interrupted his thoughts.

"You may stay, if you wish. I understand if you wish to leave, but I would not ask you to." He turned back to his observation of the fire.

"And me?" Allyn ventured. "What will become of me? You have taken from me my future as Queen of Frandia."

He did not answer her, for he knew not what to say.

Roger Boyd spoke from the corner. "You could still be queen, Your Highness. It would not be the first time His Holiness granted such a request from a king."

Phillip shot him a look that clearly said: "*Are you mad?*"

"That will not be necessary." Allyn replied. "His Majesty is not my uncle. The late king was not my father."

Phillip and Roger looked to the queen in surprise. She in turn looked at Allyn. "How did you know?"

"I overheard your confrontation with my father and his wife. I know you sent me to my chambers but I could not go when you looked so frightened, so I hid in the next room."

Allyn turned to Phillip. "I beg Your Majesty, do not think ill of my mother for she was never unfaithful to the king."

Thoroughly perplexed, Lord Boyd excused himself from the room. He did not wish to possess such knowledge as he was certain would follow.

Phillip eyed Allyn suspiciously. He did not think her deceitful by nature, but he was hesitant to believe that she might really be unrelated to him.

"Allyn," Lavinia interjected, "are you certain you wish to do this?"

"Yes, mother. The queen can attest to the truth of what I am about to tell you. I am not a princess of Frandia. I am the bastard daughter of Lord Geoffrey DeFord and a lady-in-waiting to Her Majesty by the name of Anne Beauville." Allyn gazed at him meekly, throwing herself on his mercy. Her fate, for good or bad, rested in his hands.

Phillip pondered silently. She was not his niece. But his revolution had resulted in the death of the man she had known as her father. Warring emotions battled for supremacy. "If you truly wish to be my wife, and if the queen has no objection..." He looked to Lavinia who was looking at Allyn expectantly.

Allyn's eyes filled with tears. "I would not have you offer to wed me out of a sense of obligation. I challenge you, upon your honor—tell me once and for all: do you love me?"

"Yes, I do." He said.

She needed no other confirmation. She turned and walked out of the room.

"Allyn, where are you going?" Lavinia was shocked at her daughter.

"I must rest mother. I have a wedding to plan." She said simply.

"I have not asked you to wed me." Phillip reminded her.

"Well of course not. But you will." She smiled faintly as she strolled away. Lavinia sent Phillip an apologetic look and followed her.

Phillip smiled, knowing that Allyn was right. He would wed her. He had no choice, for if he did not she would be far too dangerous an enemy.

William had finally found his way to Moreen. She was sleeping; their child snuggled close against her side. He leaned down to brush a kiss across her brow and her eyes fluttered open.

She smiled. "Will. Are you here, or am I dreaming again?"

"I am here." He walked around the bed to lay beside her. "And what have you named my son?"

"Chauncy." She smiled down at the sleeping bundle.

"Where on earth did you get such an outlandish name?" He asked.

"His name is Chauncy, and I will not change it." She lifted her chin slightly as she spoke vehemently. "After the stable boy who gave his life to protect us."

Will knew it was useless to argue with her. He supposed he would become accustomed to the name. "Which stable boy was that?"

"You don't remember? He was the one who took your horse the very first night you brought me to Thornhill—the first person to greet me really. And he and Agnes would have been wed, but he would not let the king's soldiers take us."

"It would seem he failed in that respect." Will observed sarcastically.

"Will, he gave his life to keep me and our son from harm."

"I am not arguing. Chauncy DeFord. It's sounds rather nice actually. And how are you, my love?" He kissed her gently; thankful to have her in his arms again.

"Weary. But very happy to have you and our son. Oh Will, he is so beautiful." She stared down at her babe, enraptured by the soft sounds of his breathing.

Will leaned over her to get a better look. He had hardly any hair, a chubby little face, and tiny fingers. Not exactly what he would have called beautiful, but he had seen far less attractive children. Just as he would have looked away, little Chauncy opened his eyes. Will was fascinated by his son's gaze. His eyes were deep blue, like Moreen's.

"Chauncy, this is your father." Moreen carefully eased herself up to sit and handed Chauncy to Will. She had never seen such a frightened look on Will's face. How could a man who faced down countless armed men in battle be terrified by his own baby son? "You will not break him. But he is not yet strong enough to hold up his head, so you must do that for him."

She watched as Will gradually grew more comfortable with their child. He began to talk to his son. "Chauncy. You are much smaller than I thought you would be, but I can see by the way you are paying attention that you will be an obedient child. Just do not tell anyone that you were named for a stable boy."

Baron Spencer, followed by Agnes, came in the room as Will handed Chauncy back to Moreen.

"Lady Moreen are you...?" Agnes stopped when she saw Moreen's contented smile.

"I am well. Thank you." She smiled and cooed at her son. "Agnes, would you take him to Berta please? I believe he is growing hungry."

Agnes took little Chauncy, and Moreen laid back against her pillows.

Baron Spencer offered his congratulations and went in search of King Phillip.

Moreen smiled wearily at Will. "Isn't he wonderful?"

"Spencer? He is a good enough sort, but not quite what I would call wonderful." Will lay down beside her again. "You are wonderful."

"But what do you think of our son?" She insisted.

"I'm not certain, but he seems pleasant." He kissed her forehead. "Thank you."

"For what?"

"For our son...and for loving me." He closed his eyes in contentment.

"Will?" Moreen turned. "When Chauncy is old enough to be fostered you won't send him away, will you? Could he not stay with us? You can teach him to fight."

He opened his eyes again. "We will decide that when the time comes. Sleep now." She snuggled against him and drifted into peaceful slumber. Will watched her for some time. As sleep finally overtook him, he had one last thought. *Thank you God, for everything.*

Epilogue

Shortly after Phillip of Arbandeur succeeded in his quest to gain the throne of Frandia he journeyed to Rome to visit His Holiness Pope Benedict IX and request a papal dispensation to wed Princess Allyn. Queen Lavinia and Princess Allyn had journeyed with Phillip, and Lavinia relayed the truth of Allyn's parentage to His Holiness. Phillip and Allyn were wed in Rome and returned home to be crowned King and Queen of Frandia. Their marriage helped to further legitimize Phillip's claim to the throne, as under Frandian law in the absence of a legitimate male heir the man who wed their princess would have assumed the throne after King Gustave's death.

The kingdom settled into a tentative peace which was broken in 1403 when the Landigson family, along with a few others, waged war on the crown in hopes of avenging the death of Baron Jasper Landigson, who had been jailed for the murder of King Gustave six years before and spent his last days in the dungeons of the royal palace. Jasper's son claimed that his father had been poisoned and persuaded several minor lords to join his cause. The only battle took place in central Frandia, near the town of Relsa, and the "war" was decided within a few hours' time. King Phillip prevailed and the Landigsons and their allies were stripped of their titles and lands.

Lord William DeFord was mortally wounded during the battle of Relsa. Lady Moreen managed Thornhill in her husband's stead with help from Lord Stanley St. Robert. Chauncy DeFord, only six years of age at the time of his father's death, was fostered with Lord Roger Boyd. The proximity of Glenbrae to Thornhill allowed Moreen and Chauncy to see each other frequently. William and Moreen had no other children.

Anna Sinclair and her children were often at Thornhill after the death of Anna's husband Thomas, and occasionally visited Glenbrae with Moreen. Eleanor Sinclair married Andrew Boyd.

Jeanette Raivaux had married Henry Allemand, a man of the minor nobility, during the summer of 1396 and managed to advance him to a position of some importance to the crown after the revolution. With Jeanette's assistance Henry rose to the rank of lord before his untimely death—Lord Allemand fell down several flights of stairs shortly after the birth of his son. The child had bright blue eyes, and Lady Allemand named him Geoffrey.